FURY GIRL

ELAYNA MILLER, BOOK TWO

Jill M Beene

Book Layout © 2016 BookDesignTemplates.com

Cover Design and Illustration Copyright © 2016 by Kari Joy Hodgen.

Fury Girl/Jill M Beene. -- 1st ed.

ISBN 978-0692820704

Contents

For Kari.

Prologue

Years ago, I went to Milan for a case. I arrived on a private jet and was greeted on the tarmac by a town car. I wore a black Chanel pencil skirt, a ruffled white silk shirt and black Louboutin heels. My hair was pulled back into a demure knot at the base of my neck. A two-carat brilliant diamond stud protruded from each ear, and my eyes were hidden behind black designer shades that would have made Jackie O proud. I was trailed by a nervous assistant named Emily who had fluttering hands and a tripping run of a gait. I didn't know why she wore heels if she couldn't walk in them properly.

It was all part of my cover, and the most important part of that cover had just pissed in my twenty-thousand dollar Hermès Birkin bag.

"Oh, poor little sweetums," I crooned to the prize-winning Chihuahua show dog as I slid into the sumptuous leather backseat of the town car. My nervous assistant shut the door behind me with a solid thunk, and since no one could hear me for a few seconds I added, "You worthless little rat of a dog. Bruno never would have taken a leak in my purse."

When Emily slid into her seat beside me, I coolly handed off the purse with the dog still inside.

"Muffin had an accident," I said in a bland voice.

Emily was ready with wet wipes and paper towels that she pulled from the massive pleather tote she carried everywhere. I leaned back and pretended to enjoy the view, but my mind was on the case I was working. Child molesters were both my least favorite people on the planet and my absolute favorite people to eliminate. My target this time was Randall Themes, a retired sixty-year-old from family money whose second passion was collecting prize show dogs.

His first passion was what had put him at the tippy-top of my list.

I had been hired by his neighbor in an exclusive town in Massachusetts. Randall Themes had made the error of messing with the son of Suzanne Vermillion. Suzanne was the CEO of an acquisitions firm that was famous for their ruthless hostile takeovers. She was excellent at what she did. Suzanne was gone a lot, but she adored her only child. Randall Themes really should have known better.

Suzanne didn't want to press charges; she wanted me to bring back Randall Themes' offending body part... that had been severed when Themes was still alive.

I wasn't fond of carving off body parts. I preferred clean kills, where I could walk away from a scene instead of having to run. For Randall Themes, I was willing to make an exception. My background showed that Themes had paid off several live-in housekeepers over the years, millions of dollars to each one. Each of these women had been single mothers with young sons, and there was no sign that any of them knew what they were getting into. One had tried to press charges, but that case had been buried. That was the largest payout: three million.

Three million for a lifetime of damage, of mistrust, of heartache and being the victim of pure, undistilled evil. The thought made my blood pound in my temples anew.

"Is everything alright?" Emily asked.

I realized that I had been clenching my knee so hard I had white knuckles. I smoothed out my skirt, gave a strained smile and nodded.

"Just a headache," I said.

Emily rummaged in her bag and came up with three different kinds of painkillers and a designer bottle of water.

"Thank you."

I wished again that Camilla was along with me. But Emily wasn't just an assistant; she was a certified groomer and dog-handler. She would be the one running Muffin around the ring on Saturday morning, not me. Hopefully by that time, I would have Randall Themes' private bits in a jar of formaldehyde.

Entering a dog show was not my ideal cover. It was too high-profile for my taste. But with the exorbitant price of entry came tickets to the exclusive pre-show mixer on Friday night. It also gave me access to the rooms on Randall Themes' floor, which were reserved for diamond-level competitors. To be a diamond-level competitor, you had to pay a lot of money and have a diamond-level dog.

Suzanne Vermillion didn't even blink at the added costs.

The reception that evening was like every other event I'd ever attended with this type. The lighting was dim, the clothing understated but of the finest quality, and the comparisons rampant. Banal conversation flowed over the top of crystal rims of champagne glasses and the untouched seafood canapés. It could have been a chic funeral; there was very little laughter. Everyone was too uptight, clinging with one hand to their current social rung while grasping upwards for the next higher one.

At events like these, I always had the impulse to yell something wildly inappropriate, just to stir things up. I wondered what the response would be if I called out: "Hey, y'all! How about a game of charades?" In my mind, I always accompanied this loud announcement with a manic grin and jazz hands.

I never would do it, obviously. The point of my expensive crepe de chine cocktail dress and my italian leather pumps was to blend in. I frowned after each sip of my delicious champagne to let everyone know that I was accustomed to a better vintage. I waved off the sumptuous bites presented by waiters even though that itchy, rebellious part of my brain wondered what would happen if I yanked a silver tray out of a server's hand and demanded a fork.

I arrived on time, which broke the rule of the upwardly-mobile: acting like you didn't care. I survived an hour of appraisal disguised as boring conversation before Randall Themes arrived. He strode in with the quiet confidence of someone who was assured of his status. His dogs had won previously, and he was from the kind of old money that absolves sins and terrible personalities. He mingled: evil draped in the thick cloak of expensive manners and higher education.

I watched him from afar, careful never to let the social bubble surrounding me to merge with his. He was a small man, five foot four and slender. His custom suit was cut to add breadth to his shoulders and tapered at his trim waist, and I was certain that his leather dress boots contained concealed lifts. I wondered about the psychology of that: a man trying to appear bigger than he was, who also abused those smaller than himself. I felt like it was a clue of some kind, but I wasn't here to try and rehabilitate him. I was here to end him altogether.

Randall Themes projected an air of cultivated ennui. He left at the first sign of party disbursement. Another rule of the elite: don't be the last one to leave a party. It implies that you might have been enjoying yourself, which is tantamount to admitting that it wasn't beneath you.

He entered the elevator and I ran up the stairs. It was only three flights, and I couldn't chance someone placing us in the elevator together. The stairwells were sparse, with no cameras. I emerged from the stairs and followed him down the hallway, my shoes sinking into the plush red carpeting. We were alone, and I had everything I needed for the job in my tasseled Yves Saint Laurent clutch.

I let him enter his room and close the door behind him with a reassuring click. I was ten or so paces behind him. When I arrived at his door, I heard his voice on the other side.

"Is that the best you can do?" There was a pause, then Themes said, "Fine. But I don't like waiting."

I wasn't concerned. Room service at this hotel took ages. I had at least a half an hour. I waited several more moments, until I was convinced that he had ended the phone call, then used my duplicate key card and was in the room behind him. A glance showed me that his cell phone was off and on the desk. Half-shrugged out of his jacket, he stared at me. I tripped a bit as I approached him, blinking slowly as if I were drunk.

"Why are you in my room?" I slurred.

I stumbled again, and he held out an arm to stabilize me on instinct. I let him catch one of my arms, and in one smooth motion with the other, I stabbed a syringe into his flesh and depressed the plunger. That much paralytic that quickly had to sting like a bitch, but it didn't leave him much time to react, either.

He flailed and I yanked the collar of his coat further down his back, trapping his arms. His eyes went wide and his mouth gaped: a fish out of water. He slumped against me. I scowled at the contact and pushed him over onto the bed. Themes couldn't move, couldn't speak... but he could still feel.

I dragged him into the marble bathroom, dumped him into the bathtub, and yanked his trousers down until they bunched around his ankles. His head lolled and I positioned it so that he could see. I injected him a second time; this one was a blood thinner.

I explained the special request that Suzanne Vermillion had made on behalf of her son. Then I sat on the counter, checked my email, and waited to give the blood thinner time. With his racing heartbeat, ten minutes was more than enough. If I was being honest, I was dragging it out so that he would feel the helplessness and terror that his victims had felt.

I wasn't looking forward to this next part, but I had stalled long enough. I took a pair of gloves out of my clutch and pulled them on up to my elbows. I set a small jar of formaldehyde on the counter with a sharp click and twisted off the top. The pungent chemical smell permeated the air, taking me momentarily back to high school biology class. I pulled out a curved blade that farmers use to cut grapes and opened it with a snick.

I made a swift cut and deposited his member in the jar, washed up with efficient movements, and waited for Randall Themes to bleed out in the most undignified way possible. The marble bathroom amplified noise. I listened to the diminishing sound of his ragged breathing, the dripping of blood down the bathtub drain, the sound so similar to the end of every bath I'd ever taken... a soft knock at the hotel room door.

A jolt of adrenaline set my heart thumping. I slunk from the bathroom to the exterior door and glanced through the peephole. He stood there, his facial expression looked bored, but I saw the jumping pulse in his neck, the tightness of his jaw as he clenched it. I knew why he was there, and I was surprised he couldn't hear my teeth grinding through the door.

When I was a senior in boarding school, I wrote my thesis paper on the effect of gun control on violent crimes against women. It was too ambitious a topic- I scraped by with a C and felt lucky to have it, but for weeks, I walked around touting statistics.

"Did you know," I asked one girl in my class whose hair was up in a sleek ponytail, "that rapists usually target women with long hair, especially if it is in a bun or a ponytail?"

"Why on earth would you think about things like that?" she asked, her glossed lip curled.

I had stepped back, my teenage head confused, my teenage heart embarrassed at her reaction.

I've thought a lot about that conversation in the years since, and I've decided that there is a fundamental difference between people like me and people like that ponytailed girl. She is content to believe that nothing evil would ever dare graze its filthy fingers against the clean fabric of her life. She will never look evil in the face; she will never turn over the rocks of society to see what is crawling around on the other side.

But me? I can't *not* look.

So when that fifteen year old boy knocked on that hotel door in Milan, I thought about ignoring him. I thought about waiting in silence until he turned around and went back to where he came from. I thought about it, but there wasn't really a choice for me. I answered the door.

I slept in the next day, all the way through the dog show. It had been a long night. Muffin piddled on the show floor and didn't place. I didn't care. My driver was loading my luggage into the trunk when two blue and white polizia cars pulled up to the hotel, lights rotating. I was already ensconced in the back-seat of the car, out of reach in so many ways. On the way back to the airport, I chatted with Emily about whether Muffin should start seeing a dog massage therapist to help him get over his performance anxiety, then I faked another migraine so I could have some quiet.

I didn't see the city as we drove. My mind was on the private plane winging toward Sydney that had taken off three hours ago. It had taken longer than

I liked to cobble the plan together. The Belgian only arrived with the forged passport and other documents an hour before the Sydney flight was to leave. He was a short fellow with bags under his eyes, and grumbled about the late notice despite the fifty-percent fee increase I had paid to get him there in the first place.

The hired guard, a pale British woman with a crew cut, chain-smoked in the background of the parking garage while I paid the Belgian in cash. The boy watched from the back of the car with suppressed intelligence. He was used to being treated as chattel, but this night was different. I hoped that he could heal. There was a program for kids like him on a huge ranch an hour outside of Sydney, one that would offer counseling and education.

"Do you want out?" I had asked him in that hotel room, where his would-be abuser was still draining on the other side of the bathroom door.

I already knew the answer was yes. He was missing the tip of one finger at the knuckle that proved he had already tried.

What I really wanted to offer was: "Do you want me to kill them all?"

Of course I went back and did it anyways.

Chapter 1

I felt like I was seeing Milan for the first time, now. It was stunning in the morning hours. Lights winked everywhere, like diamonds catching the light at the throat of a grand old woman. They illuminated the cobblestone streets, the luxurious shopping centers, the ancient churches and stonework. Shopkeepers flicked their signs over and banished dirt from the sidewalks with brusque brooms while cafe owners arranged still-warm pastries in gleaming glass display cases. The morning commute was in swing, a mix of small cars and motorbikes, here and there punctuated with a sleek sedan.

Hyde and I were here for a well-deserved vacation. Our last case had looked straight-forward enough. My team had been hired to find a smuggler hidden within a produce company, but before we could get the intel we needed, my team was double-crossed by the woman who had hired us. Our ocean-front house in Mexico was blown up, Frankie and Camilla were traumatized, Hyde joined the team, and our tech guy Wu was sucked into the CIA. By the end of it all, the entire team was in hiding for months while a traitorous enemy in the agency was found, tried and convicted.

Milan was gorgeous. I saw the beauty, but I was too miffed to enjoy any of it. It had been four hours of travel time from the Tennessee airport to New York City, then a layover, and another nine hour flight into Milan. I was tired and I felt that familiar post-commercial-flight sheen of grime covering my body.

Hyde and I were packed into the back of a small Fiat taxi, trundling towards our hotel. My suitcase sat between us on the back seat, and it was jammed in my side, digging into me with every bump we hit. The windows were up and the controls in the back seat were broken. The air was stagnant with the smell of the unwashed, hairy man in a tank top who was driving us. I didn't understand how the taxi driver couldn't smell himself. It wasn't a scent that I had gotten used to in the past twenty minutes.

My sweaty discomfort wasn't the sole reason for my irritation. It had been almost a full day since I had told Hyde that I was interested in him the same way he was interested in me. Armed with that knowledge, Hyde had chosen to do... nothing. He hadn't so much as held my hand. If anything, he was keeping his distance more now than ever before. I crossed my sticky arms and looked out the window in pointed silence.

Hyde pushed all my buttons. He was gorgeous, in a rugged way. If GQ decided to do a sexy lumberjack photoshoot, Hyde would make the perfect model. He was a little over six-foot tall, with light olive skin, broad shoulders, large biceps, and long muscular legs. And that was just his body. His face was equally as impressive. A wide, soft mouth rested under a masculine nose. His eyes were the color of melted milk chocolate, and dark brown hair was swept back off his forehead.

He caught me staring, and gave a little smirk. "What?"

"Nothing." I turned to look out the window again.

With traffic, it took over an hour to reach our hotel. When we pulled up, I allowed the driver to stop, park and open my door. I took his help in getting out of the taxi, thanking him and wiping the residual sweat from his hand onto my jeans once he released me. Hyde wrestled my suitcase from the backseat while the driver unloaded another from the trunk.

I grabbed the handle of one of the bags and made for the door. I left Hyde outside to deal with paying the driver and hauling the remaining luggage. I was met with a welcome rush of cool air in the cavernous lobby. Large palms in huge ceramic planters swayed in the air conditioning. Overhead was an elaborate glass and iron dome, and I paused for a moment to look, thinking that it must be amazing inside when it rained.

The desk clerk was an elegant brunette who was so heavily made up that I could not tell whether she was twenty or forty. She raised a flawless eyebrow as I approached, and I knew that she was taking in my bedraggled state. I was wearing cheap jeans and a t-shirt that had met it's wrinkle threshold about eight hours earlier. My hair was pulled back into a greasy ponytail, and I had sweat my drugstore makeup off somewhere over the Atlantic.

Despite my appearance, she was nothing but efficient and courteous in greeting me and getting us checked into our rooms. Hyde came up behind me with the rest of our luggage while the desk attendant was issuing our keys. I felt like she was handing over gold when my fingers closed around the thin plastic cards. I could almost feel the suds and the water from the shower I was going to take. It could not come soon enough.

The ride up in the wood paneled elevator was quiet except for the whoosh of the efficient mechanics and Hyde's repeated yawns. The silence seemed comfortable on his end, but was sullen on mine. I just wanted to be alone, wanted time to soak in my feelings of embarrassment and rejection.

A discreet ding, and we were on our floor. I handed Hyde his key. Our doors were next door to each other. We paused at my door, the key in my hand. I found it ironic that before I told him that I had feelings for him, we had shared numerous hotel rooms. Now he felt it imperative that we have separate spaces. I sighed.

"What is wrong, Elayna?" Hyde said, his voice heavy with weariness.

"What is wrong with me?" I snapped. "What is wrong with you?"

He crossed his arms and waited for me to explain.

"You told me you wanted to date. You told me you were all in," I said. "Then I tell you I feel the same way, and you don't do anything about it. What is that about?"

Hyde shook his head, and smiled. "When a beaten puppy sniffs your hand for the first time, that's great, but it doesn't mean it's ready for you to tackle it to the ground and wrestle with it," he said. "I'm taking things slow."

"In this scenario, *I'm* the beaten puppy?" I asked, crossing my arms, my eyes narrowing.

"Yes. The only man you've ever had a serious relationship with ended up breaking your heart. Then you had to kill him."

"And you think this will be serious?"

"It already is serious, Layna," he said, his voice low and soft.

I made a small noise of derision and swiped my key card to open my door.

Hyde continued, "You told me that the ball is now in my court. You can't give up control in this area and then just take it back. Not with this. I won't let you."

I narrowed my eyes. "You think I gave up control?"

"Didn't you, though?"

I rolled my eyes and wrestled my suitcase through my door. This conversation was going nowhere, and I felt embarrassed in the exchange.

"Under the circumstances, retreat is a good tactical decision." Hyde chuckled, a muscular arm propped on either side of my open doorway. "I'm going to get some sleep, but see you for dinner around seven or so?"

"You're a little shit," I grumbled, shutting the door in his amused face.

The shower felt even better than I had expected. The hot water cascaded down through my hair and turned my bare skin pink. The soap and hair products were expensive and lathered wonderfully.

By the time I finished rubbing myself down with a fluffy towel, I felt like I had washed off the residue of the last few months of my life. Losing Wu to the CIA, the failed mission in Mexico, Frankie's tears, Camilla's bruises, Rowan's gurgled final breath, and the torture Hyde had inflicted on the man sent to kill me all faded into the past. The memories were still there. They always would be. But I was ready to move on.

I felt energized and determined, and decided to start checking things off my long-dormant to-do list. My first call was to an architecture firm in the Hamptons. I put my phone on speaker and talked while I got dressed.

"Phillips and Berkin," a familiar, cheerful voice answered.

I smiled. "Anna? It's Elayna Miller. How are you?"

"Fantastic! How are you? How is the house?"

"That's why I am calling," I said. "I need you guys to build me another one."

"We would love to work with you again. Mr. Berkin says that he wishes all clients could be as easy as you," Anna gushed. "Do you have a site picked out already?"

"Um, it's the same lot. Same site," I said, wincing.

There was a long pause. "Is something wrong with the first house?"

I sighed. "It's gone, Anna. There was a horrible fire. The whole thing is leveled."

"No! Oh, Elayna, I'm so sorry," she said, a slight tremor in her voice. "Did the sprinklers fail?"

"Well, the fire was more like an explosion."

"Oh my goodness!"

"It's alright," I said. "No one was hurt. I was hoping you guys could build another one, and I want you to start immediately."

"We are just finishing up a big project on the east coast, and I am sure that we can get you in next. Should I patch you in to Mr. Berkin?"

"That's not necessary," I said. "If you could just jot a couple notes. Tell Mr. Berkin that I need the basement to be restored to it's original dimensions, but I want it to be much more plush and comfortable down there. Still one big open space, but more like a living room than a basement. I want the house to be one story. Other than that, tell him that he has carte blanche."

"Excuse me?" she squeaked.

"Tell him that he can do whatever he wants. He knows what I like. Lots of windows, wood floors, the whole deal. And tell him that I want it done as soon as possible. Within ten months, but I would prefer six."

I could hear the furious scribble of a pen from the other end of the line.

"What's the budget?" Anna asked.

"Keep it under three million."

"I think we can do that." Her voice rose an octave.

The last contract I had with them was for one and a half million, so I knew this was a step up. I smiled. These were good people, and I liked being able to give them my money. Well, it wasn't my money. I had billed the CIA three million for my house. My insurance had kicked in another two million. That was in addition to the millions in penalty that Geraldine Lawrence had signed over prior to her death. And my ex, Rowan Linney, had left me everything in his will, which admittedly was a little awkward, 'cause I was the one who had killed him.

"I will need the same setup, in terms of living space, at least four other bedroom bathroom combinations. I want one to be very feminine, two to be more neutral, and one to be more masculine."

"Alright," she said, sounding flustered and breathless. "When do you need to see mock-ups?"

"I don't," I said.

"What?"

"The only constraints I am placing on Mr. Berkin are the budget and the time frame. I know his aesthetic, and he knows mine. When you have bills, email my assistant Camilla and she will send you the money."

"You don't want to see mock-ups," Anna repeated dully.

"No. I'm on vacation."

"We will still need you to sign a contract," she said, now sounding a little anxious, like this was all too good to be true.

"Sure," I said. "Once you have a set of plans finalized, give me a call and I will tell you where to fax it. I had the lot cleared a month ago, so it's ready when you are."

"Alright, Elayna. I will pass this on to Mr. Berkin." She sounded like she was in a good kind of shock.

"Thanks, Anna," I said, hanging up.

I had finished the conversation in my bra and blue jeans. I flopped back on my bed and smiled. It felt good to be proactive. I had been on the defensive for the last few months, and it wasn't a feeling I was accustomed to. I was itching to get things headed in the right direction again, to reclaim control over my life as much as possible.

I called Frankie, my computer expert. It went straight to voicemail, which wasn't a surprise to me.

I didn't even know where she was. She and my munitions expert, Howard, had started dating in the middle of our last mission. They were in the middle of a tour through Asia and Europe. Last I heard, they had been in Hong Kong and were headed to Thailand.

She could be going without cell service for days at a time. I shot her an email instead, knowing that she would be checking that regularly. It was only a couple lines, letting her know that Hyde and I were in Italy, and that we planned on spending another month on vacation. At the end of that month, I wanted to get back to work. I told her to make a list of pro-bono cases that could use our special brand of attention.

I finished getting dressed, threw my hair in a ponytail and wheeled my suitcase to the front desk. I was painfully aware of how my unhighlighted roots and Walmart shoes clashed with the expensive lobby of the hotel, but the concierge had a polite smile for me all the same.

"How may I help you?" He spoke in English, pegging me as a tourist.

"If I go shopping and have things sent to the hotel, will you put them in my room for me?" I asked.

"Of course."

"It's my first time in Milan. Could you recommend a good place to go shopping?"

"What are you looking for? Clothes? Souvenirs? There is a lovely open market with art just down the road," he said.

"I need new clothes. Nice, expensive clothes."

He leaned forward and smiled. "You have come to the right city for that. I will call you a car."

"I would like to donate these." I pushed my suitcase at him. "I was hoping you could get them to a local charity, or someone in need."

To his credit, he didn't even blink in surprise. "How generous of you."

Chapter 2

It was still morning, and there was little traffic in the shopping district. The black sedan dropped me off at the first upscale salon I saw. The facade of the building was white marble, and a brass doorbell was inset near the tinted glass of the front door. I doubted my ability to get a walk-in appointment, but I rang the bell anyways.

A tiny, tan woman wearing a crisp black apron answered the door. She had a shock of luxurious curls on the top of her head, but the sides of her hair had been buzzed. Somehow, she managed to make this look chic and elegant. She certainly had the cheekbones for it.

"Appuntamento?" she asked crisply. Her voice was huskier than I had imagined for someone so small.

"No," I said, trying to seep my voice with apology. "Do you speak English?"

"Yes," she answered, her gaze raking me from split-end hair to ragged cuticles.

"Do you have time to fit me in?"

"For what?" she asked, raising her sculpted eyebrows and still blocking the door with her slight frame.

"Everything," I said. I sounded desperate, even to myself.

She pursed her polished lips, and then winced. "Our prices, signora..."

I pulled my black American Express card out of my back pocket and relinquished it to her.

"I don't care about your prices," I said. "I really don't."

She smiled at me, and it was the same smile I had often made before taking a shot with a sniper rifle, when there was no wind and my aim was true.

"I am Francisca," she said, sweeping the door open. "Please, come in."

I spent the next three hours being trimmed, highlighted, buffed, extracted, waxed, plucked, powdered and polished. My spirits rose with each treatment, with each fresh glimpse in the mirror. Some of the time, I had no idea what they were doing, but I was feeling more human with each passing minute.

Francisca and her team were efficient and ruthless when it came to the removal of my body hair. They showered me with compliments in English, but muttered to each other in guttural Italian. I wasn't offended. Spending two months on a houseboat in the backwoods of Tennessee was relaxing, but the hygiene products I had access to consisted of a package of men's razors and a combination shampoo and conditioner that didn't clean or condition.

It was noon by the time I exited the salon, and traffic had picked up. I looked and felt much better, but I was still dressed in cheap jeans and a t-shirt. That was my next mission. The boutique next door to the salon had a headless mannequin in the window that was wearing what looked like a hand-painted silk skirt. It was knee-length and a little voluminous, and was paired with espadrille sandals and a white, structured, midriff-baring top that toed the line of sexy without being skanky.

I ducked inside, and approached the two sales women behind the counter. They smiled and greeted me in Italian-accented English.

They were wildly in love with me within fifteen minutes. They chucked items over the door of my dressing room with abandon, and I bought nearly everything that fit. I bought three filmy skirts that swirled in a beguiling way when I walked. I bought two classic cocktail dresses, one red, one black. I bought three sun dresses, two short, one long. I bought the outfit in the window and wore it out of the shop, ditching the jeans and the t-shirt in the dressing room. When I left, the ladies were wrapping my purchases for delivery, and said the packages would be in my room within the hour. Apparently, this was a common thing in Milan, package delivery to an expensive hotel.

Next door, I bought a complete suite of bras and panties from La Perla, most of them little more than scraps of the finest lace. I ditched my cheap, ill-fitting bra in that dressing room. I bought four sets of silk pajamas with lace. A couple shops down, I bought four pairs of Louboutin heels, two pair of espadrille wedge sandals that laced up my ankles gorgeously, and three pairs of flat, jeweled sandals. I thought the little shopkeeper might weep with joy. He kept calling after me as I left, "Bella, bellisima!"

I did so much damage to my credit card balance that I didn't know who was going to call me first, American Express or Camilla. The credit card was black and made of titanium and carbon fiber. Supposedly, it had no limit, but I had never tested that theory the way I was testing it today.

Next up was swimwear, something I was prepared to face after the wax at the salon. I bought a black suit that was complicated to put on. It was technically a one piece, but there were so many geometric cutouts and straps that it was as revealing as a bikini. I bought one of those too, for backup. And I had to have a cover-up, a long, flowing silk gown. And a sun hat. I'd never been a hat person before, but hey, I was in Milan, why not?

The next three stores were a blur of more dresses, skirts, designer jeans, silk and cashmere. I made friends with shop attendants wherever I went and decided Italians were exceptionally friendly people. I found a menswear store and bought enough to elevate Hyde's wardrobe. To cap it off, I stopped in at Louis Vuitton and bought a set of luggage to hold my new purchases. And a couple purses. And a wallet. And some sunglasses.

By the time I returned to the hotel, it was late afternoon. I was sated, and I thought I might have achieved a better understanding of Frankie's psyche. This whole 'shopping as a therapeutic outlet' thing had it's merits. I stepped into the lobby, my skirt swirling around my knees, and felt a thrill of satisfaction when I commanded the admiration of every man in the room, at least for a second.

The concierge greeted me by name. I think he was relieved to see me. If I was there, I couldn't be sending any more packages to the hotel. As it was, I rode up in the elevator with a harried-looking porter who was toting bags and boxes from familiar stores. I smirked and tipped him well once he had unburdened himself in my already very full room.

For the next hour, I unwrapped and packed my new clothes into my new suitcases. When I was finished, my room was swamped in tissue paper, empty bags, boxes and ribbon. I slipped off my shoes and sprawled across my bed for a moment to rest before I met Hyde in the lobby for dinner.

"What in the heck?" Hyde said, waking me.

I cracked open my eyelids and then shut them again. "Go away. I'm taking a nap before dinner."

I heard his low chuckle, then heard the crunch of tissue paper as he waded over to my bed. The bed jostled as he sat next to me. He brushed my new hairdo off my face.

"It's seven-fifteen, Elayna," he murmured, placing a small kiss above my ear. "I was waiting down in the lobby. It was very clear to the concierge that I had been stood up."

"Shit. Sorry," I mumbled, raising my head from the pillow. "I'm starving. Let's go."

He watched me with a smirk of amusement as I sat up and stretched. The strip of midriff that my shirt exposed increased dramatically until I lowered my arms.

"Nice shirt," Hyde said, swiping a warm finger across the band of bare skin.

I swatted his hand away. "Knock it off. I need coffee."

"Traditionally, espresso is served after a meal, not before."

"I don't care about tradition."

Hyde looked around my room again. "What did you do? Buy everything you saw?"

"Pretty much," I admitted. "It was loads of fun, though. And I bought you presents."

I gestured at the pile of boxes and hanging bags near the door.

"Well, thanks."

I shuffled next to him on the edge of the bed and began strapping my wedge sandals to my feet.

"Ugh," I said, fumbling with the clasp of the first sandal. My mind was foggy, and my body felt like it had been hit by a truck. "In retrospect, I should have slept more and shopped less."

Hyde pulled the sandal out of my hand and swung my feet into his lap. He deftly clasped my feet into my shoes and then pulled me up.

"Do you have a foot fetish?" I asked.

"Huh?" He looked surprised, his eyebrows raised.

"You're always messing with my feet. Rubbing them, putting on my sandals," I said.

"I rubbed your feet *one* time," he said, leading me through the wads of tissue paper and empty bags. "And helping you with your sandals was selfish. I want food, and you are moving too slowly."

"I need food, too," I grumbled. "I'm going to get the biggest bowl of pasta in Milan. And if I'm still hungry, I'll order another."

Hyde laughed.

Exiting the elevator in the busy lobby, I once again was the recipient of a lot of male attention. Hyde put his hand on my lower back, and I smirked. My new tactic was working already. I was going to try not to bring our relationship up again. I was just going to bait Hyde in the best way I knew how, and part of that was inspiring a little protectiveness, a little harmless jealousy. There is nothing like a well-dressed woman to make a man want to act like a gentleman.

We ate dinner at a corner cafe, and I ordered espresso and a bottle of wine together, much to Hyde's amusement and the chagrin of the waiter. I ordered a huge plate of mushroom ravioli and ate the whole thing. I ordered a tiramisu to go.

"Did you get enough to eat?" Hyde asked with a teasing smile.

"I didn't eat lunch, and I was up all day."

"Shopping."

"Shopping," I confirmed.

"What did you buy for me?"

"Pants, shirts, shoes. A coat," I said, yawning. "I want to buy you a suit, but you have to be present for that. Maybe tomorrow."

"A suit?" Hyde asked. "The little village we are heading to isn't a suit kind of place."

"I know, but I thought we could stay in Milan awhile before we head out. I haven't hung out in a city in forever," I said. "Do you mind? Is that alright with you?"

He smiled and patted his flat stomach. "Fine with me. As long as there is lots of pasta, I'm good."

"It doesn't bother you, does it?" I said, frowning. "That I bought you clothes, I mean."

"Nah, sometimes a guy needs a bit of help in that area. At least, I do."

"Good. Cause I've recently discovered that I *love* shopping."

"Frankie and Camilla will be proud," he said, taking a sip of wine. "A convert to the church of fashion consumerism."

I laughed.

The walk back to the hotel was perfect. It was clear and stars twinkled above. Hyde threaded my arm through his. We didn't speak, but I felt the air warm between us. It seemed to thicken with a tempting promise. Hyde was walking me back to my room from something that now felt very much like a date.

He held my hand in the elevator, his thumb skimming over my knuckles. I had been trained not to show any outward signs of how I was feeling when I felt vulnerable. I hoped that Hyde couldn't hear my rapid heart rate. At my door, he paused, so close to me that I could smell his cologne. He pulled me into a quick embrace, and pressed a quick, chaste kiss to my temple.

"Goodnight, Elayna," he said, letting me go. "See you in the morning."

He turned to unlock his door, and I turned to do the same so he wouldn't see the surprised let-down I could feel written on my face.

"Goodnight," I mumbled as I stepped through my door.

I leaned against the door with a frustrated sigh. In my mission of getting Hyde to pay romantic attention to me, this night was a bust.

Someone had cleaned up the miles of tissue paper and packaging while I was out. Ninja maids. All the best hotels have them. I undressed and took off my makeup, pulled on a ridiculously expensive camisole and went to bed, hoping that when I woke up in the morning, Hyde might want me the way I wanted him, or that I wouldn't care as much.

Chapter 3

I felt galvanized in the morning, waking almost at first light. I did a circuit workout of plyometrics and bodyweight exercises until I was sweating. I decided to skip the shower for now, and instead took twenty minutes putting on the strappy black swimsuit. It seemed even more scandalous in my room than it had in the shop, but I threw my shoulders back. It was Milan. I was going for it. I slid the sheer cover-up over my skin, slipped on some jeweled flat sandals, and donned sunglasses and my floppy sun hat.

I grabbed my cell phone and a tawdry romance novel that I had taken from Tennessee, and headed out to the pool. It was a large classic rectangle tiled in azure blue. At each corner, a different stone maiden poured water from her outstretched jug into the water below. Large black and white striped cabanas stood in intervals around the perimeter, and huge palm trees waved from massive blue and white painted pots. I was the only one there, alone except for a young attendant in a crisp white shirt who looked startled when I stepped out from the double doors.

I smiled and waved at him, and the over-appreciative look he gave me made me doubt my swimwear choice even more. I straightened my spine and walked to the farthest cabana, slipping off my sandals and out of my cover-up. The attendant was right there, offering me two enormous, fluffy white towels.

"A drink, madam? Some fruit?" he offered.

"A peach bellini and a water," I said. "Thank you."

He retreated and I stepped into the pool. The water was crisp and refreshing, but far from cold, and I wondered if it was climate-controlled. I did thirty laps, letting the calming monotony of the activity clear my mind. A bottle of water and a sweating peach bellini were sitting next to my chaise when I emerged from the water.

My bellini was half-empty and I had just settled back into the insipid story of Katrine and Renaldo, (she of loose morals, he of bulging biceps and low IQ), when my cell phone chirped. Frankie had emailed me back. I was glad for the distraction. Katrine had just swooned into Renaldo's arms for the third time, and I was only halfway through the fourth chapter. I was starting to wonder if Katrine had undiagnosed blood sugar issues.

Elayna,

I've been keeping an eye on the news wires on a daily basis. Thought that a few months off might be all that you could stand, and I've been waiting for your email for a few weeks now. It came later than I expected...you must be having fun with Hyde? ;)

To business... In the LA Times, there was this little blurb about a bomb threat in a Judge's office. Turns out there was no bomb, but they charged the mother of a molestation victim with the threat. She says that Justice Michael A. Shelly keeps letting molesters go free, or giving them unusually light sentences. I looked into it, and the mother is right. His case record towards every other offender is normal, but when it comes to molesters, he lets them off with probation, light sentences every time. Hacked into his private computer. Turns out he shares their proclivities. I have his internet history and hard drive copied; tell me what you want me to do with it.

Kansas City, MO.- A battered women's shelter was burnt to the ground, two killed. Looking at police logs, they have focused their attention on one guy, but they don't seem to have enough to move on him. This is a recent case, and it is still under active investigation.

Oakland, CA.- There are reports of a new gang on the streets. There was just a blurb, but I found it really interesting, so I looked into the police files on the case. Turns out that this gang seems highly organized, highly trained. They are going up against the other gangs in the area, but don't seem to have a real motive. They will burn drug stashes instead of robbing them, shoot gang leaders from a distance with precision and not take credit. No tagging, no boasting, no drugs, hookers, etc. Can't really tell how they are funding themselves. Very strange.

Portland, OR.- An honors college student who was being stalked by her ex-boyfriend is in the ICU, critical condition. She was sexually assaulted and stabbed fourteen times. On the 911 call, and before she went unconscious in the ambulance, she made a statement that "Jay did this." Detectives have questioned the ex-boyfriend, Jason Kollins. He claims he was home during the attack. But he had violated the restraining order several times, with each instance being more brazen than the last, and this is the second ex of his that has ended up hospitalized. First one would not make a statement, too scared. Police did a search of his place, came up with nothing, and the judge says they cannot arrest him for it, since she did not use his full name in her statement. His lawyer is arguing that "Jay" could stand for anyone's first initial, or she could have been delusional from loss of blood. If nothing else happens, he is going to get away with it.

In world news, the leader of the Almeida cartel in Brazil died a week or so ago. It is the largest organized crime group in South America, and they are expecting some sort of power vacuum. So don't go down there right now. Things are going to be ugly for a while.

Let me know if any of these float your boat. See you soon,

Frankie

I wrote her back immediately.

F,

In the LA case, anonymously forward everything you have on the Judge to the FBI's Violent Crimes Against Children Task Force. They are the ones with the power to go up against a Judge. If nothing comes of this legally, we might step in, but I think that being disbarred and spending quality time in prison as a former judge would be a better (and longer) punishment for him than what I would do to him. Have our lawyers in LA defend the bomb-threat mother, telling her it is pro bono. Tell them to bill us for it.

In the Kansas City case, let the police do their job. This one is too fresh to take up. Let's hope they can solve this one on their own, but keep eyes on it.

For the Oakland thing... I don't see the bad side of what you are telling me. There is a highly-trained, highly-organized group taking out the high-ups in street gangs, getting drugs off the streets, with seemingly no illegal activities? Tell me how I can buy these guys a beer.

Portland is the winner for me. If she wakes up and can make a statement to police, terrific. If not, keep that asshole in your sights. I want to meet him.

Keep the case ideas coming. I want to have a stack of them to whiz through when I get back to reality. We aren't planning on going anywhere near Brazil. Italy is beautiful and my bellini is delicious.

Wish you were here. - E

The email exchange with Frankie was what I needed to feel normal again. I had only spent a little over forty-eight hours feeling out of balance with Hyde, and it was too much for me. Waiting for him to make a move felt pathetic, needy, made me feel like I was out of control. Which, if I was being honest with myself, in the romantic area of my life, I was. That didn't mean I couldn't be a take-charge badass in all the other facets of my existence.

Two bellinis later, the sun was starting to beat down at just the right temperature, and the pool was seeing more traffic. At some point, I fell asleep, my book face down and open on my chest, my hat pulled over my face. I woke up to someone jostling the end of my chaise lounge. I lifted the brim of my hat and saw that Hyde was kicking my chair. He was wearing exercise clothes, was dripping sweat, and clutched either end of a towel wrapped around his neck.

"Hey," I croaked, stretching.

"Hey, yourself," he said with a wry smile.

"What time is it?" I asked redundantly as I reached for my cell phone to check.

"Nice suit," Hyde said.

"Thanks."

"That's going to be one hell of a tan line," he said. "And I don't think that I'm the only one who's noticed."

I glanced around, and saw what he meant. There were a disproportionate number of men down at my end of the pool. Some were lounging, and a couple were typing away on laptops in the sun. A businessman with a hairy chest and a watermelon-sized paunch gave me a hopeful smile when I glanced his way. A lone woman herded her three children past us and shot me a dirty look as she went by.

"It's not that scandalous," I said with a shrug. "It's a one-piece."

"Yeah, and your outfit last night was just a skirt and a top."

I frowned. "I thought you liked my outfit last night."

"Oh, I liked it. So did every other guy who set eyes on you. It's kind of like this swimsuit, here," he said, nudging my chaise with his foot again. "If you're a straight male, what's not to like?"

"I bought this suit for me, not for the men who might see me in it," I said.

He leaned down swiftly, one arm braced against the backrest of my lounge chair, his eyes only a foot from mine. He studied me for several long moments, and I fought to keep my breathing even, keep my face impassive. Then he grinned, and pressed a fierce kiss to my cheek.

"I know what you're doing," he said, a hint of laughter in his voice. "And it's not going to work."

He straightened and turned to leave.

"Well, maybe not on you," I snapped.

He turned back toward me, and his face had lost all its warmth.

"You don't want to play games with me, Layna," he said, his voice serious.

"Isn't that what you are doing with me?"

"Not at all," he said in an even voice.

"Then what are you doing?"

"I'm waiting for you to be ready," he said.

"Ready for what, exactly? I'm a grown woman, Hyde."

He sighed. "Come get lunch with me."

I shook my head at the rapid change of subject. "What?"

"I'm hungry, and this isn't a conversation we should be having in public, anyways," he said, glancing around.

I saw several heads turned in our direction, watching our exchange with unabashed interest.

"Fine," I said, gathering up my stuff.

Hyde held my elbow as we walked to the elevator. The contact, so far from what I wanted, irritated me. I yanked away, and he let me go. But as soon as the elevator doors closed, Hyde pushed me back against the wall of the elevator, pressing his front to mine, and spread his large fingers across my back. One of his hands snaked up behind me, grabbed my hair and pulled gently, tilting my head back. His lips claimed mine fiercely and I responded, but just for a moment, before he pulled away.

His eyes were dark, his voice low when he said, "Is this what you want, Elayna?"

"Maybe," I said, sounding a little too breathless for my pride.

"That's the problem," he said. "That's your only goal in this. And I shouldn't be surprised. That's all you've ever let yourself have."

I took a shaky breath and opened my mouth to speak.

"No, let me finish," he said. "We could have that, and it would be... incredible. But that's not going to be enough for me. Not with you. And I don't think you're ready for more than that, not yet."

I pushed him away, angry at my pulse for racing at his nearness, mad that he could affect me that way, and I didn't seem to be able to get to him.

"And you are the one to decide that, are you?" I snapped. "Oh, please, wise one. Tell me how you have decided that I'm not ready for this."

"No need for sarcasm," Hyde said lightly. "I know you aren't ready for more because of how hard you are pushing the physical angle. Like that's the only way you know how to feel connected."

I crossed my arms and looked away from him. I was ashamed at his words. They made me feel small, cheap. I felt like an idiot for wanting him when he obviously could take me or leave me. More than that, his words hit me somewhere hidden and vulnerable. I didn't want to admit it, but part of me whispered that he was right. I was dismayed to feel tears prick at the corners of my eyes. I bit the inside of my cheek until it hurt, narrowing my focus on that pain until my emotions were under control.

"Fine," I said, pleased to hear how even my voice sounded. "Well, when you decide you aren't going to damage me by moving forward, let me know. But until you stake some sort of a claim, make some sort of declaration, as far as I'm concerned, I'm still single."

The door dinged and swung open, and I walked down the hall towards my room, head high, back straight. I didn't look back to see if he was behind me or still in the elevator. In my room, the door closed against him, I decided some things.

First on my agenda was going to stop giving a shit if Hyde ever made a move or not. He didn't owe me anything, and from his actions, I could only surmise that he was one of those guys who really wanted something until they had it. Like a kid who begged for months for the latest, greatest toy and discarded it after ten minutes of play on Christmas morning.

Second, I was in Italy, and I had never spent any real time in Milan. And here I was, like one of those women I despised: pathetic, clinging, waiting for a man's actions to make things bright and enjoyable for them. I had never been tied that way before, and it irritated me that I had spent the last couple of days with my mood in someone else's hands.

I called the concierge, got what I wanted, and dressed in a sweeping sundress and flat sandals. Ten minutes later, I was knocking on Hyde's door. He answered, his hair still wet from the shower.

"Are we going to get lunch, or what?" I asked cheerfully.

"Um, sure," he said, his brow furrowed.

I could tell he was thrown by my change in attitude. Inwardly, I smirked. Outwardly, I kept my face friendly. That's what he wanted, right? To be friends? I was ready for that, ready to be chums, best buddies, for as long as he could stand. I wasn't going to show him weakness in this area again. Let him put his heart on the line next time. I was done with that.

We found a cafe a few blocks away from the Milan Cathedral. It was early afternoon, and the crowds on the sidewalks were as thick and disorganized as flies on carrion. Hyde and I had a sidewalk table, so we had a great view of them walking by, heads on a swivel to catch the sights, or pointed down towards the free tourist maps they had picked up at their hotel kiosk.

Most of them were in groups, parents herding children, young college students on vacation. I noticed a man standing alone to the side, studying the map in his hand. The sight of his tanned skin and brown eyes made me miss Camilla. I wondered how she and Bruno were doing.

"You've been quiet for too long. Penny for your thoughts," Hyde said.

"I was just thinking of Camilla and Bruno. Wondering how the cabin is treating them. I'm ready to get everyone back together," I said, smoothing the cloth napkin over my lap.

"You miss them?"

"Of course. I emailed Frankie this morning and asked her to assemble a list of cases that look promising."

"How soon did you want to head back?" Hyde asked.

I shrugged. "I figure that a month of vacation would be enough. Then I want to hit the ground running. I need to get back into the swing of things."

I took a sip of water and the ice cubes tinkled against the glass as I set it back down.

"You excited to go back to work?"

"I'm ready to feel like things are normal again. I haven't really felt like myself since Wu was taken."

"I know," Hyde said. "That's one of the reasons I don't think we should rush whatever it is between you and me. I don't want to be the thing that you use to distract yourself from feeling out of control. I don't want this to be disposable to you."

I sighed. "Hyde, I don't want to talk about that anymore. I don't understand your thought process, but I don't need to. You're right, at least about one thing. I don't enjoy giving up control in any area of my life. So whatever. I'm ignoring the whole thing for now. You figure out what you need to figure out."

Hyde was spared having to respond by the waiter arriving with our plates. I had ordered a salad. Hyde had ordered fish.

I wrinkled my nose. "You aren't sick of fish yet? I thought Tennessee would have cured you, at least for awhile."

"That was freshwater bass. This is branzino," Hyde said with a frown. "They are different fish."

"They're both bass, Hyde."

"Branzino is a salt-water fish," he argued, holding a fork-full out to me. "Try it. You will taste the difference."

I obediently took the bite.

"That's good," I admitted.

"Maybe you just have a problem with freshwater fish," Hyde said.

"Or maybe I would get sick of anything if I had to smell it being cooked once a day for weeks on end."

"Could be," Hyde said with a grin.

After lunch, we walked down to the Duomo and stood in the square looking up, just like every other tourist. As the breeze caught my hair and skirt, I stood there trying to memorize every facet and crevice of the impressive building. I tried to think of what it looked like while it was being built, tried to imagine the faith of the architects who first envisioned the final product.

What would it be like, to know that you were promising to deliver something that depended on others' work? What would it be like to command the life's work of hundreds of artisans, and then, when you were too old to continue, to hand off control to another man? It happened over sixty times, that transfer of control, that passing of the torch. And each time, it must have been a frightening thing. But necessary, if the work was to ever see completion.

I thought of what Hyde was saying about me, about us. That I was willing to give him my body, but I wanted to retain control of my heart. Because that, the letting someone else in, having faith in someone else in that way... that had the potential to break me. And I knew myself well enough to know that if I had been one of the architects working on the cathedral, they would have had to pry the torch from my hands. I wouldn't have handed it over willingly. I don't trust people.

I realized that Hyde was studying my face in the same way I was looking at the cathedral.

"You're right," I said. "I'm not ready for that yet."

Hyde looked back towards the building.

"I know," he said.

The walk back to the hotel was comfortable, simple, and I was grateful. Things felt normal. Hyde left me at my door.

"Dinner and a movie, later?" he asked.

"Sounds good."

Chapter 4

We met later to discuss our limited movie options. There was only one theater that had showings in English, and neither one of us liked subtitles.

"Too much work," Hyde said.

I agreed.

"No, not that one," I said about one of our options. "I've heard of it. It's supposed to be this steamy romance, but let me tell you what, if some guy tried to get his jollies by beating on me, he'd be in for one hell of a surprise."

"I've never understood the appeal of that, myself," Hyde said. "Abuse is still abuse, even if the abuser gets turned on by it."

"For *reals*," I said.

"The post-apocalyptic one, then," Hyde decided. "It starts in an hour."

We made it to the movie right as the previews were starting. We slid into our seats and soon we were well into the plot, our fingers greasy with buttered

popcorn. The main character was predictably beautiful and willowy and I had to force myself not to roll
my eyes at her perfect eye makeup and her loose,
bouncing curls in the middle of a desert battlefield.

I couldn't control my snicker when she shouldered
a high-caliber rifle and took a dramatic shot. With
her tiny frame and lack of muscles, she would have
been blown over backwards from the recoil.

"What do you think?" Hyde whispered, leaning
over. "A dislocated shoulder?"

"At least," I whispered back. "And I call bullshit
that she would even able to lift that rifle with those
twiggy arms."

We were able to contain our sarcasm until the
final battle scene, where the main characters were
pinned down by heavy fire with only the blade of a
front-loader for cover. Her hair was still perfect, even
though she had been running and fighting for her
life for two hours straight.

The male character turned to her. "I guess this is
it," he said.

"Just one kiss," she said, grabbing the front of his
tight tank top.

He stopped returning fire and enveloped her in his
large arms, which had been oiled down for the scene.
The kiss lasted for almost a full minute, complete

with panning camera angles and a swelling crescendo of music.

"You think someone on the other side would use this time to flank them and put all of us out of our misery," Hyde whispered.

"Seriously," I said. "How did this ever become a cliché? I want to know if ever, in the whole history of the world, someone in the middle of a firefight has ever stopped to make out."

"I can't ever say that it was an option that I seriously considered in the past," Hyde said. He rose his eyebrows speculatively. "But next time we get the chance, maybe we should give it a go."

I laughed, and was promptly shushed by someone a few rows back.

"Also," I whispered to Hyde, "how come bad-guy hired guns can't ever shoot? These guys couldn't hit the broadside of a barn if it were painted red."

The movie ended like movies should: the guy got the girl, the bad guys were splattered throughout the desert wasteland, and there was new hope for humanity.

"Why was that the only place they could drill for water?" I argued as we left the theater. "Wells draw water from a water table, which is accessible from lots of different places."

"It's called suspending belief," Hyde said wryly.

"I don't like crucial, unexplained questions that poke serious holes in the plot line, that's all," I grumbled.

"You're just going to have to let it go," he said, patting me on the back.

"How was it?" A middle-aged man asked as we walked by.

"Hilarious," Hyde deadpanned.

I laughed at the man's confused look.

The next day, Hyde and I spent the day drinking, eating, and reading by the pool.

"Again, absolute horse-shit," I said in disgust, flopping my novel down on the small table between our chaise lounges.

Hyde laid his book down across his chest, open to his spot.

"What is it?" he asked patiently.

"Ok, so the character's an heiress who is set to inherit a massive fortune if she marries this stupid old guy named Marley, who her father chose," I explained. "But she's fallen in love with the poor stable boy. He doesn't have a penny to his name, but he's really burly and beautiful."

"So, like me, then," Hyde quipped.

I ignored him and continued, "Like an idiot, she goes to her father and announces that she loves the stable boy. Her father says, if you marry him, I'll disown you. So now they are planning on running away together."

"So what's your problem with this plot line?"

"She would never choose the stable boy over her fortune. She's not cut out for a life of poverty. Half this book is about her silk gowns," I said, waving the novel at him.

"Maybe she is trying to be virtuous," Hyde suggested.

I scoffed. "Yeah, she's been virtuous with him twice in the stables and once in her bedroom already."

"So what would you have her do?"

"She should marry the old coot, keep the stable boy on, and wait it out. Her husband will die at some point, and then she would have the money and her love interest."

Hyde just raised his eyebrows.

"She probably wouldn't even have to sleep with him. He's like seventy, and they didn't have Viagra in the eighteen-hundreds," I said.

"I can tell you've put a lot of thought into this," Hyde said, trying to hide a smile.

"Well, yeah," I said. "If her husband stays healthy too long, she could always, you know, help it along."

"Is that what you'd do?"

"Of course," I said with a shrug.

"I hope you understand that's not a real encouraging sentiment for me to hear."

"Don't feel too bad for him. Any man that age who goes after a seventeen year-old girl deserves to get a big dose of nightshade in his hot toddy."

"Nightshade?" Hyde repeated.

"It was a poison available during that time period," I said.

"Where did you pick up that tidbit of information?"

"History of Poisons, 101," I said.

Hyde picked up the book and studied it for a moment.

"I hate to tell you this, but I have very little sympathy for you after seeing the cover," he said. "It's not like it looks like it's going to be an intelligent read."

"I didn't have a lot of options at that Tennessee grocery store slash bait shop," I snapped, snatching my book back.

"Yeah, but the cover artist didn't even get his eyes pointed in the same direction," Hyde pointed out.

I examined the book again.

"Shit, you're right."

"So, in this case, you *can* kinda judge the book by it's cover," Hyde said.

We walked back to our rooms in the late afternoon.

He asked, "Are we getting dinner?"

"I'm seeing an opera tonight. So it will have to be early," I said. I added as apology, "They had just the one ticket at this late notice, and I didn't think you were the opera type."

He laughed. "You thought right. What time do you want to meet?"

"In an hour? Down in the lobby."

Back in my room, I curled my hair, wishing that it would grow out faster. It only just brushed past my shoulders when it was straight. When I curled it, there was a half-inch of clearance. I wore the black cocktail dress and high heels, praying that the opera in Milan wasn't a ball-gown kind of affair. I didn't have a ball gown. To compensate, I wore extra make-up, smudging my eyeliner and glossing my lips. It was the best I could do.

I tucked my ticket into my jeweled clutch and went to meet Hyde for dinner. He was waiting for me, and his eyebrows raised when the elevator doors opened. He put a hand on my lower back and guided me through the open door towards a waiting sedan.

"I called a car," he said. "Made a reservation for dinner near the opera house."

"Thank you."

"You in that dress is making me rethink whether I'm an opera kind of guy, after all," he said.

Chapter 5

Hyde dropped me off after dinner, making me promise to call if I needed a ride afterwards. The Teatro alla Scala was lit up, and a steady stream of glamorous cars pulled to the curb and released their even more glamorous occupants. The interior of the theater was lit with huge, glittering chandeliers, and I could hear the sounds of the orchestra warming up in the pit. An usher guided me to my box, pulling out my chair and offering me a tasseled program.

Only moments later, the lights dimmed and the prelude to *Aida* began. Five minutes into the opera, I heard the other occupants of the opera box arrive. I glanced to the side and noticed an elderly couple beside me. Two men sat in the row behind us, but I didn't get a good look at either of them.

Soon I was swept up in the tragic love story enfolding on the stage. At intermission, the lights rose. The elderly couple rose, and I thought they were most likely heading for the bathrooms. I stood and stretched a little, watching the workers change out the set.

"Ti piace l'opera?" A voice said behind me.

I turned, and saw an attractive middle-aged man sitting in the row behind me. His eyes and hair were brown. He was tall and lean, and wearing a very expensive suit.

"I'm sorry, I don't speak Italian," I said, turning back towards the stage.

I wanted to know how the stagehands were going to move the massive pillars. Were they on wheels, or maybe some sort of pulley system?

"I said, do you like the opera?" he repeated again, in a heavily accented voice.

The man next to the speaker was younger and seemed uncomfortable that the man was speaking to me. I wondered fleetingly about the dynamic between them, but couldn't figure it out. Not lovers, as I first had thought. But more than friends.

"Yes," I said, looking back towards the pillars.

Hydraulics, maybe?

"Have you seen Aida before?" he said.

"Twice before, but never here."

"What are you staring at?" he said.

He came to stand beside me and joined me in peering over the balcony.

"The pillars," I said. "They weren't there for act one, so I know they can be moved. But they look solid, so I am trying to figure out...ah."

The stagehands, four to a pillar, were finally moving them. One pulled on a rope, using a pulley system to lift each pillar, and the other three slid them along. The pillars were on some sort of track system.

"I've never seen someone who is as fascinated in the mechanical workings of the stage as they are in the actual story," he said, cocking his head and looking at me with interest.

"Well, this is my third time seeing *Aida*. This is the most impressive set I've seen yet."

"I am a patron of this opera house," he said. "I could force some poor stagehand to answer all of your mechanical questions, if you like."

"They probably don't get paid enough to put up with my questions." I laughed.

"I'm Umberto," he said.

"Elayna," I said, shaking his offered hand.

"So what brings you to Italy? Business or pleasure?" He turned and leaned on the balustrade, facing me.

"I'm on vacation," I said.

"Where are you staying in our beautiful city?"

I raised my eyebrow. "South of here."

He grinned. "Ah, a challenging woman. How rare. Have you seen the cathedral yet?"

"Yes, today. It was lovely."

"Many people do not think so," he said, watching me. "It is called an overworked monstrosity by some."

"I don't see how you can think it is ugly, even if you don't like the aesthetic."

"What do you mean?"

"Even if you don't like how elaborate it is, how can you look at something that took so much time and work, and call it a monstrosity? Think of the history, of the lives' worth of work that went into it. Or look at it purely from an architectural standpoint. It's a feat of design. It's amazing what people accomplished before they had modern machinery."

"It is amazing," he said, his eyes drinking in my profile. "Would you like to see more of it? The inside? Places that the public does not see?"

"What? Are you a benefactor of the cathedral as well?" I asked, meeting his eyes.

"Of sorts," he said.

"I shouldn't," I said, turning back to watch the stagehands change the backdrop.

"There is a man?" Umberto asked.

"Kind of," I said.

The lights flickered, signaling patrons to return to their seats.

"Kind of is not a yes," he said with a smug smile.

"It's not a no, either," I said firmly.

"Very well. Lovely meeting you, Elayna," he said, pressing a chaste kiss to my cheek. "Enjoy the rest of the opera."

I did, very much. As the doomed relationship came to it's final, shuddering close, I was unable to blink back tears, and the elderly woman next to me offered up her purse-sized tissue container. I took a couple, and her answering smile was just as watery as mine.

I lingered for long moments after the applause had faded and the lights came up. I wanted to avoid the inevitable rush of people leaving the opera house, and I wanted to see how the crew would break down the massive stone set pieces that had appeared out of nowhere in the fourth act. I was a little disappointed when they retracted into the floor. Umberto and his friend were still there when I turned to leave. They followed me out, but Umberto did not make an additional attempt to speak to me, just gave me a smile as I passed.

The lobby was deserted, and I hoped that I would be able to find a cab now that the crowds had dissipated. As I stepped out the front door, however, I realized that there was a mob... of photographers yelling in Italian. The cameras flashed rapidly in my face and I was blinded. I stood there for a moment, holding my purse up to cover my eyes, trying to regain my equilibrium.

"What the hell?" I said.

I tried to move forward, but they were pressing in, not allowing me to take a step. Above the flashes of cameras and the yelling, I heard Umberto's curse behind me. I instinctively turned toward him as he reached me. He slipped an arm around my waist and yelled something to his friend, who began parting the crowd. The other man was a bodyguard. I should have recognized that before.

"I am sorry," Umberto yelled toward my ear as he guided me through the mass of bodies with cameras flashing staccato beams of light where faces should be.

Then we were at the street, the mass of photographers following us, taking pictures and striving to be louder than each other. A sedan lurched to a stop at the curb, and the bodyguard flung open the door. Umberto hustled me into the back seat and slid in next to me, slamming the door behind him.

The heavy tint of the windows reduced the flashes of the cameras to mere flickers, and the volume of the shouts became no more than a distant murmur. A car door up front slammed, and the car squealed away from the curb.

"What the hell?" I repeated.

"I am sorry," he said, breathless. "I don't know how they found out I would be there."

"Who are you?" I asked.

"I'm next in line for the unofficial throne," he said.

"Which country?" I demanded.

"One south of here," he said with a smile.

"I didn't know that unofficial royals garnered this much attention, just for going to the opera," I said.

"I recently broke off my engagement," he said, wincing. "When she realized it was really over, my ex-fiancee went to the papers, claiming there was another woman. They have been following me ever since, trying to catch me with someone."

"So now I'm..." I said, my words trailing off into understanding.

"Yes. You're the other woman."

I opened my clutch, pulling out my cell phone, and dialed a number. I felt a sharp thrill of relief when she answered, sounding sleepy.

"Frankie, it's me. I'm about to receive a lot of unwanted attention. I need you to change the name on my reservation at the hotel, right now. Erase all traces of my real identity. Choose a name I've never used before," I demanded.

Umberto's eyebrows shot up at my request.

"I'm on it," Frankie said, all business.

"Thanks," I said, hanging up.

"Who was that?" Umberto asked.

"Where are you taking me?" I said. "Where are you headed?"

"If no one is following us, we can drop you off at your hotel," he said. "Which is it?"

I told him, and he pressed a button and repeated the information to the driver.

I dialed again, and Hyde answered.

"Hey," I said. "I got into something at the opera house, and we need to get out of Milan before I am photographed again. I'll be at the hotel in fifteen, can you meet me out front? I'll explain when I get there."

I listened to his consent and then hung up. Umberto was watching me carefully.

"You have people," he stated.

"I'm sure that you do, as well," I said.

"Yes," he said, smiling. "But I'm a future unofficial royal, after all. That means something."

I gave a polite smile. I wasn't amused by him or the situation.

"Because of your reaction to the publicity, I'm thinking that it would be pointless for me to ask you to dinner," he said.

"My job requires a large degree of anonymity," I said.

"I can be anonymous," he said, wiggling his eyebrows at me suggestively. "For instance, the back of this car is very anonymous."

I laughed at his exaggerated come-on.

"Alright, alright," he said with a chuckle. "First you say that you cannot date me because of a man. Then you claim it's because of your job. It's all very mysterious."

"It's not nearly as interesting as it sounds," I said. "The corporation I work for doesn't appreciate a lot of attention."

"Do you work for organized crime?"

"No, nothing like that," I said. "And there is a man, too."

He sighed. "We are star-crossed lovers, just like in the opera."

"I think you'll be just fine," I said, rolling my eyes. "Something makes me think that a future almost-royal doesn't need to pick up random women at the opera to get a date."

"You are right," Umberto said, looking satisfied with himself.

Chapter 6

The car stopped, and we were at my hotel. The tinted windows had made me unable to see where we were. Umberto opened his car door and helped me out. Then, he looked to the left, and pressing me back against the car, kissed me. I felt the rich wool of his suit brush my bare skin, felt the smoothness of his chin against mine. It was all wrong, and I wrenched my face away. The kiss lasted no more than the length of the camera flash I saw, and then Umberto's weight was thrown from me.

Hyde was there, looming over Umberto's prone form. He reminded me of one of the heroes carved into the marble of the cathedral's facade. His face was twisted with anger, his muscles taut with restrained fury. To the left, a camera flashed as fast as a strobe light. Umberto's bodyguard came running from the passenger side of the car, yelling at Hyde in Italian.

"Come on," Hyde said tersely, holding a hand out to me.

I took it, and he whisked me into the lobby, away from the camera. He hurried me past the curious looks of the front desk staff and the guests who had seen the interchange. We didn't speak until we were in the elevator. Hyde was breathing hard, like he had just sprinted a mile.

"What was that?" he asked. His voice was low and rough, like his throat was filled with gravel.

"I have no idea," I said. "He's some kind of royal or something. I met him at the opera, but I don't know why he kissed me. I told him I was unavailable."

"He knew that camera was there," Hyde said.

"Yes, I think so, too," I said, feeling dazed.

I wiped the smeared lipstick from my face.

"I wanted to beat the crap out of him," Hyde said. "I still do."

"It's going to be very inconvenient to get out of Italy now, that's for sure," I said. "That fucker used me for a publicity stunt. Asshole..."

Hyde interrupted me by pressing me up against the elevator wall and kissing me deeply. His lips were angry and insistent on mine, his strong hands splayed against my back, clasping me to him. The scruff on his chin scratched my face and his familiar smell surrounded me. My fingers flexed into the front of his shirt and grazed the muscular expanse of his chest, and I didn't know if I was trying to pull him closer or trying to hold myself up.

"So that wasn't you," he said when he pulled away from me by an inch.

"No!" I said, breathless and feeling a bit drunk from the kiss. "I told him..."

Again he stopped my words with his mouth, his lips gentler this time, one hand tangling into my hair, one hand sliding lower, gripping my rear. He leaned into me until there was no space between us. The elevator dinged, the doors opened, and they started to close again. Hyde's hand shot out and pushed it back open.

"Fuck it," he said, his breathing ragged.

In one smooth motion, he hauled me up and threw me over his shoulder.

"Seriously?" I said. "This is happening?"

He slapped my butt as he strode down the hall. "Better believe it."

He swiped the card to his room and dropped me inside.

"Hyde," I said. "You said you wanted to wait until I felt the same way."

"I have ways to make you love me," he said, his eyes dark on mine while locking the deadbolt behind us. "Just you wait and see."

Hours later, I breathed in the scent coming off his warm skin, and nuzzled deeper into the crook between his arm and chest.

"I love you, Elayna," he whispered tenderly against my hair, then kissed my head.

I sighed and was grateful that it was dim and that my hair was a screen to hide my face.

"It's too soon," I whispered back, reluctantly. I didn't want to break the spell, but I wouldn't lie to him, either.

"I know it is, for you. But I will love you enough for the both of us, for now. I can carry that."

He fell asleep long before I did, and I lay there listening to his deep breaths, thinking.

I woke up early, zipped up my dress in the dark, went back to my room and called Frankie.

"Hey there, lovebird," she said.

I started at her words.

"What?" I said.

"It's all over the internet, that the royal heir of Italy has a new lover," she said, laughing. "I love the pictures when he tries to kiss you. You should see your face! And then Hyde coming in like that to protect your honor; it's just too delicious."

"Good morning to you, too," I grumbled.

"I had your new IDs delivered to the hotel this morning," she said. "So you are now Theodora Bellinci, and Hyde is Thomas Mack. Don't worry. Your hotel must be discreet; the press doesn't even have your fake name yet."

"Perfect. Thank you, Frankie."

"Now, if that's all, I need to get back to Howard and this massive bloody mary in front of me. It has bacon in it. Can you imagine?"

"That's actually not all," I said, my voice unsteady.

"Alright," Frankie said.

I steeled myself.

"I'm almost out of my prescription, and I need it renewed," I said. "Sent to a pharmacy close to the hotel."

Frankie laughed. "So the Italian prince did get lucky."

"Um..."

"Unless Hyde is dipping his pen in the company ink, so to speak," she said.

"You're not one to talk about *that*," I said, feeling a blush settle over my cheeks. "It doesn't matter, can you do it or not?"

"Don't insult me," she said. "Give it an hour. I will put a rush on it. And tell Hyde my money was always on him. From that day we got drunk together in the hotel, I knew it was all over. He was half in love with you even then."

"Shut up and love you, Frankie," I said. "You're a life-saver."

"Love you, too. Drive careful. Make good decisions. Practice safe sex. Don't talk to any more strangers, especially Italian princes," she said.

I hung up, laughing. I turned to find Hyde leaning in the entryway, wearing sweat bottoms and no top. After last night, I knew I should probably be used to the view of his bare chest, but it still sent a thrill of warmth through me.

"You left," he said, his voice still thick with sleep.

"I had to call Frankie," I said, feeling shy for some reason.

Things were always different in the light of morning. I wondered if he had regrets, because if he did, then I did, too.

"Did you brush your teeth?" he asked, walking over to me.

"Yes," I said, puzzled.

"Super."

He pulled me to my feet and unzipped my dress.

"This feels a lot like deja vu," I gasped as he kissed my neck.

"It's my favorite kind of deja vu," he said.

I didn't make it to the pharmacy near the hotel until early afternoon. By that time, I needed to get some air, some distance. I extricated myself from Hyde's heavy limbs and showered while he slept. At least I thought he was sleeping, until he demanded I bring back cannolis and coffee before I slipped out the door.

Hyde's love was passionate and engulfing. Even now, on the street, alone, it hung around me like some sort of invisible tether. I was his, for the time being. I felt it. Surprisingly, I didn't mind that feeling. We were equals in the way we made each other respond physically. I liked that equality, even if we were out of balance in the emotional expressions department.

My trip to the pharmacy was uneventful, but when I stopped in the corner coffee shop, the grey-haired, pudgy woman behind the counter put her finger to the side of her nose and winked at me. A tabloid was spread open behind the counter.

"There was a time when men fought over me," she said with a smile. "Now they just fight over my pastries. In this season of my life, that's enough for me."

I laughed. "Do you have any advice?"

"Don't choose Umberto," she said. "He's no good. Too smug. That other one, though... but then, I like an overprotective man, myself."

"I think I do, too," I said.

She grinned and packed two extra cannolis into the box before looping and tying brown string around it with deft movements.

"Enjoy," she said with a wink. "The cannolis, too."

Chapter 7

We rented a car that evening and headed out of Milan. It was two hours to the village outside Portofino, but we stopped in Genoa for dinner. The salt-scented air swirled around us as we walked along the waterfront. Hyde held my hand. It felt sweet to be with someone in a way that lasted past the awkward morning hours. A host of a small restaurant settled us at a table facing the bay while the long rays of the sunset played on the water and the fishing boats came in to dock.

Our waitress was maybe nineteen, her skin soft and clear, her long brown hair pulled back with a leather strap. When she first saw us sitting at our table, she gave a small yelp and disappeared back into the open doorway of the cafe. She reemerged in a few moments clutching a folded newspaper and a pen.

In broken English, she said, "Will you... write your picture?"

She smoothed the newspaper out, and there we were, Hyde and I, with Umberto sprawled on the ground in front of the hotel. In the photo, I looked shocked, and Hyde looked absolutely lethal. I took the pen that she thrust toward me, and I signed my fake name over the picture.

"And here," she said, flipping the paper over so I could see the photos below the fold.

I glanced at them, but paused over the photo of me leaving the opera. There, in the crowded background, I recognized someone.

"Hyde," I said, handing him the paper. "Second picture down. See anyone familiar?"

"The guy from the day at the cathedral," he said.

"I was hoping that I was wrong," I said with a sigh.

But there he was, the same man I had noticed when we ate lunch in Milan, the one whose tanned skin had reminded me of how much I missed Camilla.

"He doesn't have a camera, either," Hyde said, pointing at the picture. "He's not a photographer. He was there for you."

"Bloody fucking hell," I said.

"Nathaniel's in prison. Do you think he got a contract out again, even after they put him in solitary?" Hyde said, scribbling something over his picture and handing the paper back to the still-hovering waitress. She skittered away, holding the paper to her midsection protectively.

"There's no way," I said. "The first security breach was a personal insult to Senator Mathers and the security engineer. There's no way he could ever do it again."

"Then who?" Hyde said.

"I worked a couple of cases here before, but I was very thorough. There isn't anyone left to come after me. To my knowledge no one else wants me dead."

"Who says that guy is trying to kill you?" Hyde said, tearing off a hunk of the warm bread that had been placed on our table. "Maybe he's just watching you."

"Why?" I said.

"No idea, but you bet I'm going to ask him nicely next time I see him."

"I saw your idea of asking nicely in Tennessee," I said with a raised eyebrow.

"Hey, now," he said, sounding hurt. "That was a completely different set of circumstances. That guy was actively trying to kill you."

"I know, Hyde," I said, my hand covering his on the table. "And I appreciate you for taking care of that."

I laughed.

"What's so funny?" he asked.

"I was just struck with how surreal this conversation is. I'm thanking you for killing a guy to protect me. Most girls thank their boyfriends for flowers."

"So I'm your boyfriend now?"

I rolled my eyes.

"Good to know," he said smugly.

Our waitress got the courage to return to our table, and I amused Hyde by ordering their special, branzino.

The small village outside Portofino was as lovely as Hyde had claimed. Multi-hued buildings clung to the hillsides ringing the peaceful bay. They looked like a brightly-dressed crowd jostling for the best view of the ocean. The beaches on the small inlet were pristine and unpopulated during the week. Hyde was right; the tourist masses were ignorant of this small paradise. The longer we stayed, the more I hoped that this village would remain a secret.

Our second week there, I was basting in the sun on the beach, my floppy hat pulled down over my eyes to block the glare. The beach was fine white sand, the sun was just a bit too warm, and my lounge chair was pushed back at the perfect angle. I was debating whether it was worth the energy to turn over when I heard a familiar voice.

"Shit, Layna," he said. "You make me want to re-apply sunblock just looking at you."

"Howard?" I squealed, pulling the brim of my hat up.

"In the crispy flesh," Howard said. "I'm not going to be able to be outside for long, not in this sun."

He frowned up at the flawless blue sky. Howard was the explosives expert on my team, and besides Hyde and Camilla, he was my closest friend. He was about five foot eleven and lanky, with pale, freckled skin and reddish blonde hair that had recently been cut in a very trendy style. It was shaved short on both sides of his head, with the top piece left long and wavy. His goatee had been trimmed as well. It suited him, and I would bet my whole bank account that Frankie was the one behind the style update.

"Where's Frankie?" I said, sitting up to get a better look around.

"She's directing Hyde, who is dealing with her luggage." He smiled ruefully. "That's been my job for the last few months and let me tell you what, it's nice to let someone else lug it for once."

"So how's it been going?" I asked, sliding over on the lounger so he could sit.

"Other than the luggage, it's been awesome. I saw things I never thought I'd see, ate things I shouldn't have eaten. I lost ten pounds off some sort of fish in

Thailand. Still not sure what the name is, but you can bet I remember what it looked like, going in *and* out."

"Thanks for that, Howard. That was a fantastic mental image."

"You got any sunblock? I can feel the melanoma setting in. This freckle right here's looking mighty suspicious."

I rolled my eyes and handed Howard my sunblock.

"So how are things with you and beefcake?" Howard asked, squirting at least half a cup of sunblock into his hands. He slathered it on his face, neck and arms with wild abandon.

"Good," I said. "It's easy."

"I guess this is as uncomplicated as it can be, for someone in your position," Howard said. "No secrets, no lies. Mutual understanding, and all that."

"Yeah," I admitted. "It's nice not to have to lie about who I am, and what I do."

"Not that you could have ever told the truth before," Howard said. "I mean, most people would think you were delusional if you told them half the stuff you've done."

"If they believed me, they would call the police."

"Yeah, there's that," Howard said. "Frankie tells me that we are going to be working some new pro-bono cases when we get back?"

"I have a good amount of money saved up, and I want to do some cut and dried, straight-forward missions," I said. "I need to feel like I can make a *positive* difference in the world again."

"Elayna," he said, his voice serious. "I don't know anyone who has had a bigger positive effect on the world than you."

"Thanks, Howard." I was touched, and reached out to grip his sunblock-slick hand. "That's really sweet of you to say."

"I leave you guys alone for five minutes, come back, and you're holding hands," Hyde said.

I craned my neck to look at him, and winked. Frankie was standing next to him, carrying her shoes. Even after all this time, I was still a little surprised that a hacker and computer expert could look the way she did. Frankie was gorgeous. She was Indian, about five foot three, with long thick hair that was curled into her trademark bombshell waves. She loved fashion, and was wearing a bright turquoise halter dress that contrasted with her olive skin beautifully. Numerous delicate gold bangles were stacked on both wrists so she jingled slightly when she moved, and she had topped the whole look off with a pair of enormous Chanel sunglasses that shaded her face.

I stood and hugged her.

"So glad you're here!" I said. "We are going to have so much fun!"

"Nice suit," Frankie said, hugging me back.

"I discovered shopping," I said with a grin.

"Then we really *are* going to have fun," she said. "There's not a lot of shopping to be had in Thailand street markets."

"Yeah, except for the four hundred beaded purses you bought, not to mention the thirty pounds of silver jewelry we sent back."

"He's not exaggerating," Frankie whispered, hugging me again. "That was the weight of the box I shipped home."

Chapter 8

We slipped into an easy rhythm the next few days. Every morning we met on the hotel terrace, a terracotta-tiled expanse that overlooked the marina. While the sun and gentle sea wind had a friendly battle over the temperature, we would order breakfast. Then, over bellinis and mimosas, the four of us worked on a list of cases to tackle once we got back to the States.

The inn keeper, a short, swarthy man named Signor Mancini, couldn't believe his luck. Two of his rooms were filled with people who wanted nothing more than to recline in the sun on his balcony and ring up a huge food and drink tab every morning. He was sweet and effusive in his thanks, but there was no need. He made a mean peach bellini, and his chubby wife's roasted potatoes and sausages were so good that I mentioned them to Camilla when she called one morning to check in.

"Better than mine?" she asked, trying to sound casual. I wasn't fooled; her voice had risen almost a whole octave with the question.

"Hmmm...." I said, pretending to consider.

I was spread out on a chaise lounge, a stack of files and a cold bellini on the table beside me. Hyde was watching the street, and Frankie and Howard were at a metal patio table, working.

"You're terrible," Camilla said, figuring out that I was baiting her.

I laughed. "You know no one can cook like you, Camilla. She just got so *close* that I thought it was worth mentioning."

"You're forgiven, then," she said, sounding mollified. "Are you guys coming up with any good cases for when we get back to work?"

"Too many, actually," I said. "A couple that are right in our backyard, too." I was thinking of the therapist who was raping at-risk women in San Diego, and the executive who was murdering prostitutes in Los Angeles.

"I know you are focused on pro-bono cases right now, but I'd be remiss if I didn't at least mention that our work inbox is filling up," Camilla said. "When you're ready for it, there are a lot of people who want to pay for your services."

"Send out a form email letting people know there is a three-month waiting list right now. Except for any molestation or child abuse cases. Forward those to Frankie."

"None of those on the docket right now," Camilla said. "Oh, and your mother is wanting to know when you will be back from your European buying trip."

"Tell her it will be another month." I sighed. "I'll try and call her tomorrow."

"She thinks you are holed up with a man. She thinks you are hiding a relationship from her. She keeps asking about your boyfriend that I mentioned last Christmas."

"Thanks for the warning. Where are you this morning?"

Camilla had begun the long drive back from the lake house in Canada with Bruno. We had agreed that we would all meet up back in California in a couple weeks to get to work.

"Winnipeg. I decided to do a little tour of Canada while I'm already up here. Plus, the Canadians just love Bruno. Everywhere we go, he gets spoiled with attentions."

"I miss him. I miss you," I said, feeling a little pain in my heart from being away from them for so long. "I'm glad you guys are having fun."

"Don't worry. Bruno hasn't forgotten you. In fact, he's nudging the crap out of my leg 'cause he hears your voice on the phone."

"Really?"

"You want me to put the phone up to his ear?"

"Um, sure," I said, darting a quick look at my terrace companions. They were occupied. I sat up, swung my bare legs to the side, and turned away to help hide my voice. I heard a snuffle on the other end of the line, then heavy panting that would have made any phone-perv proud.

"Hey, buddy," I crooned. "I miss you. That's a good boy."

There was a pause, then Camilla came back on the line, laughing.

"What did you say to him? He is wagging like crazy."

Camilla had to go after that, so we said our good-byes, and I turned back to the task at hand and realized that I was being watched. Howard looked incredulous, Frankie was blinking at me with her eyebrows raised, and Hyde was chuckling, still watching the street.

"What?" I asked, my voice sounding a tad more defensive than I liked.

"Were you just talking to Bruno?" Howard asked, his eyes round, his mouth open and curling into a devious grin. He looked like someone had just given him an unexpected gift.

"Keep in mind that if you make too much fun of me, I literally can kill you in your sleep," I groused.

At that, Hyde laughed out loud. He had been distracted during these meetings, leaning against the railing, peering over the balcony at the surrounding buildings, looking in windows and noting every person that walked by. He was the only one out of us who wasn't drinking. He was alert and ready, and I knew he was looking for the man in the photograph, the one following us.

"I've got access to Umberto's emails and texts," Frankie said, sitting straighter in her chair.

"How did you do that?" Howard said.

"You know how these famous people are... they claim to hate the limelight, but hunt down every story that has their name in it. I sent him a link that supposedly showed compromising pictures of him with a woman."

"Let me guess... there weren't any photos."

"There were, but they weren't of him. The link gave me access to everything on his smartphone. It seems that Umberto had a very good reason for using Elayna to try and throw the press off his trail."

"What's that?" I said.

"He's been sleeping with his younger brother Durante's new wife," Frankie said. "Apparently the brother was getting suspicious, and the wife was pressuring Umberto to find a way to draw Durante's attention away from them."

"Is there any proof of their affair?" I said.

"Loads," Frankie said. "Pictures, emails, texts, a very unfortunate video that I would like to scrub from my memory..."

"Send it all to Europe's biggest gossip magazine. Anonymously. Let them do the rest," I said.

"The nuclear option," Howard said. "Wow."

I ticked the reasons off on my fingers. "I told Umberto no and he still kissed me. He knew the press would be there... heck, he probably called them. He used a stranger to cover for his affair. He could have ruined some innocent woman's life. That jerk had no way of knowing I would have the resources to fight back."

"When you put it that way..." Howard said, "the nuclear option starts to seem downright reasonable."

"Give me half an hour," Frankie said. "I'm glad that little mystery is solved; I still have tons of backgrounds to do for our case files."

So far, as a group, we had decided on fifteen firm cases, and we had about two dozen more in the pipeline that were just too new to tell. We had to give the authorities the chance to dole out justice. We only stepped in if the system failed. Unfortunately, the system failed often enough for us to have a decent-sized list.

Michelle Yessup, the graduate student in Portland, had died a week ago. She never regained consciousness after the ambulance ride, so police were not able to get a follow-up statement from her. There was no additional evidence that her ex-boyfriend was the one who had murdered her. Frankie got her hands on internal emails between the detectives. There was one detective, Penelope Givens, who had pushed the case so hard that her boss had told her to stop.

There either is enough evidence, or there isn't, one email had read. *Until we get a new lead, or until there is new evidence to present, we have other cases we can work on. Focus on the ones you can win, Givens. The sad fact is that this case might not be one of them.*

Detective Givens had done everything right. She had worked to the very extent of the law, and had come up with nothing. She had questioned Jason Kollins so many times that he filed a harassment complaint with the department. She had subpoenaed every video surveillance camera within a three-block radius for the evening that Michelle Yessup was murdered. But the crime had taken place in a mid-rent, residential neighborhood. It wouldn't have taken much for Jason Kollins to avoid the camera at the corner liquor store and the one at the small bank tucked in between two apartment buildings.

There were no witnesses that saw anything suspicious. One neighbor reported seeing a male jogger in the area, but there was nothing strange about that. The neighbor couldn't even give a specific description, other than the fact that he had been wearing black running shorts and a grey sweatshirt. No markings, nothing distinctive. Nothing to go on, not even a definitive skin color. But someone knew what had happened to Michelle, and I was betting that person was Jason Kollins.

The problem with cases like this one was that I didn't have the evidence I needed. I hadn't been wrong yet on a case, but I wanted to keep that clean streak alive. In some cases, I was able to have Frankie hack into systems that were not available to the police, in order to get the evidence that I needed. In this case, I believed that the evidence I needed lied within a person.

Detective Givens had spoken to the first ex-girlfriend, Thalia York, by phone. Thalia lived in Minneapolis now. She had moved right after she had been released from the emergency room in Portland a couple of years earlier. She had refused to make a statement in her own case then, and she refused to help Detective Givens now. Looking at phone records, the first phone call from Detective Givens to Thalia York lasted barely five minutes. The next three phone calls went unanswered, unreturned.

Detective Givens had put in a request to buy a plane ticket to fly out and question Thalia York in person, but it had been denied. *Have a local Detective go out and ask your questions,* her Captain had written back. *If she won't talk to you on the phone, a trip out there would be a waste of time and resources.* Detective Givens made a request, but Thalia York refused to even open her apartment door to the Minneapolis Detectives.

So that was going to be one of our cases, we had all agreed. Jason Kollins was near the top of our list. He was my personal favorite, at least. I felt the familiar rush of blood thrumming through my veins as I looked at photos of his smug face. It was the precursor to contact, this feeling. It was the beginning of the dance between predator and prey. The grazing gazelle had not yet scented the lion that was crouching in the bushes. Jason Kollins' hourglass was getting close to empty, but he didn't know it yet.

I loved this part.

I looked up to find Hyde watching me as I studied photos of Kollins. He gave me a knowing smile and a wink, and returned to scanning the street. I was aware, in that moment, probably more than any other moment before, how much Hyde and I had in common. Frankie and Howard were always on the fringes of death. They contributed to the bodies I dropped. Frankie found them and covered my ass from a safe distance. In the rare event that Howard actually killed someone, the act was camouflaged in a loud noise and billowing smoke.

But Hyde and I? We knew the noise and smell and tension of a final breath. We knew the crunch of a windpipe under our thumbs. We were familiar with the stuttering failure of a pulse under our fingers, and we knew to stand back from the gush of a freshly cut throat. We were intimate with the desperation of the victim, the personal emotions that came afterwards, the inevitable letdown and depression that was the price paid for a job well done.

I didn't have to hide any of myself with Hyde. He had the capacity to understand me better than anyone I had ever known. He was the only one able to lock eyes with the deepest darkness within me without looking away. I stared at the solid line of his muscled back for long moments, trying to let that knowledge take hold deep in my heart.

"I got him," Frankie said.

"Huh?" I said. I was entrenched in my own thoughts, not paying attention.

"Flannerty," she said, squinting at her computer screen. "The idiot used his mother's maiden name on an apartment rental in Boca."

"Oh?" I said, trying to remember who Flannerty was. We had been over at least twelve cases that morning, and they were all starting to run together.

"Ha! Got his accounts, too," she said. Her nimble fingers sprinted over the keys.

"The swindler?" I asked.

William Flannerty had been an investment advisor for about thirty elderly people in Pasadena. Over and over, the story was the same. He visited retirement homes and gained his victims' trust with his honest face, pressed suit, and plain promises. He listened to their life stories, doted on pictures of their grandchildren, and lingered over decaf coffee and stale cookies.

Then he drained their accounts and disappeared.

The story hadn't gotten a lot of attention from the media. In their defense, there are lots of other newsworthy things happening in Los Angeles. It was only a month before the lead detective moved on to bloodier crimes. That had been three months ago.

"Yes. I can either contact authorities or take the money back and give it to the investors," Frankie said, brushing brown curls back from her face. "What's your pick?"

"Is most of the money still there?" Hyde asked.

"Ironically, after he stole it, he invested it. Looks like there is more than he took. He's been doing well. Maybe he should have stayed a legitimate investment advisor."

"Too late for that now," I said. "Robin Hood the money plus whatever interest back to the victims. Once that's done, contact the LA detectives and give them an anonymous tip on his address."

"With pleasure," she said, and she was busy for an hour.

Chapter 9

It was past noon when I snapped my laptop shut with a decisive click. I was in serious danger of succumbing to the inertia of the internet. My mind was starting to reel with all of the potential cases out there, and I felt the subtle tugs of depression on my psyche. These cases weren't light reading by any means. We were trolling through the stinking, murky waters of the worst of the worst, hoping to reel in the prize catch of the cesspool.

"Let's call it for the day," I announced. "Let's go do something fun."

"Lunch?" Frankie suggested, closing her laptop in agreement. "There's that place down by the water that we haven't tried."

"Yeah, I think that's the only one left that hasn't benefited from our vacation-induced alcoholism yet," Howard said, swigging back the last bit of his bellini to illustrate his point.

We carried the files and computers back to my room and locked them in the metal room safe. Then we were off down the narrow, creaking stairs and past the check-in desk and kitchen, waving at the Mancinis as we passed.

It was bright in the little street, and we donned our sunglasses. The lane was narrow, so Frankie and Howard walked in front of me and Hyde. The light reflected off the white stucco buildings and shone through the petals of the bougainvillea flowers, making them look neon pink. It was not a bad place to wear a sundress and stroll along with friends, while holding the hand of a handsome man who loved me.

I gave a little sigh of contentment, and Hyde looked down at me. His brown eyes were hidden behind sunglasses, but his eyebrow quirked up and his wide mouth stretched into a questioning smile.

"Yeah?" he asked.

"Yeah," I said, giving his large hand a little squeeze.

"It's nice here," he said. "I am starting to understand your preoccupation with Italy, I think."

"Random question time," Howard said, turning his head and speaking back at us.

Hyde groaned, and I laughed.

Frankie said, "Hey, I'm just glad that you guys are here to share in my misery. This is way better than him asking me a random question, me answering, and then listening to him pick apart my choice for twenty minutes."

Howard ignored all of us. "If you were a super-hero, what superpower would you choose?"

"Bullet-proof skin," Hyde said.

"Omniscience on the internet," Frankie said.

"You have to choose something you don't already have, Frankie." Howard sighed. "We've been over this."

"Fine, then I would choose supernatural patience to put up with these questions," she grumbled.

"Elayna?" Howard prompted.

"Crap, I don't know," I answered after a few moments. "Teleporting? Telepathy? The ability to see an individual's moral compass at a glance? Can't choose."

"Telepathy?" Howard repeated. "Worst choice, ever. Can you imagine overhearing Hyde thinking that your ass looks fat?"

"Her ass is fantastic, but you better not mention it again," Hyde said, seriously.

"What about you, Howard?" I asked, squeezing Hyde's hand again and smiling.

"Underwater breathing," he said.

"That's oddly specific," Frankie said.

"Yeah, what made you choose that?"

We were at the end of the alley, and I didn't hear Howard's answer because Hyde squeezed my hand hard. My head jerked up to look at him, and saw that his attention was focused across the street. I looked.

"I see him," I said.

Unfortunately, the man saw that we had seen him, and he began to walk, faster than a casual pace, up a different street.

"Layna, what's wrong?" Frankie had turned and was watching me.

"Hyde?" I asked, but he was already away from my side, heading across the lane of traffic, his movement punctuated by the shrill sound of a car horn.

"That's the man who we told you about," I said to Frankie and Howard. "Go get us a table at the restaurant. If we aren't there in thirty minutes, eat without us."

I could no longer see the stalker, and a second later, Hyde disappeared up the same narrow, cobblestoned street. I moved to follow at a safer pace, considering how much champagne I had consumed that morning. It occurred to me that I was experiencing the first downside to my relationship with Hyde. Instead of thinking about the target, his motivations, his actions, moves and countermoves, I was preoccupied.

I was thinking of Hyde. Rationally, I knew he was more than capable of keeping himself safe. He was sober, skilled, armed, and had been waiting for an encounter with our stalker. But here I was, fighting the welling panic in my gut, tamping down the compulsion to follow Hyde instead of cutting over a few streets and working back, like I knew was best.

I resisted the urge to protect Hyde and headed up a side street. Adrenaline and fear had cleared my head somewhat. I wasn't one hundred percent, but I wasn't that far off, either. The road I hurried up ran almost parallel to the one the target and Hyde were on, but nothing in this town was straight. The village had appeared on the hillside over time, and it was built in the age when a large boulder or tree had been enough to change the route of road.

My street seemed more modern than the rest, but it took an unexpected turn up the hill, when I was hoping it would run straight and connect to the others. I looked at the buildings separating me from the two men. There was a small pottery shop open in the row of buildings, and I ducked in and headed to the back like I owned the place. A surprised shopkeeper with grey-streaked hair just had enough time to give me a questioning glance before I was through the back and out on the other street.

Hyde was about a block up, scanning an intersection. I jogged to catch up.

"I lost him," Hyde said in a low voice. "I didn't see him at all once I got to this street."

"So he either ran, or he ducked into one of those buildings," I said, scanning the street behind us.

"Either way, I lost him," he said. He was tense, the muscles in arms pulled tight like guitar strings.

"*We* lost him," I said, rolling my eyes. "It's no wonder. He had quite the head start and knew where he was going."

"I think we should cut this short," Hyde said.

"What?" For a bizarre, earth-tilting moment, I thought he was talking about our relationship.

Hyde looked down at me quizzically. "Our time in Italy. If this guy is intent on following us, let's make him meet us on our own turf."

"I agree," I said, silently chastising myself. "I'm ready to get back to work, anyways. I'm sick of lying around, eating and drinking. Howard is right. My ass is getting fat."

Hyde gave an easy laugh. "No, it's not."

"You're biased. You're supposed to say that," I said, turning back down the street, towards the restaurant.

"I might be biased, but I'm also right."

"Did you get a better look at him?"

"You mean better than the photo we already have of him?" Hyde raised an eyebrow.

"That's not what I meant," I said.

"Nothing stuck out to me about how he moved. Just that he was fast, and he had a head start. I didn't see anything that screamed military training, or anything like that."

"I don't know if that's a good thing, or a bad thing," I said.

"Me neither."

Over lunch, the four of us went over the options again. It was a familiar conversation, well-worn like the cover of a much-read book. We had discussed all of this before.

"He can't be Italian media," Frankie was saying to Howard. "Remember, he started following them before Elayna was photographed with that Umberto guy."

"What if the first sighting was just a coincidence?" Howard argued.

"No such thing," Hyde said. "Besides, if he was media, he would be more aggressive. He'd be trying to get photographs or an interview. This guy is careful. He was waiting for us, and already had an escape route planned."

"In light of this, Hyde and I are going to cut our time in Italy short. If you guys want to keep your vacation going, that's fine, but I would recommend moving on from here," I said. "We don't know who he is, or what this is about, but I don't feel safe with any of us staying. It would be better for him to meet us back home, where we have resources."

"At your blown-up home?" Howard suggested in a sarcastic voice.

"Hey, they are supposed to start work on the new house this week," I said. "I signed off on the plans a few days ago, and they rushed the permits. I kind of thought I would camp out at the office until my house is habitable again."

The thought was a little depressing. As plush as our basement office was, it was still a basement.

"We're coming with you," Frankie stated. "We already decided to stick with you once we met up with you here. We're ready to get back to work when you are."

"Yeah. I haven't blown something up in ages," Howard said seriously. He sounded depressed.

Hyde laughed.

"Let's just keep moving the next few months on cases," I said. "Frankie, when we get back to the hotel, can you work on grouping the cases geographically, and then we will figure out our first target area? I'm thinking it probably should be the Pacific Northwest, since that is where my favorite man on the planet lives."

"Hey," Hyde protested with a smile.

"Jason Kollins?" Frankie guessed.

"Yes, sorry. That was my sarcastic voice, which sounds a lot like my regular voice," I said.

"Noted," Hyde said.

"What other cases do we have up there, does anyone remember?" I asked.

"There's that one with the nurse who was offing her patients," Howard suggested. "Felicity Werther? She's in Seattle, I think."

"Frankie, did you finish the statistical analysis on that?" I said, stabbing a plump ravioli with my fork and swirling it through cream sauce.

If this was one of the last meals I was going to have in Italy, I was going to ignore the protests of my already-full stomach and indulge my mouth by eating the whole damn thing.

"Yes, and while it isn't good enough evidence for a court of law, I am certain that she killed those people," Frankie replied, over her salad.

"How certain?" I mumbled, my mouth full.

"Deaths on her shift were four standard deviations above the mean."

"Dumb it down, please," Howard said.

"The chances of that many people dying naturally during her shifts were one in one point five million.

She's either the unluckiest nurse alive, or she was up to no good."

"That's putting it lightly," I said.

"She took a second job," Frankie continued, her volume increasing. "Even though she was financially stable, she took a second job. Neither employer was aware of each other."

"Why did she do that?" Howard asked.

"So she could kill more without getting caught," Frankie snapped. "She was smart enough to realize that someone was going to notice that people were dropping like flies if she increased her kill ratio at her first job."

"That must be a strong compulsion," I said. "To put up with more work, and all the bullshit that entails, just to kill more."

"You're one to talk," Howard quipped.

I raised my eyebrow at him.

"So where are the police on this?" I said.

"There's no *proof*," Frankie said passionately. "She was fired from her jobs, and they looked into her, but she was cleared."

"How did we get wind of this, again?" I asked. I had finished my pasta, and was considering whether I could squeeze in some tiramisu.

"I went through the state medical complaints files. They're like internal affairs for nurses," Frankie said.

"You're amazing, Frankie," I said.

"Thanks," she said, a slight flush of pleasure appearing on her cheeks.

"So what is Nurse Ratched up to these days?" Hyde asked.

"Werther moved and got a new job," Frankie said. "She's going to be working in a pediatrics intensive care unit."

"Excuse me?" I said, sitting straight up in my chair.

"She starts Monday," Frankie said.

"Fuck that shit," I said, loud enough to garner a disapproving glare from the tourists a table over. "Kollins is bumped down a notch. She's number one."

"If we leave tomorrow, that's what, five days to recon?" Hyde said.

"If we fly straight into Seattle, yes," Howard said.

"Then that's our plan," I said. "Frankie, can you get us first class? It's a long flight."

Chapter 10

It was cool when we walked back to the hotel. The sea breeze was cold and salt-scented, and I shivered. Hyde lifted an arm obligingly, and I tucked into the warmth of his side. There was someone trying to keep tabs on us here, but in this moment, I felt safe. I put away the events of the afternoon for later consideration, and snuggled closer to the sweet, lethal man who would kill or die to protect me.

The town was silent around us. Unlike the large cities that did not pay heed to the circadian rhythms of day and night, this small fishing village lived by the sun. When the sun went to bed, so did they. Even the hotel was shuttered for the evening when we returned. Our lunch had turned into dinner, and we had closed down the restaurant with our last round of limoncello. We knew that it was going to be our last night in Italy, and we had lingered in our farewell. The owner of the restaurant was glad of our business, but very happy to see us go.

The front door of the hotel was locked when we got there, but Signor Mancini had told us where to find the key hidden under the doormat. We let ourselves in. At the narrow landing at the top of the worn staircase, the four of us said our muffled goodnights.

Hyde and I knew at the same time that something wasn't quite right in our room. The lock mechanism seemed to fight against the key for a moment when I inserted it, and there was a lingering smell of stale sweat in the air when the door swung inward.

Hyde grabbed my arm. "Layna, let me go first."

I was halfway into the room already, so this required me to do an awkward shuffle back into the hallway. Howard and Frankie had gone up the stairs first, and they were already in their room. I could hear their pleasantly inebriated lack of conversation. The walls of this hotel were thin. I blocked it out, focused all of my attention on our room.

"It's clear. But our files..." Hyde said.

I went up on tiptoe to peer over his shoulder. The closet door had been left open, and the safe had been pried. Our paperwork was strewn across the bed. Still organized, I noticed. Still grouped into cases. But the last page of each case file was on top. Someone had taken the time to photograph each one, I guessed. It would have taken a while. At least ten minutes.

"Why didn't he put it back?" I asked.

Hyde was checking the safe. "It's an old safe. No way to break in without marks. He knew that we would see that someone had been in there, anyways."

"So I guess I should see it as a twisted sign of respect that he didn't even try to cover it up," I said.

"Think it's the same guy?" Hyde asked, his brow furrowed.

"I would hate to think there's more than one person after us," I said, raising an eyebrow.

"True. We are on vacation, after all."

"He get in through the door, or the window?" I wondered out loud.

Hyde was examining the door, running his fingers along the door jam.

"Door," he replied. "But no pry marks that I can see."

"A lock like that would just take an old-school pick set," I replied, stating something we both knew.

It hadn't bothered me before, the lack of security. I had found the inn charming. Maybe we should have chosen a more modern hotel, with more eyes and electronic keys. Maybe we should have left Italy the moment we knew someone was following us. Maybe I had put my team at risk just for a vacation. Maybe I was stupid, thinking that someone in my line of business could ever take time off to relax.

Hyde took gentle hold of my elbow and gave my arm a little shake.

"Whatever you're thinking, stop it," he said. "This isn't your fault."

"This couldn't be his end game," I said, sweeping my arm towards the strewn paperwork.

"No," Hyde said. "He was following us before we ever chose any of those cases."

"So it's more likely that he wanted to just gather more intel on our operation."

"Maybe," Hyde said. "Maybe he just wanted to see where we were going next."

"It makes no sense," I said, sitting on the edge of the bed. The files and papers slid towards my weight in a tiny avalanche, and I didn't care. "He has been restrained, just keeping tabs on us. What does he want? What's the point in this?"

"I don't know," Hyde said, sitting down next to me and tucking my limp hand into his strong one.

"If it was a kill contract, he would have made a move by now. It's not like our team's been on high alert, or anything. We've been lounging around on a rooftop patio for a week now. He could have taken a headshot from like five different directions."

"I was waiting for something to happen," Hyde admitted. "When nothing did, I figured that he was on a fact-finding mission, and not supposed to engage."

"Yes, but why? Who wants to know more about me?"

"I've been trying to figure that out," he said.

"It's not the government," I said. "They already know all there is to know. If they wanted to take me down, they could."

"Yeah, I'm sure there is still a copy of that video floating around, somewhere," he said.

I nodded. I had recently been coerced into killing my ex-boyfriend, a CIA agent, and it was recorded by his boss. Officially, I had been cleared by a Senate committee, but unofficially, the video was still excellent leverage.

"So, not our government," I said, ticking the list off on my fingers. "No enemies, that I'm aware of. I haven't had a mission go bad on me in the recent past, with one glaring exception. But Nathaniel's in prison, and he's not able to get any messages out."

"Couldn't see the point, even if he was able to," Hyde said. "He doesn't have any money, and no influence left with the agency."

"So, I'm stumped," I concluded.

"Me too. I thought maybe that asshole Umberto had sent someone after you, but that doesn't fit, either."

"No," I agreed. "He got what he wanted from me, which was a whole bunch of media attention. This started before him, anyways."

I sighed. This conversation was so far past stale, it fairly crunched each time we had it. I was sick of it. I resented the fact that someone had an angle that I wasn't seeing, that I was part of something that wasn't of my making. It was rare that I was the target, and I didn't like it.

"Breaking in doesn't help him, any," I said. "There are thirty different cases, here. He couldn't possibly know which ones are high priority for us."

"I'm not sure about that, Layna," he said, pulling a couple files over to him. "He will be able to tell which of the case files are the thickest. We have put more time into researching the cases that we decided would be highest priority."

I nodded. "He can't be in three different places at once. I don't think that we can let this change our plans. Well at least, I can't."

I was thinking of the pediatric ward, the sterile beds filled with tiny people fighting for their lives. Even if I had to shoot my way through a team to get to her, Felicity Werther was going to die before she touched another patient. I thought also of Thalia York and Michelle Yessup. They deserved justice, too. Their grief weighed on me, since I had the means to bring justice to Jason Kollins, the one who had taken so much from them.

Those were only the first two cases. Each file on the bed contained a deep well of pain and grief from tragedies and crimes that had already taken place. I wasn't preventing anything; I was just trying to clean up a bit afterwards. I wasn't someone who could prevent the plane from crashing into the ocean. I was the person who skimmed the debris off the surface of the water after the fact. My shoulders slumped, and I ran a hand through my wind-swept hair.

Hyde squeezed my hand. "I know."

For the first time, we didn't make love that night. Hyde held me close and we lay under a thin blanket. Our window was brazenly open to the cool sea breeze, as if to invite in the trouble that was following us so we could face it together. Neither of us slept well.

We were woken the following morning by loud thumps in the hall. Hyde was up with the door cracked to check on it before I even mumbled my complaint about the abrupt awakening.

"Stupid suitcases," I heard Howard huff. "What does she have in here... rocks?"

"Need a hand?" Hyde offered.

He stepped into the hall and shut the door behind him. I flipped back the covers and started to put myself to rights. I took Howard's struggle with Frankie's luggage as a sign that she had booked us a flight and we would be leaving soon.

I was dressed and packed before Hyde made it back into the room. He was chuckling to himself.

"You should hear the creative four-letter word mash-ups that Howard is doing over that luggage," he said.

"I can imagine."

The drive to the airport was long. We were too late booking our flight to get first class seats, so we sat in the back with the rest of the human cattle. I slept for most of the flight to JFK, but Hyde woke me up when we landed. We had forty-five minutes before our next flight, which was just enough time to grab dinner and regret our food choices. Frankie and I got limp lettuce salads, and Hyde and Howard got fried chicken sandwiches.

"Just like mama made it," Howard proclaimed after he took his first bite.

"Really?" I asked.

"Well, in theory," he said. "If I'd had a mama, and if she'd made fried chicken, it might have tasted like this."

The flight to Seattle was uneventful, which is the biggest compliment that can be paid to modern air travel. When it came time to disembark in Seattle, however, it was the same, familiar clusterfuck as always. And we were sitting in the back of the plane.

"Why don't they just sit down and wait their turn?" I said to Hyde. "It's an eighteen-inch wide aisle. There is no passing lane. We all want to get off this thing."

"I wonder if there's ever been a study done on why it takes so long to empty a plane," Frankie said, turning around in her seat to talk to me. "I mean, it has to be a psychological phenomenon, like rubber-necking at an accident."

"What?" Howard asked. "What do you mean?"

"You know, when you're on the freeway, stuck in traffic, and you can see that there is an accident on the side of the road, but it's not blocking any lanes. Everyone is pissed that they have to wait for the traffic caused by people looking. But once they get up there, they feel like they've earned time to slow down and look, too."

"My theory is that the way air security and airlines treat their passengers makes everyone revert to their baser instincts," Hyde said. "Everyone's just had their toothpaste confiscated out of their carry-on; they're on the defensive, waiting to get screwed over, so they go into 'every man for himself' mode."

"Like the guy who tried to sit in my window seat on the flight out of Milan. He had his earbuds in, and pretended not to hear me the first two times I told him he was in my seat," I said. "Usually I need extensive background information on someone to feel like doing my job. But that guy had me in the zone almost instantly."

Hyde laughed, his brown eyes crinkling.

Chapter 11

Four days later, Hyde and I were sitting in our rental car, a blue Hyundai. The ubiquitous Seattle rain tapped on the roof and spattered the windshield, producing a rhythm that threatened to lull me into a stupor. The last few days had been spent on recon and research. Hyde and I had discussed it, and decided that tonight would be Felicity Werther's last night.

We were going to wait for her to get home from her weight loss meeting, eat the pint of ice cream she bought herself afterwards as a reward, and go to sleep. Hyde would go in the back patio door while I came in through the garage, into the kitchen. We would sneak into her bedroom together.

The plan was for Hyde to hold her torso while I jabbed a syringe between her toes. We had learned from medical records that Werther had been diagnosed as pre-diabetic, so I was going to give her a huge dose of insulin. The coroner would deem it a natural death, brought on by Werther's fasting before her meeting to see the scale move, and then the huge rush of sugar from the reward ice cream, which would be the only thing in her stomach during the autopsy.

We had hours to wait. Werther had left for her meeting twenty minutes earlier and we weren't going in until midnight. Werther was plump, but blonde and pretty, which would surprise most people. I've found that most people believe, at least subconsciously, that people are consistent all the way through. But in my experience, evil souls sometimes wear the loveliest shells.

Hyde and I watched the target location. Werther lived in a charming brick house with grey shutters that was ensconced in a nice neighborhood with large lawns and double garages. It was hard to imagine that someone who lived this kind of lifestyle had any pressing reason to kill innocent strangers in their hospital beds.

"I would love to know why," Hyde said, echoing my own thoughts.

"Me too," I said. "I doubt she even knows the reason for it. There doesn't seem to be a sexual, financial, or revenge motivation to her murders. Once you have ruled out those three motivators, you have wandered into the realm of mental illness."

"So which is it for you?" Hyde teased.

"At least two of the three." I gave a cheeky wink and he laughed.

My phone buzzed where it was resting on my thigh. I swiped the screen and held it up to my ear.

"Hey, Frankie," I said, then I was cut off.

"Elayna, Jason Kollins just booked a flight to Minneapolis. He leaves in three hours, and will be there in the morning."

"Are you kidding me?" I sat forward, tense.

Hyde's eyes were sharp on me.

"No," Frankie said. "It's worse than that. He found Thalia York, was Googling information about her neighborhood."

"He got a taste of killing, and now he wants the one that got away," I said. "Shit."

"I thought you should know."

"Thanks, Frankie. Get me and Hyde on a private charter, out tonight. Maybe eleven or midnight, we could be at the airport?"

Hyde raised his eyebrows. Our timetable on the killer nurse just got pushed up by about five hours. I ended the call.

"Kollins?" he guessed.

"He's going after Thalia York in Minneapolis," I said.

"If it comes down to Werther or Kollins, who gets priority?"

"Kollins. Werther probably won't kill her first day on the job. She will most likely be on some sort of training or shadowing program for at least a few shifts. Someone will be watching her."

"Hopefully," Hyde said, echoing my own thoughts.

"Hopefully," I repeated, thinking of the children who would meet a monster tomorrow if I didn't do my job well tonight.

Suddenly, the rain no longer sounded lazy and comforting to me. It was a ticking clock, and I was on edge. I bounced my leg up and down, trying to dispel my rush of nervous energy. I hated feeling pressured for time. The missions that I'd had go wrong were those where I felt a time crunch.

"Take a deep breath," Hyde said, looking out the window towards the pretty house. "We will get them both."

"I know. I just don't want them to take anyone else with them before I get to them."

"What's the worst case you ever worked?" Hyde asked.

I knew he was trying to distract me from staring at the clock.

"A serial molester," I replied immediately. "He was a hoarder."

"You didn't think about that one too long."

"Didn't have to," I said, peering out into the rain. "I can still smell that house. I washed my hair six times before I got the odor of cat pee out of it."

Hyde winced. "Is that the only thing about it? The smell?"

"No. He heard me coming. It's very difficult to be stealthy in a house that's carpeted in trash."

"What happened?"

"He picked up the closest thing and chucked it at me. It was a bottle of pee."

"Cat pee?"

"No," I said. "His pee."

"Yuck."

"It hit me in the face and broke. I got a black eye and I had to throw all my gear away afterwards 'cause it stunk so bad."

"How did you end up finishing the job?"

"I pulled a full bookcase over on him and lit the place on fire," I said.

"That'll do it," Hyde said, smirking.

"I figure I saved some poor coroner from having to dig through that rubble to get the body out," I said. "Believe me, the fire made a huge improvement to that house."

"I don't doubt it," Hyde said.

"What about your worst case?"

"I had the flu."

"You hate puking," I said with a smile.

"That wasn't it," Hyde said. "I was all ready, but got sick for a few days. He got someone else while I was laid up watching MASH reruns."

I nodded in understanding. "I've had that happen. Had a list running, and he was number three. Didn't get to him before he got to my client."

"Took me a long time to get over that one," Hyde said. "I had to keep reminding myself that I couldn't control everything. That it wasn't my fault. Bad people do bad things, and even though there are lots of systems and safeguards in place, sometimes they get away with it."

Hyde's features were lit dimly by the streetlight up the block. I turned to study his face.

"In your mind, is what we do one of the systems or safeguards?" I asked.

"Of course."

"That's not how I see it, actually. I think of what we do as above and apart from the conventional justice system," I said.

"It's more of a symbiotic relationship than you would admit," Hyde said.

"How do you figure?"

"Think about it. You let the cops have first dibs on every case we do. If you can, you send in confidential information to help them along. You use them, and in some ways, they use you, too."

"They don't even know I exist," I argued.

"Yes, but that doesn't mean they don't benefit from you removing some of the worst criminals from the playing board."

"I doubt anyone notices at all, actually," I said.

"You're kidding, right?" Hyde twisted in his seat to face me.

"Asking if people notice the absence of crimes that would have been committed is like the whole tree-falling-in-the-forest-when-nobody's-around question. There's no way to know," I said.

"You don't even believe that, yourself," Hyde said. "You know that what you do matters. If you didn't think it did, you wouldn't be so stressed about getting to Werther before she gets to those kids."

"I do think it is important," I admitted. "I just don't think anyone notices. And I don't think that I am some invisible arm of the same legal system that fails so often."

"That's the hard part of that thought for you, isn't it? The failure part?"

"Maybe," I said, shrugging.

"You put so much pressure on yourself to be perfect, to be above and beyond law enforcement. The truth is, you are a human, just like them. You are trying your best, but you make the occasional mistake, just like them. The only difference is that they have to work within the law, and you have the dangerous freedom of working outside the law."

I thought for long moments about his statement. Then I decided to ask about the easiest thing he had said.

"What do you mean, a *dangerous* freedom?" I asked.

"Well, think about it. You're breaking the law, just like all the people in your case files that we're going to visit," he said.

"I like the way you say 'visit', like we're going to drop in for tea or something."

"My point is, the only thing that separates you from the people you kill is your morals, your code of conduct," he said.

"So first I'm like law enforcement, and now I'm the same as the people I kill?"

"We are all the same, Layna," Hyde said with a smile. "We are all human. It's our choices that are important. Choices are the only thing that determine what side of the prison bars a person's on."

"Here's where I have a problem with that argument," I said. "Because, according to you, I'm morally good. But according to the law, I should be in prison, or put to death."

"Laws aren't written according to morality," he said. "They are written around what is socially acceptable."

"Because morality is subjective."

Hyde frowned. "Some people would argue that, yes."

"You don't think so?" I asked.

"No, I don't," he said. "I think that what is morally right always stays the same. But laws have to be written as blanket statements. That's the nature of the law. Laws can't take into account all the details that you can. Laws have to be impersonal. Most of the time, the legal system does strain the crap out of society."

"Blind justice," I said.

"Exactly. The people who are tasked with upholding the law can't turn around and break the law to uphold the morality behind the law. It would be chaos."

"So that's where we come in."

"Yes. That's where we come in," Hyde said, smiling.

I sat for long moments thinking about what Hyde had said. He took a very 'we're all in this together' approach towards law enforcement and society, which surprised me. I had always looked at the legal system as nothing more than a net with gaping holes.

And society? I had never considered myself part of it, not really.

But with Hyde's words, I found my thoughts slightly shifted, altered. Just a half-click from where it used to be, like my worldview had seen a chiropractor. I was surprised what a difference it made, that small adjustment.

"So what you're saying is that I need to cut myself some slack," I said. "You're saying that I'm not the final line of defense."

"I think it would be very good for you to stop expecting perfection from yourself. You are human," Hyde said.

"I'm well aware of that," I said.

"Like this guy that's following us. I know it bothers you that you didn't see that coming, that you don't know what his motives are. It bothers me, too, but in a different way. I don't expect to know his motivations until he reveals them, whereas you seem to be thoroughly pissed off that you aren't omniscient."

I laughed.

Our conversation was cut short by Felicity Werther turning the corner in her navy Volkswagen SUV.

"I always thought those were cute cars," I said, watching her wait in the driveway for the garage door to open.

"So, we're going in early?" Hyde asked.

"Earlier than I would have liked," I agreed. "This might be a smidge more violent than planned. We'll wait until she is in bed, but there is no guarantee that she will be asleep."

"No registered firearms," Hyde said, nodding.

"Yep. And for being a murdering bitch, she sure does follow all the other laws."

"It's a perfect cover. I mean, look at this place, her life. Who would think that she could be what she is?"

"Yep," I agreed. "Who woulda thunk it?"

I put a call in to Frankie.

"She's home. Can you check her credit card, see if she made the regular purchase?"

I heard the rhythmic tapping of the keyboard, sounds that I always associated with Frankie.

"Yep," she replied. "Same amount, six twenty-three. Same as last week, and the weeks before. I got bored earlier, hacked into the store security feed. She buys a pint of cherry ice cream every week."

"Cherry?" I said. "Blech. That's the only flavor of ice cream I hate."

"See?" Frankie said. "This kill was meant to be."

I laughed. "Bye, Frankie."

While I had been on the phone with Frankie, Hyde was getting his thermo device out. It was on now, pointed at the house. I smiled. Hyde loved this toy. It was the newest version, capable of zooming in from a remarkable distance. He held it up to his eyes and fiddled with the controls on the side.

"There she is, sitting on the couch. She's eating right from the carton; I can see the cold signature," he said.

He sounded reproachful.

"Of course she's eating from the carton," I said. "She's alone."

He turned to look at me, eyebrows raised. "You eat ice cream from the carton if you're alone?"

"Yes. And I would do it in front of you, too. Loud and proud, babe."

"I guess that means the honeymoon's over," he said.

"Don't you dare start farting in front of me."

He laughed, but it sounded a little evil to me. I gave him the side-eye, which he couldn't see. He had turned back to watch Felicity.

We waited, but not for as long as I thought. It was already eight-thirty. Werther seemed to be calling it an early night, probably because her shift started at six in the morning.

"She's up from the couch," Hyde said, then paused. "In the kitchen, throwing away the ice cream...she only ate half, must have learned something at that meeting, after all."

I listened to Hyde narrate Werther's movements: turning off lights, then into the bathroom, brushing her teeth, undressing and then putting on pajamas in the bedroom. The thermal device was sensitive enough for Hyde to see the heat dissipate from her shed clothes.

"Good enough for you?" Hyde said. "We need to get moving if we are going to make our flight."

"Yeah," I said. "Let's go."

Chapter 12

Hyde and I separated at the front of the car. He went towards the back, slinking like a large shadow through the rain. I walked on the sidewalk until I was in front of her house. Then I took a quick glance around. The neighborhood was quiet, only a few lights on in the house across the street. I wasn't worried. People didn't buy houses like this if they liked the outdoors that much. And these weren't the type of people who sat on front porches in the evening, especially not when it was raining.

I walked up to the garage like I owned the place, or like I was an expected guest. So much suspicion can be avoided by acting normal. People notice people who dart about, peer into windows or otherwise act strangely, but ignore those who act like they are supposed to be somewhere.

I was on the side of the house now. I pulled out my trusty lock pick set, and the builder-grade lock in the side door gave way easily. I opened the door silently, then I was in the garage and shutting the door behind me with barely a dull click. The dark garage was filled with the smell and slight warmth of the Volkswagen SUV. It was otherwise empty, except for a wheeled trash can at the far end.

Two steps took me to the door that led from the garage into the kitchen. I ran through the plan again in my mind. Hyde and I were to meet in the hallway outside of Werther's bedroom. I would unsheath the syringe there, and then we would go in together. I took a deep breath and set to work on the door's lock. Frankie had already hacked the alarm system. It would act and look normal to Felicity, but it wouldn't transmit or set off for the next ten hours.

A few deft, silent movements later, and the door was unlocked. I turned the knob quietly and stepped through the door.

And came face to face with Felicity Werther.

She froze at the trash can, a spoon in one hand, the half-finished pint of cherry ice cream in the other. The next detail that my brain registered was that she was wearing pink flannel pajamas with bulbous clouds on them. Her mouth and green eyes were so round in their shock they were almost cartoonish. It was hard to say which of us was more surprised.

The old adage is true, that in a stressful, life or death situation, you don't rise to the occasion, you fall back on your training. And I was the one who had training. Right as she took a sharp inhale, presumably to scream, I bum-rushed her. I could have had her dead on the floor in three seconds, but Hyde and I were trying to avoid a murder investigation. I needed to subdue her without leaving suspicious marks or bruises.

I clapped my left hand over her mouth, muffling her scream, stepped behind her, and encircled my other arm around her waist, pinning her right arm to her body. Her left hand was still free, and she swung wildly up and back, and connected with my face. I exhaled sharply to express my pain, and tried to wrestle her to the ground. Her fight wasn't coordinated, but she was motivated and not a small person. Plus, she was trying to bite me.

"Hyde," I called in a conversational tone, hoping he had made his entrance. "A little help here."

Felicity and I swung around, staggering like two drunks trying to keep each other upright. As we careened near the stove, Werther managed to grab a blue teakettle with her flailing left arm and proceeded to land several poorly aimed blows to my face and head. Cold water sloshed everywhere, and I focused on her feet, finally tripping her, but not quite bringing her down. She got her feet under her again and tried to wrench free of my hold. She moaned and squealed, but because my hand was still securely over her mouth, it wasn't enough to wake the neighbors.

Hyde appeared in the doorway, and I couldn't tell if he was concerned for me, or amused by the flailing teapot aimed in my direction. After a half-second's assessment, he stepped forward and grabbed her legs, first one, then the other. Werther was suspended between the two of us, bucking her legs in and out, bringing me and Hyde incrementally closer and then further away. She was still waving the teapot valiantly. It was all I could do not to laugh.

This was exactly the wrong arrangement we were supposed to be in, on so many levels. Both my hands were occupied, and I had the insulin syringe. I couldn't get to her toes to inject her. Plus, Werther had succeeded in biting me through my glove, and I was pretty sure that I was bleeding into her mouth.

"Well, this is ridiculous," I said.

"On three, we put her down," Hyde said.

He counted off, and we sat her down on her rump. I settled behind her, and wound my legs around her torso. Hyde let go of her legs and stood, receiving a vicious but poorly aimed kick towards his crotch.

"Where is it?" Hyde asked, sliding over toward me.

Werther struck out with the teapot again, but Hyde caught her arm and brought it back in towards her chest, pinning it down. She whimpered against my bleeding hand.

"Left pocket," I said.

He reached in, found it, deftly uncapped the syringe, and slid back over towards her feet. This released Werther's left arm again, and she landed several more blows to my head. She seemed to have improved her trajectory, and I grunted in acknowledgement of the fresh ringing in my skull. She was also kicking Hyde in the face with her one free leg. For someone who loved to inflict death, she wasn't too keen on experiencing it for herself.

I felt the small jerk of her body when Hyde stuck the needle between her toes. She struggled for long moments, then slumped. I held her mouth until I no longer felt the heat of her breath coming from her nose. Then I released the body, slid back and rested against a cabinet. Hyde did the same.

"That was the perfect illustration about me being human," I said, gasping. "That was very imperfect."

That seemed enough conversation for many moments. We were both working to control our breathing, waiting for the adrenaline to recede a bit. My hand was bleeding, and I was careful to press the wound into my pants so it wouldn't drip anywhere. I was going to have at least a black eye from the stupid teakettle, and possibly much more facial bruising than that.

"Why did she brush her teeth if she still wanted ice cream?" Hyde asked.

I thought this was an odd place to start the conversation, considering the freshly cooling corpse between us.

"I think it's supposed to be a diversion," I said.

"What?"

"Like, it is supposed to stop you from eating anymore, since you already brushed your teeth."

"Well, it wasn't a very effective tactic."

"No. She should have poured dish soap on it."

"How do you know about this stuff?" Hyde asked.

"One of my targets was a weight loss instructor," I said with a shrug. "I had to sit through a meeting or two to get her alone. Why do you ask?"

"Just wondering if you used to be, you know, fat."

I stood up. I'd had enough of a breather, and our night was far from over. Hyde rose with me.

"Would that be a problem, me being fat?"

"No, there'd be more of you to love," he said, grabbing my butt with his whole hand and squeezing.

"Ew, stop," I said, swatting his hand away.

"More cushion for the pushin'," he elaborated.

"Hyde! You're grossing me out," I said. "Now help me move this dead body."

He laughed. "You have an odd sense of what grosses you out."

"I just don't ever want my weight to be an issue, that's all."

"Stop eating ice cream from the container, then."

"You're not the boss of me."

Hyde chuckled.

Without much discussion, we fell into an easy rhythm of staging the body. I pulled a bandage from my fanny pack and wound it around my injured hand. Fanny packs are a horrifying fashion choice, but very effective in a tactical situation. I stripped off Werther's pajamas, which had some of my blood on them. Hyde wiped up the water and melted ice cream from the floor and counters. He scrubbed the teakettle in the sink, refilled it, and set it back on the stove.

From my pack, I took out several alcohol wipes and worked on Werther's mouth. Some of my blood was visible between her teeth. I wiped as well as I could. I could not guarantee that some of my DNA wasn't in her mouth, but at least there wasn't any visible blood when I was finished. If they ran my DNA, it wouldn't be in any of the search databases, and I could always have Frankie go into the files and corrupt that information later.

I went to the bedroom and got a new set of pajamas. Hyde and I dressed Werther's body in flannel purple pajamas with white fluffy bunnies all over them.

"I do not understand this woman," Hyde said, shaking his head. "Daytime murdering innocents, nights in cartoon PJ's. Makes no sense to me."

"Who knows?"

"Her hair's a bit wet," Hyde pointed out.

"It will dry by the time anyone finds her," I said. "As long as it's just water, it will be fine."

We tucked the body into six-hundred thread count sheets, checked the kitchen again, locked the doors behind us, and left with a plastic bag full of evidence that would have pointed towards foul play.

"I think that you should keep those pajamas," Hyde said as we were getting back into our car.

"Like as a trophy?" I asked, holding up the visqueen bag and looking at the contents. "That's never been my thing."

"No, I mean, to wear," Hyde said, smirking.

"You think flannel pink cloud pajamas would be a good look on me, huh? Think that's my style?"

"I think you could make anything look good," he said, turning the key in the ignition.

"Nice recovery. But then again, screw you for thinking these would even fit me," I said.

Chapter 13

On the drive to the airport, I called Frankie and filled her in on the situation.

"Frankie says that she will take care of any DNA they find," I said to Hyde after I hung up. "She says that she will change the orders in the computer for any samples, try and have them destroyed by the lab before they are even tested."

"She is worth her weight in gold," he said.

"Yes, she is."

"How are you going to go about the Kollins case?" he asked.

I folded my arms across my chest and looked out at the traffic and the rain.

"I still feel like I need to at least try and talk to Thalia York," I said. "This is the most uncertain case I have worked in a while. Kollins is too arrogant to confess. I mean, he is trying to sue that detective, Givens. Most guilty targets would lie low, but he is too cocky."

"What are you going to tell her?" Hyde asked.

"I don't know," I said. "I don't have any time to build a rapport with her. I thought about just telling her the truth."

I expected Hyde to have a vehement reaction, but he nodded.

"I think that in this case, it might work," he said. "Thalia seems to have no trust in law enforcement. She's probably not going to run to them with a crazy-sounding story."

"That's what I thought," I said, gratified that he understood my reasons, that he didn't dismiss the idea without thinking about it.

"And more than that," Hyde said, long moments later. "After what she's been through, she might be open to the idea of someone killing him."

"I thought about that, too," I murmured, looking out again, towards the dark.

Frankie had arranged for us to have dinner on the flight. A cranky stewardess served us overcooked steak and a limp salad and then slumped in the chair farthest from us and started texting on her phone. Hyde and I didn't care. We ate and then reclined in the seats. We were both asleep fifteen minutes after takeoff. The landing in Minneapolis woke us. I was stiff from sleeping for a few hours in a chair, and my eyes had sleep crusties in the corners. In short, I felt disgusting.

A rental car representative was waiting for us at the airport to hand over the keys to yet another nondescript sedan. We checked into a mid-price hotel close to Thalia York's apartment, set our alarms, showered, and slept another few hours. Hyde woke me the next morning before my alarm went off. I forgave him because he had brought me hot coffee and a chocolate croissant.

"What's the plan for the day?" he asked, sitting on the bed across from me.

"I was thinking that we would get into Thalia's neighborhood as soon as possible, try and get a feel for where the cameras are, different routes, stuff like that," I said. "Frankie sent me Thalia's schedule, and she worked until five this morning. She's going to be sleeping for awhile, but Frankie is tracking her with her cell phone. I told her to let us know if she makes any unexpected moves. Frankie's also going to let us know when there is activity on the phone. I want to be there pretty soon after she wakes up."

Hyde looked at the clock. "Kollins is due in at ten, right?"

"Yes," I said. "I think that you should meet him at the airport and tail him from there. I will go meet with Thalia at about the same time. Hopefully, I won't have to wake her up."

I rubbed my jaw. It was tender, due to repeated contact with a metal teakettle the night before. Hyde winced.

"How bad is it?" I asked.

My face had only been pink last night, but this morning, I could feel that my one eye was a bit puffy.

"Hope you brought makeup," Hyde said, taking a sip of his coffee.

"That doesn't sound good," I said, then shrugged. "Oh well. I will take a bruised face over leaving the Werther case open while we work this one. I'm glad the fate of a pediatric ward isn't hanging over us while we are tracking Kollins."

"Me too," Hyde said.

We walked the next few hours, sometimes separately, sometimes together, trying to get a feel for the neighborhood. It was a cute area, with a coffee shop, a Cuban restaurant, and a small grocer's on the corner. It was also pretty standard, in terms of layout. The ten block radius surrounding Thalia's apartment was an orderly grid of streets with apartment buildings. There were alleys running along the back of buildings with reeking dumpsters and a couple of sleeping homeless men. A small park punctuated the east side of our grid, but other than that, it was all buildings.

At nine-thirty, we were back at the hotel. Hyde gave me a quick peck on the cheek before getting into the rental car and heading toward the airport. He planned on meeting up with Kollins at the baggage claim. Frankie informed us that Kollins had checked two suitcases. The baggage claim is a perfect place to start a tail. It's outside of security, and the subject is stationary for a few minutes and focused on getting their bags off the carousel. It's long enough to find them in a crowd.

At ten-thirty, Frankie called me.

"Thalia York just called for take-out," she said.

"What place delivers at ten-thirty in the morning?" I asked, curious.

"A diner called Carl's. They're twenty-four hour," she said.

"Thanks. I'll head over. Anything new with Hyde?"

"Kollins landed about twenty-minutes late, but he just turned on his cell. He is headed right towards Hyde at the baggage claim," Frankie said.

"You're the best," I said, and hung up.

Thalia's apartment building was one of the smaller ones. The facade was new brick, the shape unapologetically rectangle with no decorative design elements, but the doors had heavy locks, and you had to be buzzed up by a resident if you didn't have a key card. Luckily, I did have a key card, but mine was issued by Frankie, not the building's management. I climbed the thinly-carpeted stairs instead of using the elevator. People sometimes expect to make small talk in elevators, but no one wants to talk to strangers in a stairwell. There were no hanging pictures, but the overhead lights left no corner in shadow. I didn't think that Thalia had chosen this place for its ambiance.

I knocked on the door of 3C, and heard rustling and footsteps inside the apartment. I had carefully applied makeup to cover the bruises on my eye and jawbone, and I had left my hair down. I knew that what Thalia would see through her peephole was a non-threatening blonde lady with a hopeful smile. I heard the snap of multiple locks being thrown back, and then she cracked the door open.

"Hi. Can I help you?" she asked.

Thalia was polite, but cautious. Her thick brown hair had grown out since she had taken her ID photo at work. That was the most recent photo we had of her. Her clear, intelligent eyes were hazel, and were currently narrowed at me from behind a heavy fringe of eyelashes. No makeup, I noticed. She was a natural stunner. She was barefoot and her toes were painted a pale pink. She was wearing faded jeans and a soft Georgetown t-shirt. This was the uniform of someone on their day off.

"My name is Penelope Marsh," I said, pulling that name out of the air. "I'm Mrs. Benson's niece. She lives one floor up, in 4D? She broke her hip on the stairs and is moving into a rest home?"

"Oh yeah, I did hear something about that," Thalia said, opening the door wider.

Bless Frankie and her research, I thought.

"Anyways, I was supposed to meet Mr. Lucas, her neighbor, because he has a key. I was going to start packing up her things. The moving truck is coming tomorrow. Mr. Lucas isn't answering the door, and my cell phone is dead, and no one seems to be home," I slumped my shoulders a bit for effect, tried to look pathetic.

"You're welcome to use my phone," she offered.

"Oh, thank you so much!" I said, rewarding her with my best smile.

She opened the door, and I stepped in. Thalia York's apartment was small, but light and bright. A vintage pedestal table and four mismatched dining chairs had all been painted the same butter yellow. Beyond that, in the small living room, an over-stuffed grey couch faced two armchairs that were upholstered in a floral chintz. The only sign that things weren't maybe as blissful as they seemed were the four large deadbolts in the steel security door.

"Tea?" she said, closing the door behind me. "I was just heating myself some."

"Yes, please," I said. I noted the delivery bag sitting on top in the trash. She had already eaten, then. That was good; it wouldn't do to have her faint with shock and hunger when she heard what I had to say.

"Sit," she offered, gesturing towards the living room.

I sat down on her plush grey sofa, and a chubby white cat came to curl up next to me.

"That's Jasmine," Thalia said distractedly. "Sorry, but she's going to get hair all over you."

"That's fine," I said, petting behind the cat's ears. Her answering purring was loud in the small space.

"I'm so sorry about what happened to Mrs. Benson," Thalia said, handing me a steaming mug.

"That's alright," I said, taking a huge chance. "I don't actually know her at all. I lied to you."

Her body jerked, then she froze, staring at me with round eyes.

"Uh..." she said, her eyes flickering to her cell phone on the counter.

I crossed my legs, clutched my tea with both hands, and sat back into the couch, trying to look as nonthreatening as possible. Jasmine the cat kept rubbing her head against my thigh.

"I'm not going to hurt you, Thalia. I'm here to help you, actually."

She retrieved her cell phone and set it on the white-painted table by the armchair across from the sofa. Then she perched on the edge of the chair and looked at me.

"I believe that you aren't going to hurt me," she said, sounding surprised at her own statement. "How do you know my name? Why are you here?"

"I'm sorry I lied. I don't mean to scare you. Like I said, I'm here to help you."

"What do you mean?" Her eyebrows were drawn together in concentration.

"Do you like Minneapolis?" I asked, tilting my head to the side.

"I do," she said, gripping her teacup. "It's a big city, but it still feels small. It's not too anonymous, and it has character. I know most of my neighbors. What does this have to do with anything?"

"I was just wondering what made you pick Minneapolis when you moved out from Portland," I said.

She stiffened in her chair; her eyes met mine. "You're a detective."

I didn't contradict her. I just shrugged.

"You're here because of why I left," she said.

It was a statement, not a question.

"Yes," I said. "I'm here to help you. I'm here to make sure you're safe."

"I'm safe here," she said, eyes flicking to the dead-bolts that she hadn't locked behind us. "I've been here for almost three years without so much as a phone call from him."

I was relieved she wasn't going to lie to me, at least not about everything.

"Look," she continued. "I was so sorry to hear about what happened to that poor girl in Portland."

She paused for a moment to compose herself, her lips pressed together, her foot tapping an erratic rhythm on the floor.

"Her name was Michelle Yessup," I offered, taking a sip of my tea.

"I know," she said desperately, tears welling in her eyes. "When that detective called me, I asked her. I asked her if my testimony about what happened to me would be enough to put him away for Michelle's murder. She told me that it wasn't, but that it might help."

Her damp eyes met mine, pleading.

She continued, "But if they had enough of a case to convict him, they wouldn't need my testimony at all. And to put myself out there for nothing, to bring his attention back to me when I'm just starting to feel normal again... I can't do it."

"I understand that," I said. "But what if your testimony *was* enough?"

"Detective Givens said it wasn't enough," she said, swiping away the tears that escaped her rapid blinks as fast as they appeared on her cheeks.

"I'm not a detective," I said. "The work I do is more freelance."

"Like a private investigator?"

"Sort of, but my services are unique."

"So how could my testimony help?"

"I don't need you to testify," I said. "I just need you to answer my questions honestly, and I will take care of the rest."

"What good will that do?" Thalia asked, sniffling. "It's behind me. I've put what happened behind me."

I took a deep breath. I didn't want to say the words. I could imagine the terror they would inspire, and I knew that I would put Jason Kollins in the ground before he hurt Thalia ever again. But I also needed the information that she had.

"Part of the reason I am here right now is because yesterday, Jason Kollins bought a ticket to Minneapolis," I said.

I was looking her in the eye when I said it, so I saw the exact instant her composure broke. I saw her eyes squeeze shut against the knowledge, saw her face crumple, saw her bow forward slightly at the waist and wrap her arms around her midsection.

"He's here?" she gasped. "He's coming for me?"

"He landed about a half an hour ago," I said. "I was able to get information off his computer that shows he tracked you down. He has your address."

Her eyes flickered toward the door, and she launched herself towards the deadbolts, locking them in succession while she sobbed and leaned against the door. I joined her at the door and guided her back to her chair, rubbing her back.

"I'm sorry," I murmured. "Please believe I am going to help you."

"How can you help?" she said. "How can you stop him? The police can't."

I sat on her coffee table, our knees almost touching. I met her eyes.

"I need you to answer my questions honestly. Then I will help you. I will protect you. I promise he will never hurt you again."

"Alright," she said, looking towards the door. She shuddered. "Alright."

"First, do you think he murdered Michelle Yessup?" I asked.

"I know he did," she said, her voice gathering strength with anger. She met my eyes defiantly, as if daring me to argue.

"How do you know?"

"He was in my house when I got home after work that night. We struggled, and I hit him. He threatened to kill me. Said he was going to stab me so many times that no one was going to recognize my face. He told me that I was going to have a closed-casket funeral, that they would have to use dental records to identify me."

"So why didn't he kill you?" I asked.

Her face turned up towards mine, and I saw her fury. She began to shake.

"I saw that he meant it. I knew he would do it. He had the knife. I wanted to live," she gritted out. "So I told him that I was wrong, that I had made a mistake, that I wanted him back."

I reached forward and clasped her shaking hands with mine. They trembled like captured animals in my grip.

Thalia continued, "That's when he began hitting me. Every time he hit me, I would repeat that I wanted him back, that I was so sorry, that I didn't know before then how much he loved me."

She sobbed, and I rubbed her shoulder, my eyes pricking with unshed tears.

"Then, after he was done beating me, we had sex," she said. "That was the worst part, even though he was so gentle. That hurt the worst."

"Thalia, you didn't have sex with him," I said softly. "He raped you."

"I didn't say no," she said. "I knew he would kill me if I said no."

"You didn't want to do it," I said. "That was rape, not sex."

She nodded, her eyes squeezed shut against the memory. "He had a knife with him the whole time, even while... I knew he had come planning to use it. I was willing to do anything to survive, to live."

"You survived," I said. "That's the important thing."

"I guess," she murmured, shrugging. She didn't sound convinced. Her eyes slid to the locks on the door again. In the small silence that ensued, I glanced around the apartment once more. The bright colors and floral chintz suddenly made sense to me; these bright surroundings were Thalia's way of trying to banish the darkness of her past. This was her safe space, and I had just tainted it, ruined it with my words.

"Why didn't you testify when it happened?"

"I asked the detective who came to see me in the hospital," she said. "He told me that the maximum sentence for aggravated assault was ten years. Since Jason had no prior record and wasn't considered a flight risk, he would most likely only get a couple years in prison, if any, and then would be released on probation. But since at the beginning of the attack I had fought back, Jason got a bruise on his face. His lawyer would argue mutual combat, self-defense, and he would probably just get probation. I thought if I could just get away without making him angrier, then maybe he would leave me alone."

Tears were streaming down her face.

"This isn't your fault," I said. "None of this is your fault."

"Michelle Yessup is sort of my fault, though, isn't she?" Thalia said, her face bleak. "Maybe if Jason would have been on probation, she wouldn't have dated him. Maybe his probation officer would have seen who he really was, and had him locked up or something."

"No," I repeated. "None of this is your fault."

"So what are you going to do to protect me?" she asked.

I looked straight into her red eyes. "Is it alright with you if I kill him?"

"Yes," she said, relief flooding her face, hope smoothing her features. "Oh my goodness, yes."

Chapter 14

We baked brownies and waited. After I had given her a broad-strokes explanation, there didn't seem to be a lot to say. Thalia didn't want to talk, but she definitely didn't want to be alone.

"Do you have any vanilla ice cream?" I asked when the brownies came out of the oven. "And some Irish cream?"

"I see where you are going with the ice cream, but I'm curious to see what you're going to do with the Irish cream," she said, pulling a small bottle down from the cupboard above her fridge.

"You put the ice cream on a brownie, then pour a shot of Irish cream over the whole thing. Best dessert, ever," I said.

While we waited for Hyde's phone call, we watched reality television and ate the whole pan. I skipped the alcohol in order to keep my senses sharp, but Thalia topped her brownie sundae with copious amounts of Irish cream and chased that with two large glasses of wine.

"You know I don't even feel guilty about that," she said. "If any situation calls for tons of sugar and booze, it's your crazy ex-boyfriend coming to kill you."

Thalia laughed at her own joke, and I watched her out of the corner of my eye, trying to figure out if she was cracking under the stress. But there was color on her cheeks and light in her eyes that hadn't been there before. It was like finally talking about what had happened to her had leached some kind of poison from her veins. Or maybe it was the knowledge that, one way or another, her nightmare would be over soon.

She turned to me abruptly. "You're really going to kill him, right? You're not making that up?"

"No, I'm not making it up," I said.

"I didn't know her parents had that kind of money," she said. "At least, the papers never said anything about them being rich."

"They aren't the ones I'm working for," I said. "Past that, it's best if you don't ask me any more questions like that. It's best if you don't know."

My phone rang, and it was Frankie.

"Hyde's on him," she said. "He's on the move, close to Thalia's apartment."

"I'll call you back in a minute," I said.

When I looked up at Thalia, she was pale again, her hazel eyes wide.

"I have to go," I said, standing. "Thanks for the brownies."

Thalia clutched my arm. "What if you don't get him? What if he gets you, instead, and then comes for me?"

"He won't," I said. "He kills for fun, and I don't. I hope I don't have to tell you this, but if anyone comes and asks you about his death..."

"I don't know anything," she said, her face set in stubborn lines, her chin lifted. "Trust me, I'm good at not answering questions."

"I know," I said. "There won't be many questions. Local police might not even make the connection, and no one will be sorry to see him dead. I'll come to see you when it's done. Until then, keep your door locked. Bake more brownies."

I met with Hyde four blocks away from Thalia's apartment. He was skulking in the shadows near the mouth of an alley, leaning against the brick wall. To any casual observer, it looked like he had just stopped for a smoke, a lit cigarette was poised between two fingers. But Hyde didn't smoke, and I could tell where Jason Kollins was based on where Hyde was glancing every few moments.

"Babe," I said by way of greeting, kissing him full on the mouth.

He embraced me back and used the chance to whisper into my ear.

"He's just getting started, walking around the neighborhood, taking note of any place that might have a camera. He's good at avoiding them."

"Right," I said. "So this is his night for recon. He most likely won't go after her tonight."

"He already passed by her street twice," he said. "He paused both times, but I don't think he will let himself go there, not tonight. He's disciplined, but I could have had him three times over already."

"Thanks for your restraint," I said. "I want my voice to be the last thing he hears."

"So you're going to have a talk with him first?" he said.

"I want him to have time to be afraid," I said. "I was thinking a paralytic to start."

Hyde met my eyes. "Are you going to slice and dice this guy, or what?"

"No, nothing like that. I just want a minute to talk to him. For some reason, I want him to know why he is dying. I don't want him to think it's a mugging. I want him to know that this is for Michelle and Thalia."

"I get it," he said, his voice low. "But if it's not going to be quick and dirty, I want to go with you, as backup."

"Of course," I said, surprised that he would even need to ask. "I always thought you'd come with me."

He relaxed a bit. "Were you thinking of doing it tonight, or tomorrow?"

"Thalia is scared half out of her mind, which is understandable, considering what that fucker did to her," I said. "I want this over tonight, if possible."

"If we don't get a clean shot tonight, I can watch him until tomorrow night," Hyde said. "This guy is smarter than our average quarry. I want to do this safe."

"He may be smart, but he is still crazy," I said. "And crazy always clouds judgement."

"He's walking again," Hyde said. "Let's move."

So we followed him at a distance, arms looped around each other, looking like one of those couples disgruntled singles hate.

"How did Thalia take it?" Hyde asked.

"Like a trooper," I said. "She just wants this over. To be honest, I thought I would have to work harder to convince her I wasn't full of shit."

"When you talk about death, when you're serious, it's very plain on your face."

I thought about that for awhile. The night grew steadily cooler, our breath became visible, people became scarcer on the street, and still Jason Kollins walked back and forth, up and down, around and around.

"He's really getting on my nerves," I said.

"He needs to know the neighborhood as well as he knew Michelle Jessup's neighborhood."

"I know, but the longer he's out here, the better the chance he will see us more than once," I said. "Plus, I'm cold."

Hyde grinned. "He hasn't seen us once yet. Buck up, it's not that cold."

"He's working a grid," I said. "Let's let him do the next street alone, and catch him when he comes back."

"Sounds good," Hyde said, watching the retreating form of Kollins as he turned a corner.

My phone vibrated in my pocket, and I frowned. It was Frankie, and she knew we were busy.

"Hello?" I said.

"Layna, I don't think you guys are the only ones after this guy," she said, breathless.

"What are you talking about?"

"That detective from Seattle, Penelope Givens, was tracking Kollins' credit card payments, and she bought a ticket out here, too. She's out here, and on her own dime. And she checked a pistol."

"She was told to let this case go," I said, the hair standing up on my arms.

"Maybe she couldn't," Frankie said. "All I know is that she is risking her career, disobeying orders. I don't know that she would do that just to talk to this guy. She knows she doesn't have the evidence, and he made that complaint against her already."

"She's going to kill him," I said.

"Yes, I think that might be why she's here. She's booked on the first flight out in the morning. If she's going to do it, it's going to be tonight."

"Thanks, Frankie." I hung up. "We gotta move, Hyde. We're not the only ones stalking him."

"Who?" Hyde said, falling into a quick stride beside me.

"Detective Penelope Givens," I said. "She's just here for the night..."

My words trailed off as we rounded the corner. Halfway up the street, I saw the figure of a woman duck into an alley. She was slinking about like she didn't want to be seen, and her focus was on something further down the alleyway.

"Shit," I said, breaking into a run.

Hyde kept up with me easily, and we both ran as lightly as possible. We didn't want to spook either of them and trigger a deadly reaction. By the time we reached the dark mouth of the alley, Jason Kollins was backed up against the brick wall between an overflowing dumpster and a discarded couch.

"Say it!" Penelope Givens shrieked. Her voice echoed off the bare, cinder block walls. "Admit what you did!"

Kollins' face was smug enough that it made me want to kill him even more, which I didn't think was possible.

"What are you going to do, shoot me?" he said with a smile. "That would make you the murderer."

"Only if they catch me," Givens said, her ragged panting loud and desperate. "Isn't that what you learned? That you're only a murderer if you get caught?"

Kollins' eyes shifted behind Detective Givens, to me and Hyde, who were sneaking up close behind her.

"Help!" he yelled. "This woman's been stalking me, and now she's threatening to kill me!"

Penelope turned to look at us, her dark eyes full of despair. She winced, then her lip began to tremble. She kept her gun leveled at Kollins' chest, but her hand shook.

"I'm a Detective," she whimpered at us in explanation.

"Am I under arrest?" Kollins said. "You wait until my lawyer gets ahold of this. You're going to be paying this lawsuit off until the day you die."

"Gently," I murmured to Hyde.

When Givens' attention swiveled back to Kollins for a moment, Hyde closed the final distance behind her. He disarmed her firmly, using pressure points on her wrist to force her to drop her gun. She didn't put up a fight, and started to sob the moment she lost control of her pistol, tears sliding down her mocha cheeks. When Hyde tucked Givens' pistol into his waistband, Kollins stepped forward, a sneer on his face.

"You are so screwed," Kollins told Givens viciously. "I own you."

I stepped behind him, jabbed a syringe high into his neck above his hairline, and depressed the plunger in a fluid motion.

"No, Jason Kollins," I said, catching him as he fell. " *You* are the one that is screwed."

"What?" Penelope shrieked. "What?"

"You need to be quiet," Hyde said in a low voice, squeezing her upper arm.

I slid Kollins into a seated position on the alley floor, and leaned him back against the grungy wall. His head lolled against his shoulder and he made a vague spluttering noise with his mouth.

I rounded on Detective Givens. "What were you thinking, coming here like this?"

"You don't understand," she said, brushing back long, dark strands that had escaped her ponytail. "He killed a woman in Portland."

"Yes, we know," I said calmly. "But why are *you* here?"

"I..." she said, looking back and forth between us, as if for help. "I thought if I could get him to confess..."

"This wasn't about a confession," I said, angry at the obvious lie. "You know anything he said would be inadmissible in court. You already made your determination of guilt, otherwise you wouldn't have come here to kill him."

"Why are you here? Who are you?" she asked. "You know his name."

"We know a lot more than that," I said. "We are here to do the same thing you were planning on doing, but we are going to do it clean."

"I wasn't..." she started.

"You checked your registered firearm onto the plane with you," I snapped. "Got a hotel in your own name. I thought you were smart!"

"She needs to go," Hyde said, watching the mouth of the alley. "We have thirty minutes."

This isn't where either of us would have chosen to do this, but we had no choice. Hyde emptied her pistol of ammo and handed it back to her.

"Penelope Givens," I said, watching shock cross her face at my words. "Go back to your hotel and take a shower. Then go to sleep. Tomorrow morning, get up and go to the airport, catch your flight home. And don't ever, ever do something like this again."

"Who are you?" she repeated.

"It doesn't matter," I said. "What should matter to you is that now *we* know who *you* are. If your suspects start turning up dead, even years after the fact, I will find out. Then *you* will be the one in an alley getting my special brand of attention. Do you understand?"

Penelope nodded, fear in her caramel-colored eyes.

"Now do as I say," I said sharply. "You have to work within the parameters of the law, otherwise, what good is the law? You almost took a non-refundable trip tonight. Do not do something like this ever again. We will be watching you."

She nodded again, sparing one last look for Kollins, then turned and ran from the alley. I dialed Frankie.

"Frankie, track Givens' cell phone and make sure she goes back to her hotel and stays there. If she turns around or goes anywhere else, I need to know."

I clicked my phone off and took a few deep breaths. Coming clean to Thalia was one thing, but Detective Givens was an investigative pit bull. If she decided she needed answers, she might be a problem. I shook my head, trying to focus. Hyde watched the mouth of the alley as I turned my attention to Jason Kollins. I squatted down to look him in the eye.

"Hi there, Jason," I said. "My name is Elayna, and I am going to kill you."

His only response was a tear that coursed down his cheek. I pulled a knife from my waistband. It was nasty looking, eight inches long with serrations down one edge.

"This is the one, right?" I asked Kollins, holding it at his eye-level. I ran a finger down the flat of the steel. "This is just like the one you threatened Thalia with. This is the same kind of blade you used to carve up Michelle. And why? Because you are a narcissist. Because you believe women are *things* that you have an inherent right to."

His body was limp, but his eyes were alive and following the movements of the blade. I set the edge of the blade against his cheek.

"Maybe I'll stab you in the face, so many times that they will have to use dental records to identify your body," I said, repeating the words that he had used to terrorize Thalia York. I slid the blade lower, towards his crotch. "Or maybe I'll start by taking away the one weapon you have left."

I pressed the edge of the knife between his legs. I wasn't going to cut him, but Kollins didn't need to know that. I kept the knife there and let the fear build until his pants bloomed with moisture and the stench of fresh urine pierced the air.

"So typical," I sneered. "Don't worry, I'm not going to be as cruel and violent as when you killed Michelle Jessup. I'm not a monster, after all."

I held my hand out to Hyde, and he handed me a second syringe.

"Remember how you got booted out of community college for dealing cocaine?" I said. "Well, it turns out that you didn't ever kick the habit. It's not uncommon, you know, for an addict to relapse years after they got clean, and then overdose because their resistance isn't what it used to be."

I flicked the syringe, bringing the air bubbles to the top. I picked up Kollins' limp right hand and placed it around the syringe several different times.

"Fingerprints," I explained. "And it can't be too perfect. Before you go, I wanted to tell you that this is because of what you did to Michelle Jessup and Thalia York. I am going to go see Thalia after we're done here, and she's going to let me into her apartment, the one that she shares with her gorgeous boyfriend. Then I'm going to tell her how you are gone, and she is going to sleep so well tonight, and every night for the rest of her life. Well, she'll sleep well after she's done screwing her boyfriend."

I pressed the syringe into the crook of his left arm, piercing the largest vein there, and squeezed the plunger down quickly.

"Bye now, Jason. No one will miss you."

We stood there long enough for his breathing to cease, for a small amount of bloody foam to crest on his lips. I took a picture of his slack face with my cell phone and we left the alley. All in all, it was an anticlimactic death. I loved those.

"What was that bit about Thalia having a boyfriend?" Hyde asked as we walked back to Thalia's apartment.

"Oh, just something I made up to piss him off," I said. "Possessive, control-freak that he was... I just wanted to inflict as much pain as possible. I figured that imagining some guy throwing it to the girl you're obsessed with wouldn't be much fun."

"Now that's just mean," Hyde said, smirking.

I laughed.

Thalia stared at us through her peephole for a full minute after we knocked, and when she finally undid the deadbolts, she greeted us with a heavy meat cleaver in her hand.

"No need for that anymore," I said, taking it from her gently and putting it back in her knife block.

"Really?" Thalia said. "It's done?"

"Yes, I killed him," I said, clicking my phone on and showing her the picture of Kollins, his eyes barely open, foam on his purple lips.

She broke down, and I comforted her for long moments.

"I need a favor," I said, after her crying had subsided.

"Anything," she said fervently.

"If anyone ever calls to ask, I need you to tell them that Detective Givens came to your door this afternoon, but that you refused to open it, and that you refused to talk to her."

"Alright," she said. "What time was she here?"

"Around three," I said.

"Right when we were eating brownies," she said, looking at the empty pan in the sink.

"Hey," I said. "I was never here, remember? That means you ate that whole pan of brownies by yourself."

Thalia laughed, then surprised me by nearly throttling me with a hard hug.

"Thank you," she said, weeping again. "Thank you for giving me back my life. Thank you."

"That was a good ending," I said, once Hyde and I were back on the sidewalk.

He pulled me into a tight embrace and kissed me.

"I love you," he said.

I didn't respond, because I never did when he told me he loved me. I didn't quite know how. That didn't seem to bother Hyde, at least not yet. We held hands on our way back to the hotel and had dinner in the lobby. I called Penelope Givens the next morning.

"Hello?" she said, sounding tense.

"I met you last night," I said.

"I remember," she said.

"If anyone asks you why you were here, tell them that you came to see if Thalia York would speak to you. You went to her apartment at approximately three o'clock in the afternoon yesterday, but she refused to open the door or answer any questions. Understood?"

"Yes, but what if they question her?"

"It's taken care of," I said sharply.

She sniffled. "I wasn't wrong, was I?"

"No, you weren't. That is no excuse. Remember what I told you last night. I will be watching."

"I know," she said, her voice steadier. "It won't ever happen again. But is it over?"

"Yes," I said, then hung up.

I broke the phone in half, snapped the SIM card, and threw them away in a trashcan in front of a liquor store.

Chapter 15

On the private flight back to California, I didn't feel like talking at all. I had refused to get fully presentable. I had showered and pulled my wet hair back into a ponytail. No makeup. I had slipped on yoga pants, a t-shirt, and a large cashmere cardigan that I pulled around myself defensively. I refused to be baited by the way our flight attendant looked and smiled at Hyde. I inserted my earbuds doggedly, and turned on my favorite playlist.

I was drained. I had been running on hotel food and adrenaline for the past forty-eight hours straight. In some ways, doing my job got easier with time, but in other ways, it was still hard. It's an unnatural thing, cutting someone else's life short. I usually took time after the conclusion of a case to reflect on the good that had come from performing my service. Now I had two cases to reflect on.

I tried to focus on the good. Felicity Werther wasn't walking the halls of a pediatric ward this week. She wasn't pretending to care about her small patients. She wasn't paying attention to who got the least amount of visitors, who might be missed less than those who were always surrounded. She wasn't a wolf in disguise, wandering a plain filled with injured sheep.

Jason Kollins wasn't lurking around Thalia York's neighborhood, figuring out the gaps in schedule and security that would allow him to slip through and get to her. He wasn't able to go over Michelle Yessup's last moments in his mind, caressing the memory like a favored pet at his leisure. I hoped Thalia York slept well last night. I hoped that in time, she started to forget to lock all of her deadbolts. Maybe someday, one lock might be enough for her.

I always kept tabs on when the body was found. The cable shows got one thing right; usually if a suspect was identified, it was done in the first two days. If there was going to be a problem with a case, it often came up right away. Frankie knew the drill. She was watching both situations.

I wondered if someone at Werther's new job had called the authorities yet, or if it would take longer since they didn't know her. I wondered who would miss her, if anyone. As for Kollins, garbage service wasn't until Wednesday, but someone would find his body before then. According to Frankie, there wasn't law enforcement activity at the house in the suburbs of Seattle, or in the alley in Minneapolis.

Not yet.

I thought most of all about how I had chosen to deal with Thalia York and Penelope Givens. In the space of a day, I had told two people the truth about what I did. I had broken one of my very few rules. And worse, I didn't feel like it was a mistake. Was I getting too confident in my own abilities? Was I starting to feel untouchable, like I couldn't be brought down by anyone, that I was out of reach of the justice system?

I had needed Thalia's testimony to prove to myself that Kollins was a valid target. But she had already given me the information that I needed before I told her. Did I need her validation? Was I looking for appreciation for a job well done? Was telling Thalia the truth a vanity thing? In the moment, it felt like the right thing to do, but now I couldn't rule it out that I was looking for approval.

That one I might be able to write off, but telling a cop to her face that I was going to kill her murder suspect? That was what concerned me about my own actions. I was starting to trust people with the information that could make me vulnerable. But what else could I have done? Detective Givens was going to kill Jason Kollins in that alley, I knew. She hated him more than I did. But there is no real coming back from your first unsanctioned kill, even if you think there is.

I thought about my first kill. It was my senior year in college, my third year of interning for the agency. My boss was a guy in his early thirties named Clark who always smelled vaguely of mothballs and sweat. He pulled me into his tiny office and handed me a file. I thought it was another research and intelligence case, as I had been working those for awhile. I was good at it, finding vulnerabilities and identifying the best time to hit a target.

"When do you need it by?" I asked.

He looked earnest and was sweating more than usual, which tipped me off that something was a little different about this case.

"Deadline is two weeks," he said, leaning forward.

"Two weeks?" I asked, my forehead scrunching. "I can have it for you in a few hours, if you want."

"You're working a different part of this case," he said. "Take a look."

I opened the file and found that someone had already done the research and intelligence portion of the case.

"You mean..." I trailed off, flipping through the paperwork.

"Yes, your first field case," he said. "Let me know what you think."

I began to read. The target was forty-one, attractive, married, two kids. He was an executive of a company that had an office in Beijing, and one in Los Angeles. Whoever had done the research had done an excellent job when it came to potential weaknesses and openings to get the kill. The analyst thought that the best chance of success was in the parking garage of his gym in LA, in the airport club lounge at LAX, or on a flight to Beijing.

I shook my head at the last one. I did not want my first kill to be in a plane. It was an enclosed space, where I couldn't run if something went wrong. It made me feel claustrophobic, trapped, just thinking about it. The club lounge might have too many witnesses. Waitresses and bartenders coveted those spots; there wasn't a lot of turnover. Who knew how long it would take me to infiltrate there? I didn't have enough time for that. I had a Grecian Art final on Thursday.

"The gym parking lot," I decided out loud.

Clark was watching me closely, sweat beading in the bays of the coastline of his receding hair.

"And?" he prompted.

"A taser, put him in the trunk, drive him out to the desert, shoot him poorly, take his cash, jewelry. He drives an Audi. I'll have it chopped downtown."

"So you're angle is to make it look like a carjacking?" Clark asked.

"Yep," I said, snapping the file shut.

I had been training for over a year. I was confident.

"Anything else?" Clark asked.

He looked like he was expecting something. I frowned, thinking.

"No," I said carefully.

"Great," he said, smiling. "Let me know when it's done."

I watched the target for two days before I got my chance. In the end, it was almost too easy. The parking garage was dim, dingy. He came out of the elevator, smelling of fresh sweat and heat-activated deodorant, headed to his car. I wondered briefly what kind of person works up a sweat in the gym only to take the elevator two floors down. I had one of the techs disable the cameras. There wasn't any live security, but when they reviewed the tapes, they would find they hadn't been turned on that night.

I was wearing teensy workout clothes, my hair pulled up in a perky ponytail, a small gym bag slipped over my shoulder. I looked fresh, like I was on my way to the gym. He gave me a polite smile as we passed each other. This surprised me, since what little I was wearing was skin tight. Most men would have at least taken a second look. No matter. I had timed it so that he would arrive at his trunk just as I was walking past.

I heard the jingling of keys and I whirled, jabbing him with 50,000 volts of electricity in the small of his back. He arched, grunted deeply, and fell despite my clumsy efforts to catch him. I retrieved his keys, unlocked the trunk, and started lifting him, torso first, then his legs. It took about thirty seconds, but I got him in. My heart was pounding, there was a slight ringing in my ears. Everything felt too loud, too slow. I disabled the trunk release latch with pliers, and slammed the lid.

The drive out to the desert was slow, and I heard him wake up and start yelling. But there wasn't anyone who could hear him above the noise of traffic. It was hot, and everyone had their windows up, AC on. He had quieted by the time I pulled off the road. I unholstered my pistol, and opened the trunk. He was disheveled and he had a bloody lip. He raised his hands at the sight of the gun leveled at his chest, but he made no attempt to fight, to flee. His face was calm; he seemed resigned.

"Why?" he asked, his lip trembling but his voice steady.

I realized that I had no idea.

In lieu of an answer, I gave him two poorly-clustered bullets to the chest.

I followed through with the motions of the rest of my plan, just as I had said, taking his money, his watch, his wedding band. I turned the car over to a part of LA that was as efficient to a stolen luxury car as an expert butcher is to a pig. I walked away with seven hundred dollars in cash and pulled my hoodie up around my face.

Three blocks away, I dropped all the money, the watch, and the ring in a bum's shopping cart. Sharp eyes stared at me over a bushy beard. He gave me a solemn nod, like he saw everything, understood me without asking.

I walked all the way home, getting home with the first light of dawn. Then I showered until the hot water ran out.

Clark wanted a full rundown on the case when I got in at eight that morning. He leaned forward, his fingers steepled. I wondered if he had seen the gesture in a movie and thought it made him look important.

"So?" Clark said, raising his eyebrows.

"Everything according to plan," I said, determined to be as taciturn as he was.

If he was going to ask a non-question, I was going to give him a non-answer out of spite.

"No chance of exposure?" he asked.

"No."

"Did you wipe the car before you handed it over?"

"Yes," I said, trying to seep the word with indignation.

"What did you do with the jewelry?" he asked.

They were the identifiable items, the only things that the police could track.

"Disposed of, close to the garage," I said. "They will probably be in a pawn shop by noon."

"Good," he said, then added, too casually, "Any qualms in closing this case?"

"Just some curiosity," I said. "Why was the target selected?"

Clark pressed his lips together, then answered in a tight voice, "You know that's above either of our pay grades."

"So the when, where, and how are at our pay grade, but the why isn't?"

"Yes," he said, as if daring me to challenge it.

I got up and dusted invisible spots from my jeans.

"Whatever," I said.

"For whatever it's worth, you did an excellent job," he said.

I was surprised to hear that he sounded sincere.

"Thanks," I said.

"You know the drill," he said. "You can expect to experience a week or two of slight depression. If you don't experience this, or if these feelings don't let up after fourteen days, tell me. I can put you in contact with the staff psychiatrist."

"I think I would feel fine if I knew the reason he was a target," I said, trying a different tactic. "I think it would help me have closure, to know why it was necessary."

"You're asking for information that would help you make a judgement call about your actions," Clark said.

"Well, yes," I admitted.

"That isn't the point of your position," he said. "Your job is to carry out the judgement calls of others."

Although I had always known this, I found acting on this hard truth to be much different from knowing it. It rankled me, deeply. It felt like my soul had just been petted backwards. Clark seemed to sense this, or maybe he saw something on my face that gave away my intrinsic dissatisfaction with this arrangement. He tried a different angle.

"What makes you think that the information you want would make you feel better?" Clark said, leaning back in his chair.

"What?"

"You are assuming that the targeting precursor information would help you feel better. What if the 'reason' wasn't good enough for you?"

I didn't have an answer for that. I shrugged.

"For the next couple of weeks, you will go back to research and intelligence," he said.

I opened my mouth to argue, but he cut me off.

"Don't be offended; it's standard operating procedure after an agent's first field case. It gives both of us time to evaluate whether field work is something you still want to pursue."

"What if one of us decides it's not?" I asked.

"Then you go back to research and intelligence indefinitely," Clark said.

My thoughts snapped to Carla Trope, a forty-something research and intelligence agent. Those of us in training snickered about her in the break room, joked about when she would be assigned her first case. Now I knew she had already gotten her first case. I wondered what had gone wrong.

"In the meantime, it's better if you keep yourself from wondering about the 'why'," Clark said.

He stacked a few files, rapped them loudly against his desk to put them in line. I knew a non-verbal dismissal when I saw one, and I made for the door.

"That's what you were waiting for me to ask," I said on the sudden thought, turning. "When you gave me the case."

"Your psych profile suggested we might have some problems with you getting in line with the agency's needs," he said. "We saw how you reacted to that dog thing in your preliminary testing. But I guess it wasn't a problem until after."

I succeeded in my mission. The kill was clean. Rowan and the ever-smaller group of people who remained in our cohort congratulated me. There was even a cake with a smoking gun frosted on top. But I went home that night feeling like I had failed. I had been so excited to be given a chance that I didn't ask the most important question of all: 'why?'

Now, on the plane, I knew that central problem, the question of motivation, was one that I had been able to bury beneath the surface at the time. Still, it was like I added a new bag of luggage to a very small closet every time I did a job for the agency. At some point, I could no longer shut the door on my objections. That's when the CIA and I parted ways.

I thought again of Detective Givens. Of how she had planned to kill Kollins. Of how she had acted on her plans. And now she knew about me. The question I was faced with was whether to tie up that loose end now, or to wait for it to unravel first. Was Givens' intent of killing Kollins enough to justify me in making her a target? Would this even be an issue if I didn't feel like I had exposed myself to vulnerability by telling her what I was there to do?

I sighed, and Hyde met my eyes across the table between us. He smiled and looked out the window. He was reading my mood correctly. I wanted to be left alone, didn't want to hear someone ask, "what's wrong?" and then wait for a detailed explanation, all the while acting like they were doing you a favor by listening. I pulled my earbuds out, closed down my music app, and dialed Frankie.

She picked up on the third ring, "How's the plane?"

"Still in the air, so that's a good thing," I said. "I need you to do a full workup on Penelope Givens."

Hyde was watching me, listening.

"How detailed do you want me to go?" Frankie asked.

"Treat her like a target," I said.

"Is she a target?" she said.

"I don't know. Depends on what you find," I said. "I want you to look at her unsolved cases, or cases where the outcome wasn't optimal. See if any of those suspects died under suspicious circumstances, or disappeared."

"She's only been a Detective for about two years," Frankie replied. "Shouldn't take too long. Anything else?"

"Get into the Internal Affairs files. See if Givens was ever implicated in any excessive use of force complaints, anything like that."

"Will do."

"Thanks, Frankie," I said, ending the call.

"You think that Givens may have done this before?" Hyde asked.

"With the way her hand was shaking in that alley, I'm pretty sure that was her first time," I said. "It's more like I kind of hope she did."

"Feeling a bit exposed?" he said.

"I'm not in the habit of outing myself to strangers who work in law enforcement," I said. "I don't even know why I did it."

"What else were you going to do?" Hyde asked. "She wasn't going to leave without an explanation, and you couldn't let Kollins leave the alley. It was about containment and mitigation at that point."

I watched him carefully. "Are you sure that's what it was, or are you just saying that to make me feel better, since we're sleeping together?"

Hyde raised his eyebrows. "Really?"

"Yes, really."

"There's so many things wrong with that statement, I don't even know where to start," he said. "I will start with the surface issue. Us 'sleeping together', as you put it, will make me examine you more closely and be harder on you. It's not going to make me glaze over issues. Don't think I would compromise my beliefs for a bit of tail. Your actions and decisions are more important to me since we're *sleeping together.*"

He pressed his lips together and looked out the window.

"Ok, then," I said, frowning.

I moved to put my earbuds back in.

"You really piss me off sometimes, you know that?" Hyde said.

"What?" I said. "Why?"

"You weren't the only one compromised in that alley, you know," he said. "Remember me? The guy you're *sleeping with?*"

"You're mad because I didn't call you my boyfriend in that question? Is that it?"

"No. I don't care how you put things. I care how you think about things."

"I've always been honest with you, Hyde. I've told you from the beginning that I might not be able to give you everything you want," I said. "You said you were ok with that, for now."

"Yeah, for now."

"Well, nothing's changed between us," I said, feeling unsettled.

"Right," he said, shaking his head. "Detective Givens was on the street for five years before she was promoted to Detective. I would be surprised if she didn't have any Internal Affairs investigations."

I was surprised by the rapid change in topic, but figured that if he wanted to change the subject, I should let him.

"Valid point, but I still have to check," I said.

"What if you find something?" he said. "Is she going to be a target?"

"Depends on what I find out," I said.

"I don't think that you are going to be able to tie this up as neatly as you'd like," Hyde said, turning away toward the window.

And I wasn't quite sure if he was talking about the problem with Detective Givens or our relationship.

Chapter 16

We made it to the office by early afternoon. The antique shop was stocked and staged, but the gold lettering on the door said, "by appointment only." Antiques dealing was a convenient cover, one I had assumed when I worked for the agency and never dropped. It explained the odd travel schedule. Presumably, I had a very successful business, because I was also very wealthy.

Since I didn't have a social life, this cover was primarily for my family. My parents seemed to take an odd pride in my success. Odd because they alternately chided me for dropping out of pre-med in college and congratulated my financial security. However, these compliments were always dosed with the insinuation that my success had been mostly luck.

My brother Peter didn't seem to care, one way or another, what I did for a living. His existence was small and insulated from many of the harsher aspects of what most people would consider real life. He had gone to college, paid for by our parents, gotten a business degree, picked up an artificially blonde wife along the way, had two children. He had achieved an easy success in his personal and professional life that I was alternately bored by and infuriatingly jealous of.

His wife's priority was appearances, which dovetailed nicely into my brother's desire to seem like he had more than those around him. Sybil's children wore expensive clothes and were raised by daycare providers. She was an accountant and liked to drop hints about who was having money problems after a couple of drinks at parties. She seemed to make it a policy to always like someone a few degrees less than they liked her. The only exception to this rule was me; Sybil hated me only *nearly* as much as I hated her. She had a narrow view of the world and hoarded petty social victories against others like a squirrel stores nuts.

Hyde and I stepped into the supply closet, the smell of lemon wood polish in the air. I closed the door behind us and swiped my fingerprint into the hidden sensor on the bottom of a shelf. The back wall split away and swiveled, revealing another door. I punched in the code, and the door opened to the staircase into the basement. I was only three steps down when a huge, wiggling mass of fur came barreling my way.

"Bruno!" I said, sitting down before he knocked me over on the stairs.

Bruno was a mastiff who I had rescued from being used as an object lesson by the agency when I first started. His fur was as soft as a chinchilla, and I regularly told him I was going to make him into slippers if he didn't stop drooling so much. He huffed into my hand, leaned his considerable bulk into my side, and wagged so hard his tail made a percussion sound against the steel banister.

"I missed you, buddy," I said, scratching behind his ear.

He angled his massive head to the side to allow me better access to his favorite spot. I hugged him, taking in his humid breath and his sweet doggy smell.

"Hey," Hyde said, nudging me from behind. "Forget about me?"

"Sorry," I said, standing so he could get by.

Hyde laughed. "I'm going to start paying attention to how that dog treats you. Maybe I can learn how he earned your everlasting devotion."

"It's simple," called Howard from below. "Push her around and lean on her alot, bring dead birds into the house, and every once in awhile, pee in the corner of the guest bedroom."

"Hey," I said, indignant. "Bruno is better behaved than you are."

"True," Howard deadpanned. "I *always* pee in the corner of the guest bedroom, not just on special occasions."

"Gross," Frankie said.

"Where's Camilla?" I asked.

"Kitchen. Where else?" Howard said.

"Anyone care to give me a tour?" Hyde said.

Howard said, "I forgot you haven't been here before. Come along, brother. I will show you around."

I winked at Hyde as Howard led him around the corner. I went down the opposite hall, towards the smell of simmering tomato sauce, Bruno close on my heels. The kitchen in our basement was much smaller than the one I had in my house. Well, before my house was blown to bits, that is.

It was still larger than the average kitchen, and the cabinets went all the way to the ceiling. We had bought the cabinets from a store that is famous for flat-packing all their goods because we couldn't have a contractor come into the basement. Howard swore up and down that it would be easy, but he was the first one to quit on 'put the cabinets together' night. He had cursed, thrown his weeny metric wrench at the wall and left us women to it. It had been for the best. The girls put them together, and Howard regrouped enough to hang them the next day.

Camilla was bent over the six-burner stove, stirring some freshly-chopped herb into a pot.

"Camilla," I said in way of greeting. "I missed you."

She turned, wiping her hands on her red apron. Her eyes crinkled with a large smile. I gave her a tight hug, marveling, not for the first time, at how she could look so curvy, yet feel so muscular. Camilla was Brazilian, full of sarcastic humor, amazing cooking, and accepting love.

"I see Bruno already found you," she said. "The first thing he did when we got here was to run a grid on the whole place, trying to see if you were here. Howard was impressed, started following him, wanted to see Bruno's tactical pattern. Bruno didn't like it very much."

I laughed. "Well, he found me now. When did you get back?"

Bruno was sitting in front of me, using the front of my legs as the back of his chair.

"Just this morning. I'm making your favorite," she said, turning to stir the sauce again.

"Raviolis?" I asked hopefully, walking to the stove.

Without his backrest, Bruno succumbed to gravity and slumped to the floor with a disgruntled sigh.

"I heard you were coming back tonight. Two cases with no break?" She tsked me. "I thought you could use some comfort food and some rest."

"You have no idea," I said, swiping my finger through the sauce and tasting it.

Camilla pretended not to see me, but I saw a smile twitch at the corner of her mouth.

"They were rough ones?" she asked.

I pulled a stool over, it's legs scraping over the tile floor.

"I think I made it harder than it had to be," I admitted. "The first one wasn't perfect, but it was clean enough. But on the second case, I told two different people that I was going to kill Kollins. Then I killed him. Kinda leaves me open to repercussions."

"Tell me about it," Camilla said as she put dough through a pasta machine.

So I did. At some point during the story, Camilla opened a bottle of Pinot Noir and put a big glass of it in my hand. Neither of us cared that it wasn't yet five o'clock. When you kill people for a living, some social conventions lose all their meaning.

Camilla nodded and listened, deftly making pasta. I told her my fears about Detective Penelope Givens. I told her about wanting some sort of connection with Thalia York, how strange that was for me. I told her about Hyde's words on the plane, that he didn't disagree with what I had done. I left out our strange fight. I sighed when I was finished.

"What do you think?" I said, taking a big sip of wine.

"I think that Hyde was right," she said. "You did what the situation required. From what you are telling me, that Givens woman would have smelled a bullshit story a mile away. Plus, she wanted Kollins dead, and probably wouldn't have left that alley willingly unless she was sure you were going to do it."

"You think?" I said, cocking my head to the side.

"Yes," she said firmly. "Don't forget that you did that woman a favor. She had exposed herself even more than you did. She put her career and freedom in jeopardy by stalking Kollins. She had painted herself into a corner by pulling a gun on him. Either he had to die, or she would have lost everything she cares about."

"True."

"I wouldn't worry about it," she said. "If it comes down to it, we can deal with her."

I suddenly felt a bit better.

"Ok," I said, shrugging.

"Got any wine for me?" Hyde said.

I turned to see him leaning against the doorway. I wondered how long he had been there. He ambled over and rested his arm around my shoulders while Camilla poured him a glass of wine.

"So are you two getting along now?" I asked, pointing out the elephant in the room.

"We never weren't getting along," Hyde said.

I looked at Camilla.

"That's true," she said. "We've always been on the same side."

"Camilla pissed me off with that interrogation stuff, but I understand now why she did it. She was protecting you. And there's no way I can be upset with that," he said, kissing my hair.

Camilla gave me a smug smile. I knew them both well enough to know they weren't just smoothing things over for my benefit. Something deep inside me, a tension that I didn't even know I had, relaxed.

Howard and Frankie found us in the kitchen.

"Drinking without us, again?" Frankie accused.

"Camilla, we need to order some of those ass-gas-kets," Howard said.

"What?" Camilla said.

"He means toilet seat covers," Frankie said, rolling her eyes.

"Thank you for translating," Camilla said, bewildered.

"Howard, there's only five of us living here, and we all have our own bathrooms. Why do you want toilet seat covers?" I said.

"Never can be too careful. I don't know where your butt's been lately. Not to mention Hyde's butt. He's served overseas. I don't want one of those Middle East butt diseases."

"They've been all over the news," Frankie said, in a mocking tone. "Those Middle East butt diseases."

"Why do you think they're fighting all the time over there?" Howard said. "They're all itchy and uncomfortable."

"I sure hope they get to the *bottom* of it soon," Hyde quipped.

"Maybe the doctors can *end* the madness," Frankie offered.

"They sure are falling *behind* on the issue," Camilla said.

"Stop *cracking* jokes," Howard said.

They all looked at me.

I wracked my brain for a second, then shrugged and said, "I got nothing."

At dinner, I felt better than I had in a long time. Bruno leaned against my chair. There was wine, and lots of carbs. Camilla's raviolis were plump and delicious, and the tomato sauce was better than any I had enjoyed in Italy. I think she was proving something to us. There was even tiramisu for dessert. Hyde smirked at me when Camilla served it, and I knew that he had caught on to her one-upping food game.

"What's the plan, now?" Howard asked, scraping his plate clean after dessert.

"Digestion," Hyde suggested, rubbing his flat belly.

I frowned at him, and looked down at my stomach. There was a definite post-dinner bulge happening. I had to hit the gym tomorrow.

"I mean in terms of cases," Howard said.

"Let's set a morning meeting tomorrow at eight," I said. "Frankie, have you been keeping the files updated?"

"Yes," she said, sitting up straight in her chair. "I'm ready to go over it all whenever you're ready."

"Good. Let's meet and prioritize in the morning. Set a plan of attack on the next targets," I said.

"Any sign of that guy in Seattle or Minneapolis?" Frankie asked.

"What guy?" Camilla said.

"There was a guy following Elayna around Italy," Howard said.

"You guys could have mentioned that," Camilla said, frowning at Frankie.

"Sorry, Camilla," Frankie said, looking repentant. "I completely forgot. Then we were off to Seattle and Minneapolis, and I forgot to tell you about the weirdo on vacation."

"Probably was just Italian press, anyway," Howard said.

This had been Howard's personal favorite theory of who the man was. Hyde and I shared a quick glance. Neither of us believed that the man was press. Neither of us believed we had seen the last of him, either. If he was determined enough, he might be able to track us down.

"He didn't look Italian. He looked Hispanic," Frankie argued.

"How on earth can you tell the difference? Both are tan with dark hair," Howard said.

"You've just described over half the world's population," Hyde said.

"We haven't seen him since Italy," I said, trying to steer the conversation back on track. "He didn't show up in any files that Frankie ran facial recognition on."

"Which is either a good thing, or a very bad thing," Hyde said.

"Right now, it's a neutral thing. This guy, whoever he is, is in the periphery. We aren't going to ignore the possible threat, but we aren't going to let it dictate our movements, either," I said, firmly. "Could be that he is a prospective client, taking due diligence to the extreme. We can't know until we know."

"That could be the title of my memoir," Howard said.

"I thought that was going to be called *Duck and Cover*," I said.

"Or just, *Boom*," Camilla added.

"I think *Short Fuse* would be even better," Hyde said.

"Hey, now," Howard complained, but he was laughing with us.

It was good to be together again.

Chapter 17

I was in our small gym at six the next morning, Hyde right behind me at six-fifteen. I felt fifteen-minutes' worth of superiority until he started lifting weights. Then I felt slightly inadequate. Howard stumbled in at six-thirty, mainly to chat and spot for Hyde.

At ten to eight, we had all assembled in the conference room. Camilla had decided it was going to be a breakfast meeting, and had several covered servers on a table to the side. There was quiche, sausage, and blueberry muffins, along with a carafe of fresh coffee.

"I love you, Camilla," I mumbled around my first bite of quiche.

"Camilla, you need to teach me how to make that quiche," Hyde said.

I felt a pang of guilt at his comment, but then he winked at me. I stuck my tongue out at him in retaliation.

Frankie had divided the white board into four sections, each with a photo at the top. I recognized the system; it was her favorite way to keep us apprised of all the cases that we had open. The slots were numbered one through four. Slot four was filled with a picture of the man who had been following us in Italy. There was no information written below the picture.

Frankie ran us through the cases. Case one was the Oakland issue that Frankie had brought up in an email. There had been several more shootings, but in the last one, an eight year old girl had died. She had been killed when she was standing behind her uncle, a gang leader. He had only been in the position for a few days. Whoever this gang was, they were sending a message.... whoever stepped up to the vacated leadership posts would be taken out. Frankie was the one most interested in this case.

"Frankie, this one again?" Howard asked. "Whoever this group is, they're doing Oakland a public service."

"What they're doing is illegal," Frankie said, her chin jutting out. "And they shot a little girl."

"One innocent victim, Frankie. One." Howard said. "Versus all the victims those gangs usually kill during the same amount of time?"

"She was blameless, Howard. She deserves our justice. A little girl shouldn't be labeled as an acceptable loss," Frankie said, the volume in her voice raising.

"I'm not saying that. Not at all. But whoever is doing this has thrown the gangs into a tailspin. They're confused, scattered. Business has slowed to a crawl. Drive-bys are down eighty percent," Howard argued. "Before Mikayla Johnson was killed, you were a fan of these activities. I even thought Elayna might be doing some deep undercover work. Whoever is doing this is someone like us."

"There's no one else like us, Howard," Frankie said, "Which is why we should look into this."

"Ok, but I don't think it's case number one. Look who you've put this in front of...there's Kent Sulley, a guy who is offing prostitutes on his lunch breaks, Mercer Fulton, a therapist who is a serial rapist of at-risk women, and the guy who's been stalking Elayna all over Europe. We don't even know anything about him. Don't you think *that* should be the priority?"

At his words, Camilla gave a little start. She was staring at the fourth photo as if she'd just noticed it. Frankie and Howard were too entrenched in their argument to notice. But I saw Hyde's eyes on Camilla, too.

Frankie continued, """There is something weird about this Oakland thing. I can *feel* it. *Why* are they taking out gang leadership from *all* the gangs? How are they so precise?"

"Why should we *care*, Frankie?" Howard shouted. "Whoever it is, they are doing a better job than the police force. They are making a genuine, big difference. You know how many children were killed because of gang violence in Oakland last year?"

"No," Frankie said, angrily.

"Yes you do, cause you ran the stats," Howard said. "Thirty-two. Thirty-two kids were killed. This cleanup effort has been going on for three months now, and the only collateral damage has been one eight year old."

"That's still unacceptable," Frankie said.

"Of course it's not acceptable," Howard said, exasperated. "But it's better than the previous reality. And that's what we are concerned with, right? Reality?

"I still think we should pursue the case," Frankie said. "These people obviously want to create a power vacuum. That is something to be worried about."

"I'm not saying we shouldn't. I'm just saying it shouldn't be case number one, before we figure out if these guys are on our side or not."

"This group has killed twenty-seven people, Howard. That makes them worthy of the number one slot in my book."

"Yes, but only one victim was an accident. Only one victim was innocent. And even that's somewhat debatable," Howard added, unwisely.

"What on earth do you mean?" Frankie said, her eyes narrowed in a clear warning.

Hyde and I were still casually watching Camilla, whose mouth was now clamped together, her eyes narrowed. She was still staring at the photo under the number four.

"Well, if my neighborhood was a gang war zone, you can bet your ass I'd find a different neighborhood to raise my children in."

"You think the victims are somewhat to blame, because of where they *live*?" Frankie exclaimed. "Of all the racist things I've heard you say, that one takes the cake."

"It's not racist! Sheesh. You build a few bombs for a white supremacist gang cause you are young and stupid and want to fit in, and you never hear the end of it. I killed them all, Frankie. We've been over this!"

"The people in Oakland shouldn't be punished or judged for remaining in their own homes."

"Why don't they just get on a train or a bus? Move north or south or east. There are tons of little, safe towns all across this nation where they wouldn't be shot at."

"They are often making minimum wage, Howard."

"My point exactly!" he yelled. "They could go work in some little, cheap midwest town, make the same wage, and be so much better off. Why is it acceptable to live like that? Why do they think it's normal?"

"The socio-economic system has taught them that their life *is* normal, Howard. Why should they give up their home because of gangs?"

"Because the gangs will always be there, that's why. And you can blame the education system, or the welfare system, or whatever, but no one is keeping them there. Buy a train ticket, or a bus ticket, and get to a small town. Work at a McDonald's that never gets shot up."

"That's such an oversimplified, narrow view of a complex issue, Howard," Frankie said. "Many people of color wouldn't feel comfortable living in a place where most people were white or hispanic."

"Well, *that* sounds pretty racist to me," Howard said.

"Enough," I said, firmly.

I had let their argument spiral out of control because I had been focused on Camilla's discrete shock. Camilla had recovered enough to look neutral, and it was time to move on.

"You both have excellent points," I said.

Frankie opened her mouth to argue, but I cut her off with a curt hand motion.

"Yes, Frankie. I do mean both of you. Howard is right in that so far, whoever is doing this has improved the life expectancy of Oakland residents. They did kill an eight year old girl, which is unacceptable. But that seemed to be an accident. As of now, I don't see any reason to insert ourselves into this situation. I want to see if these people, whoever they are, start to lower their standards of acceptable collateral damage before we act."

"See?" Howard said, stupidly.

"And Howard," I said. "Frankie is right that there is no other group like us. These people obviously have a selfish motive that has yet to be revealed. Once they reveal it, we will decide whether it is out of line with our standards."

"Fine by me," Howard said.

"Also," I continued, my eyebrows raised, "victims are real people, which means they aren't perfect. Victim-shaming is a dirty thing, Howard, something that is best left to skeezy defense lawyers."

"Sorry," he mumbled, looking at his hands.

"This whole Oakland situation brings up a different point," I said. "Do either of you wonder why we don't do more gang cases?"

"I have wondered that, actually," Frankie said. "Statistically-speaking, gang members should occupy the majority of our top slots. They are often the most destructive, often have the most victims."

"It's because I find it most effective to target individuals, not systems," I said. "When I take out a Kollins or a Werther, they are gone. They have no apprentice eager to take their spot. In a gang, you cut the leader off, and there are three lieutenants waiting to take his spot. And that's not the only dynamic going on there, either."

"What do you mean?" Frankie asked.

"It's like how you should eat yogurt after taking antibiotics," I said, struggling to explain. "If you reduce too much of one bacteria, the others get too strong. There is an imbalance. It's the same with competing gangs. If you eradicate one gang from a four-block radius, that area doesn't stay gang-free. Another gang is always there to take the territory."

"Which is why they should just move," Howard said.

"You ever heard how they trained elephants to stay on a thin rope?" I asked.

"No, I haven't," Frankie said.

"I have," Hyde said.

"Then you explain it," I said.

"You take an elephant from the wild, and they want to escape, so you have to tie them with a very heavy chain attached to a post driven deep into the earth. The elephant will try and try to escape, but will learn that they can't. So they stop trying, and eventually, you can keep them tied up with a tiny piece of rope and a tent stake driven six inches deep," Hyde said.

"When freedom doesn't seem possible, the elephant stops trying for it?" Howard asked.

"Yes. I'm saying that often, by the time a kid is out of high school and maybe able to support themselves, get out and have a different life, they have seen over and over again that it's impossible to have something better. So they don't even try. They've had their dreams and drive beaten out of them," I said.

"They're an elephant on a string," Frankie murmured.

"I can go up against individuals," I said. "But I cannot go up against an entire system that produces an environment ripe for gang activity. All of the factors that contribute to that kind of life-- the broken family unit, lack of positive role models, low societal expectations, drug abuse, poverty, the devaluing of education... I can't fix all of that. I also can't go up against four gangs at once, in order to reduce their numbers evenly. That's a couple of the reasons why I am interested in seeing what this group has planned. We are going to let this one set for awhile."

"I don't like it," Frankie argued. "This is right in our backyard. Shouldn't we look into this?"

"Frankie, we have other cases we can work," Howard said in a reasonable voice.

I winced.

"Oh, would you be on my side one damn time, Howard?" Frankie yelled.

She pushed back from the table and stormed out, slamming the conference room door behind her. The four of us sat in uncomfortable silence for a long moment.

"Let's break for about a half an hour," I said, and sighed.

"Yeah, I better go find her and see if my mouth is big enough for my other foot, too," Howard said wearily.

Chapter 18

Hyde nodded at me, and closed the door behind them on his way out. Camilla still sat at the conference table, gazing again at the picture on the board. I knew that she would talk when she was ready, so I waited.

"He looks different," she finally said. "Older. But that is my cousin, Fernando."

"Any idea why he tracked me down in Italy?" I asked.

"He was probably looking for me."

She paused for long moments. The creases in her face suddenly looked deeper. She looked very sad.

"Have you ever heard of the Almeida cartel, in Brazil?" she finally asked.

"Only in passing. Frankie sent me an email about a month ago, warning me to stay out of Brazil. She said something about the cartel's leader passing away, something about a messy power struggle."

Camilla nodded, "They are one of the most brutal organizations in South America. They are also one of the most powerful, mainly because they have skill-fully interwoven illegal enterprise with many legiti-mate business dealings. The cartel has funded the campaigns of the last four presidents of Brazil, and it has many loyal individuals in the Senate and the Chamber of Deputies."

I nodded, knowing that Camilla wouldn't be giv-ing me this background if it weren't somehow impor-tant to the central point.

"Their leader was Thiago Almeida," she contin-ued. "It was said that he was the only one who could keep the peace between his two lieutenants, his brother, Caio, and his own son, Alex."

"What is the problem between those two?" I asked, taking a sip of coffee.

"Caio Almeida is ruthless. He handles the gang itself, the members, the smuggling, the murders. He runs most of the illegal activities of the cartel. Alex Almeida, Thiago's son, was educated abroad in Europe and the United States. Degree in Economics from Harvard, MBA from Haas."

"So, maybe he's smart," I said sarcastically.

"A little," Camilla said, a smile dusting her lips for a second. "Alex runs the business side of things, the political affiliations, the legitimate trade operations and corporations. Caio believes that Alex is narrow-minded, and not strong enough to lead. Caio was working and fighting for the cartel while Alex was away at school. When Alex returned, Thiago handed over half of the operations to his control."

"And Caio didn't like that," I guessed.

"That's putting it mildly," Camilla said. "Caio still sees Alex as a child, as his lesser, even though Alex has almost doubled the cartel's business holdings since he took power."

"Does Alex dislike Caio as much as Caio resents him?" I asked.

"Alex is primarily a businessman. He dislikes that the illegal activities of the cartel are at all connected with the legitimate businesses. He wants to pave new roads. Alex was always arguing to Thiago that they had a better future in legal corporations than with the illegal activities. Alex sees Caio's side of the organization as a huge risk with a dwindling reward. He wants to cut Caio out altogether. In short, Caio thinks Alex is a snobby child. Alex thinks that Caio's a stupid thug. Caio has the muscle behind him, but Alex has the money and political clout."

"So the power struggle is between those two," I said.

"And possibly one other interested party," she said. "

"Who's the other interested party?" I asked.

"Me," she said, simply. "Thiago Almeida was my father."

I leaned back in my chair, watching Camilla closely.

"I'm sorry for your loss, Camilla," I said after several long moments.

It was the only thing I could think of to say.

"Because Thiago's dead?" she said, chuckling. "He was always too busy with work to pay much attention to me. Although, in my youth, I tried my best to impress him."

"How?"

"I went to work for Alex for many years. I managed two of the businesses, was liaison to several political figures. I learned a lot about the corporations, and soon became my brother's second. It wasn't because I was his sister. It was because I was good."

I nodded.

"When that didn't seem to impress my father, I went to work for Caio for a time," she said, pressing her lips together. "I had to work very hard to get respect, to raise in the ranks as a woman. But I did it."

I didn't know what to say to that. Suddenly, Camilla's innate understanding of what I needed after a tough kill took on a new meaning.

"Two years into that, Caio called on me personally to help him put down an attempted coup on his side of the organization. Many men died, and it was only later that I questioned whether they had been guilty of what he claimed."

"Why else would he have had you take them out?" I asked.

"I think now that the men were becoming too successful, that they were garnering too much support and loyalty from the soldiers, the lower ranked men. Caio felt threatened. He wanted them out of the picture."

I nodded. I had recently become acquainted with the bitter feelings that accompanied being manipulated into taking a life.

"Is that when you left?"

"No. I stayed for another couple years after that," she said. "I left when I realized that I lacked the prerequisite genitalia for attracting my father's favor."

I nodded, tried to phrase my next statement carefully.

"I've heard some comments about your past," I said. "It didn't bother me then, and it certainly doesn't bother me now."

"There is nothing I could do to change the past, even if I wanted to. Regret that doesn't inspire future change is nothing but wasted energy."

I couldn't argue with that, so I just nodded.

"What position do you find yourself in because of Thiago's death?" I asked. "Where does this leave you?"

"I didn't think that it made any difference at all. Thiago died; they buried him in a huge funeral fit for a head of state, which in some ways, he was. My brother and uncle never felt inclined to look for me before now. It could be that Caio sent his son, Fernando, to kill me. He was a sniper in the army," she said with a casual shrug.

"Why would he want you dead?"

"He may think that I will return home and side with Alex in the power struggle. Maybe Caio thinks that he can beat Alex on his own, but if two children of Thiago united against him..."

"He feels threatened," I said.

Camilla had just spelled out what Caio did to those who he felt threatened him.

"I can't imagine any other reason for Fernando being here," she said.

"So he is a threat," I said, looking at the grainy photo on the whiteboard.

"Not to you," Camilla said lightly. "You shouldn't have to deal with my family issues."

"Are you kidding me, Camilla?" I said, exasperated. "You are my family. Your family drama is my family drama. *Especially* when that drama involves guns."

Camilla smiled and murmured, "Thank you, Elayna. You're family to me, too."

"How much do you want to keep under wraps from the others?" I asked. "How much do you feel comfortable telling them about the situation?"

"Tell them everything," she said with a shrug. "I just wanted you to know first."

I recalled everybody to the meeting. By the time Frankie, Hyde, and Howard came back into the conference room, I had taken the picture of the dead girl from Oakland down from the number one slot, and posted the picture of Fernando Almeida in it's place. I carefully printed his name underneath.

Frankie's eyes narrowed when she saw that Oakland had been bumped. Howard seemed relieved. Hyde was watching me, reading my body language. Camilla and I were standing in front of the whiteboard as they took their seats. It felt strange; I couldn't remember the last time that Camilla or I had presented a case. I gave an overview of the situation, and turned it over to Camilla to answer questions.

"How many men does Caio have control of?" Hyde asked, not missing a beat when I had finished my summary.

Frankie and Howard still looked a little shocked that their kind housekeeper was one of the heirs to a multi-billion dollar criminal organization.

"At this point, I don't know," Camilla answered. "When I left, I would have estimated his loyal men to be at least a hundred. The rest could be bought."

"Are you the older sibling, between you and Alex?" Hyde asked.

"Alex is five years younger than I am," she said. "Our mother died when I was ten, when Alex was five."

"Assassination?" Hyde asked.

"Plastic surgery," Camilla said. "The surgeon told my mother that two shorter surgeries would be advisable, but she wanted to recover from both procedures at the same time. She insisted. The surgeon didn't outlive her by many days, if I recall correctly."

"That must have been a hard loss at that age," Hyde observed.

"It was harder for Alex than it was for me," Camilla said with a shrug. "The woman I consider my true mother was a nanny who passed away when I was twenty. That was right after I graduated college, and right before I entered my father's organization. Maria had always tried to keep me from getting involved in it. I think, in some ways, grief was part of my decision."

"Where did you go to school?" Frankie asked, finally finding her voice.

"Harvard," Camilla said.

"Oh, me too," Howard said in an exaggerated tone, waving his hand in an affected gesture. "Didn't you just *love* the quad?"

We all looked at him.

"Oh, you were serious," he said, eyes wide. "My bad."

"So we need to take some action on this," I said. "Frankie, I want a full run-down on the cartel, tip to tail. I want workups on all major players. I especially want to know how Fernando tracked us down in Italy, if you can figure that out."

"Of course," Frankie said, looking glad to be guided into familiar pastures once again.

"We all need to be extremely aware of our surroundings. Until we know why Fernando is looking for Camilla, we are going to assume there is a kill or kidnap order on her," I said. "Pay attention to anyone who looks like they are following you, or too interested. Especially hispanic men."

"Racist," Howard said, smirking.

I rolled my eyes and continued, "Camilla, you aren't going to like this, but I want you to stay out of sight for awhile. Hunker down here. If you need something, send one of us."

Camilla frowned. "What about grocery shopping?"

"Make a list," I said.

"But who will take the time to smell the tomatoes, to see if they are ripe?" she said. "Howard couldn't tell a head of cabbage from iceberg to save his life."

"Hey," Howard said, sounding offended. "I know that an iceberg and a cabbage are very different."

Camilla rolled her eyes.

"We are talking about your life, Camilla. This is non-negotiable. Stay out of sight," I said.

"But..." she began.

"Frankie will smell the tomatoes," I snapped. "Or Hyde will. Or me. Maybe Howard, under proper supervision. You will not risk your life for a perfectly ripe tomato."

"Fine," she said, sounding contrite.

"Today, Hyde and I are going over to the building site to check on the progress," I said. "Frankie, get that research done, and lay off the Oakland thing for now. This takes priority."

She frowned, but nodded.

"Howard, I want you and Camilla to spend some good time in the range today, brushing up on your long gun and pistol skills. I might need you in the field," I said.

"Yeah?" He sounded hopeful.

"Yeah," I said. "Especially if we are going up against one of the biggest criminal organizations in South America. You have enough material in stock if we need to make an explosive move soon?"

"Yep," Howard said. "Enough to level all of Brazil, if needed."

"Should I be nervous that we have that much explosive material stored here, where we sleep?" I asked.

He looked affronted. "Hell, no. Layna, you know my first rule is 'safety first'."

"I trust you," I said.

It was true. He never did anything stupid when it came to explosives.

"We all have our assignments," I said, in conclusion. "Let's get to it."

Chapter 19

I was processing the morning on the way to my once and future home, so I was quiet. Hyde was driving; I was looking out the window, musing.

Hyde asked, "How much of this did you know, before today?"

"I knew that she had field experience," I said. "I got a referral from Luis. He had done a full background on her but refused to hire her out as an operative because of her age. I went to him, looking for a housekeeper who could be trusted. He put us in touch, but I never asked her full history. I knew that if Luis had recommended her, she was trustworthy. That was good enough for me."

"Does this change any of that trust, for you?" Hyde asked.

"No," I said, shrugging. "We all have a past. Sometimes it rears up and bites us in the ass when we least expect it."

"Isn't that the truth," Hyde said, darkly.

"Why do you say that?" I said, laughing. "Something you need to tell me?"

"No," he said. "Nothing but the herpes."

I swatted him in the ribs and laughed.

We both grew quiet on the ride up the hill. I was remembering the last time we had been on this road. A group of CIA agents had been chasing us down the grade, a ride which cumulated in a steep drop off the side of an embankment, and the destruction of my very favorite truck.

"What did you have done with Helga?" Hyde asked, echoing my own thoughts.

"I have a guy in Sacramento working on her," I said. "The actual truck wasn't salvageable, but the console was still intact. He is making me a replica of the whole setup, should be a couple more months. He's a busy guy."

"Helga two point oh," Hyde said, smiling.

"That's the idea," I said.

Even though the last time I had seen my house it was engulfed in flames, it was still a shock when we crested the hill. The old house had been cleared. Cement barriers were up to protect the sprinkler plumbing from the earthmover parked to the side.

A new foundation had been poured, and the skeletal wooden frames of walls and roof were up. A few workers moved in the unfinished structure, unwinding spools of electrical wire. I could also see a plumbing truck and I assumed the plumber was in the house somewhere. Another team was working on sheathing the roof.

Hyde parked the car well out of the way of the entrance, near the trailer that was serving as the general contractor's office. He knocked on the door while I surveyed the large front lawn, which was brown, and the dead stubs of growth near the gate which had once been Camilla's roses. I felt a twinge of depression, and shoved it away. Another six months, and this place would be more beautiful and lush than before. This was part of the cost I paid to be in the line of work that I was.

The door was opened by a thirty-something man in clean but stained jeans and a button-down shirt. He and Hyde shared a few words at the door, and he went back inside and reemerged a moment later with a shiny green folder.

"You must be Ms. Miller," he said, extending a hand to me when they joined me at the lawn's edge.

"And you must be Mr. Trammel," I said, shaking his hand.

He handed over the folder, invited us to take a look around, and to let him know if we had any questions. He disappeared back into the trailer within a minute of emerging.

"Big talker, that one," Hyde said.

"I'd rather have it this way than have him following us all over the job site," I said. "Let's go look at it."

We entered the house through what would be the front doors. Hyde had a small copy of the blueprints in front of us, and we decided to go left to start.

"This is bigger than the last one," Hyde said, his finger walking down the hallway on the schematic as we did the same in the real house.

"I had him add another bedroom and bath," I said.

"Now that people are coupling off in the team, shouldn't you need fewer bedrooms, not more of them?" Hyde asked.

"Yeah, but who knows how long that will last?" I said, thinking of Howard and Frankie's fight that morning.

I was studying the blueprints, so it took me a moment to realize that Hyde had slipped into silence. I looked up at him, and he was gazing at me, his eyebrow raised.

"I didn't mean *us*," I said. "I was thinking about Howard and Frankie. They don't seem to see eye to eye on a lot of things."

"Hmmm...." Hyde mused. "It's a good thing for you that I'm a pretty secure person. Otherwise, your seemingly ambivalent attitude towards the future of our relationship might hurt my feelings."

"I'm not ambivalent, at all," I said. "And I wasn't talking about us needing separate rooms."

"With the way you snore, it might not be a bad idea," Hyde said.

"I do not."

"How would you know?" he said, continuing down the hallway.

I stood there for a few moments, thinking, then caught up with him.

"Do I really?" I asked, curious.

"You'll never know," he said.

"That's not nice."

The workers had all left for the day by the time Hyde and I were done touring the house's shell. It was going to be more beautiful than I had hoped. The ceilings were higher, the master bedroom and bathroom were bigger. I didn't know how I was going to fill it with furniture. I was glad that Camilla loved shopping for the home as much as she loved buying clothes. She had requested a copy of the blueprints and interior renderings so she could start planning.

"Happy with it?" Hyde asked as I took one last look around the foyer.

"Yes," I said, smiling. "I am."

"Then I am, too," he said.

"Camilla's going to go nuts over that kitchen," I said, turning back towards Hyde as we walked back outside. "About as nuts as I went when I saw the master bathroom design. Mr. Berkin knows our weak spots, that's for sure."

Hyde grabbed my arm, gave a quick jerk, and then I was standing behind him. His muscles were taut, one large arm keeping me back, the other hand under his shirt on the right side, on the butt of his pistol. I peered around him to see the threat.

A man was standing on the dug-out pathway that led up to the front door. Construction workers hadn't laid the brick there yet. I guessed he was in his very early twenties. His long blonde hair looked greasy, from not being washed or from too much pomade, it was impossible to tell. His cheap suit looked shiny in the fading light, and the plaid of his shirt was laced through with lime green. He was far shorter than Hyde, but from the outline of his body under the terrible suit, I could tell that he had spent many hours in the gym, probably trying to compensate for his height.

It was difficult for me to take him seriously. I had encountered some horrifying individuals in my time, and the truly dangerous ones didn't puff out their chests, flex and posture like this guy did. They didn't need to. He noticed my gaze lingering on his body and smirked, a look that made me want to bash his face in, make it impossible for him to make that smug expression ever again.

"Elayna Miller?" he asked.

"Who are you?" Hyde replied, almost in a growl.

I hadn't seen Hyde react this way to anyone immediately before, and wondered if he hated the man's suit as much as I did. Then again, maybe it was the man's smarmy, bad-gangster-movie attitude that had Hyde's alarm bells ringing.

"My name isn't important," he said.

"Then how do you know mine?" I asked, still leaning around Hyde to make eye contact.

I disentangled myself from Hyde's hand and stepped around him. Hyde responded to my movement by drawing his gun and pointing it at the man's head, but he let me pass.

"What kind of antiques dealer needs a full time bodyguard? Is it possible that you might not be exactly what you seem on the surface?" he said, his smirk still in place.

"No one is," I said. "But I get antsy when strange men in polyester suits show up at my house without an invitation. Now who are you, and why are you here?"

"My name isn't important," he repeated, his smug smile faltering a bit when Hyde audibly clicked the safety off. "You have a problem."

"How on earth do you figure that? You look like the only one in trouble, here."

"Tell your goon to lower his gun, and we can talk," he said, his beady eyes shifting to Hyde.

"Nope. Spit it out," I said.

"Your sister owes my boss a considerable sum of money in gambling debt," he said.

"I don't have a sister," I said in a light tone.

"Your sister-in-law. Your brother's wife. Sybil," he said, taking a couple steps forward.

I thought he might be trying to intimidate me with proximity, or maybe he thought that Hyde would be too nervous to shoot him if he was standing closer to me, but all he did was put himself in my effective range of movement. I loved it when people underestimated me. I fed off of it. I smiled.

"This interests you, you know. I looked you up; you've got money. If she doesn't come up with what she owes in three days, we are going to start picking off members of her family. Maybe we will start with her husband. Or maybe we will start with her adorable son. He probably couldn't play soccer that well without his toes."

I lunged forward and hit him in the throat with a sharp, efficient movement, then swept his legs out from under him with my foot. He went flat on his back with a sharp cough, and grabbed his neck with both hands. He writhed there, not yet recovered enough to make another sound.

"You have to be the stupidest son of a bitch I have encountered in years," I said.

I frisked him, found a revolver in his waistband and tossed it to the side. I kneeled, one knee pressed on his chest, the other close to him. His eyes were wide with fear, and I smiled at him, a feral grin. I gave him long moments of eye contact, showing him that I savored this, loved his terror.

"You come to me, not having a fucking clue who I am," I said quietly. "Then you proceed to threaten two of the very few people on this forsaken earth that I would give my life for."

His breathing came in huge, panicked gusts. His chest was heaving and he was shaking, working hard to get air under the pressure of my knee.

"I'm sorry," he spluttered.

"It's good that you are afraid," I said. "You should be. I haven't really decided if you are going to leave here alive or not."

He could see Hyde, and his eyes flicked back and forth between us.

"My boss knows where I am," he said with false bravado. "He will send people to look for me."

I laughed.

"You think I'm worried about your boss? About your boss' people?" I leaned forward and looked him straight in the eye as I said, "You came here thinking I was an unarmed antiques dealer. How big of a threat could your boss possibly be to me?"

He didn't have an answer for that. He chose to focus on Hyde, his eyes pleading.

"Oh, honey," I said, shaking my head. "You are barking up the wrong tree, there. That man wants to kill you worse than I do right now."

His panicked eyes returned to my deadly calm ones.

"Better," I said. "Who is your boss?"

"Anton Kuschov," he said.

"How much does Sybil owe Mr. Kuschov?"

"Twenty thousand," he spluttered.

"Twenty thousand?" I laughed. "You dumbass. You willing to lose your life over twenty thousand?"

"No," he whimpered.

"Good. So here is what's going to happen. I will look into the matter. If the situation is what you say, and she owes you the money, then I will take care of it. You don't do any business with her anymore, you hear me? You are not to contact or touch her or her family. Do you understand?"

He nodded, but I still saw some arrogance lingering in his eyes.

"I don't think you fully understand. Hyde, hand me that folder," I said.

Hyde handed it over, and I wiped it down thoroughly with my shirt. The glossy architecture folder was the only smooth surface I had near me. I picked up the man's right hand and pressed his fingers carefully to the folder, then repeated the process on the other side with his left hand. I handed the folder back over to Hyde, and he took a corner between two fingers.

"Now I own you," I said. "Anyone does further business with Sybil or comes near my family, I personally will come to you for answers. I will find you, no matter where you hide. And I will make you wish you were dead for hours before I kill you."

"Fuck you, bitch," he said. "My boss..."

His words turned into a scream when I tore off his right ear, top to bottom, as clean and easy as if I was pulling the tab to open a dog food bag. He screamed and clutched the bloody wound where his ear had once been. I waited for his eyes to open, for his screams to downgrade into whimpered curses, then I put his ear deliberately into my shirt pocket.

"I'm keeping this, because you came onto my property, threatened my family, and then insulted me. If you do not listen and do exactly what I told you to do, then I will take the other one. Do we have an understanding?"

"Yes," he spat, his eyes showing his fear and anger and pain.

"Excellent," I said, standing. "Get the fuck off my property, and never, ever come back. If anyone from your little group comes here again, I will kill them on sight. Otherwise, I will be in touch."

He sat up and stood, a tentative hand again touching the bleeding hole where his ear used to be. His dazed eyes went to to bloody outline in my shirt pocket, then to his gun laying in the dirt a few yards away. When his eyes met mine, I smiled slow and lazy and gave him a cheeky little wave with my bloodied fingertips, daring him to go for it. He strode over, got into his sedan, and peeled away.

I stared after his retreating vehicle long after it drove off the hilltop and disappeared from sight. It was only when the dust cloud settled that a wave of rage washed over me, and my body began to thrum liked a plucked harp string.

"Elayna," Hyde said, stepping towards me.

"Call Howard for a ride," I snapped. "Get that folder to Frankie. Tell her I want a full run-down on the entire operation. Tell her that this case is a priority."

He had a hand out towards me, a concerned look on his face, but I was already stalking towards the car.

"Where are you going?" he called.

"To talk to my beloved sister in law," I said, my face set in lines of cold fury.

Chapter 20

It took me less than an hour to reach her business, an elegant accounting office in a row of upscale, beige commercial real estate on the outskirts of San Jose. I had only been there once before, at a grand opening party seven years before. She and my brother Peter had just been married, and they used a loan from my parents to open her business. They were happy, and I was happy for them, thinking that they were doing it right, that their life would be simple and clean in a way mine could never be.

The driving time had not lessened my emotions in the slightest. If anything, I had used the time to stoke my anger into a white-hot, burning, calculated fury. Sybil had put my nephew and niece in danger. She had put my brother in danger. She had pretended to be perfect, while hiding this stupid secret that had put everything at risk. I had figured out years ago that you couldn't have a family and dangerous secrets, both. You had to choose.

I yanked open the glass door with the etched 'Miller and Associates' in a cursive font on it. Sybil's chubby assistant looked up with wide brown eyes while I breezed past.

"Can I help you?" she called nervously after me. "I'm sorry, ma'am, she's currently in a meeting."

I pushed open Sybil's office door like I owned the place.

And saw that the one-eared muscle in the cheap suit had beat me here.

He was leaning over Sybil with a grim look on his face. His face was twisted into a grimace, and he hadn't bothered cleaning up the side of his face that I had bloodied. Sybil was cowering in terror, shrinking down into her leather chair to get away from him. I didn't break stride. I grabbed a fistful of the man's greasy hair, kicked the side of his knee and felt the tendons give. I drove his face into Sybil's mahogany desk. I heard a satisfying crunch, like a walnut under a hammer.

"What did I tell you?" I said to him, tearing off his other ear.

Predictably, he screamed, his face still mashed into the desk. I added his second ear to my bloody pocket.

"I told you to go have a conversation with your boss, and not to bother my family again," I put more pressure on his head for emphasis. "Are you that stupid?"

All I got was a muffled cry in response. Blood from his broken nose and his fresh head wound was oozing like spilled syrup over the crisp paperwork on Sybil's desk. I kept hold of his hair, kept his head down, twisted his arm back, and half-drug, half-walked him out of Sybil's office, and out the front door. I tossed him out the front, where he sprawled, leaving bloody marks on the sidewalk. I locked the glass door behind me, and barely got a glimpse of the assistant's horrified expression as I stomped back to Sybil's office.

Sybil was still in the same position, but she had composed her face. My sister in law was a petite woman with faux-blonde hair that was fashioned into a chic, blunt bob. As I watched, she did an unconscious survey of her jewelry, touching both ears to ensure that her pearl earrings were aligned just so, and straightening the rings on her fingers so the glittering gemstones were positioned front and center, where they would be most visible.

"Elayna," she began, in soothing tones.

"Shut your mouth," I snapped. I propped my fists on her desk and leaned over to look her in the eye.

"What did you get yourself involved in?" I snapped. "How did you ever get in touch with those people?"

"It's just a misunderstanding," she said, swallowing.

"That man came to my house today, and threatened my brother and my nephew. Because of you."

"I doubt it would ever come to that," she said, smoothing the front of her silk suit jacket. "I will get them the money."

"Why haven't you?" I said.

"I hit a bad run, but things will turn around," she said. "They always do."

"Oh, no," I said. "You are done with that."

"This is just an overreaction on everyone's part," Sybil said, straightening the disheveled files on her desk. She stopped when she smeared some of the blood that had pooled there.

"They threatened to cut off Jack's toes," I said, my gaze boring into her eyes.

She had the grace to wince, at least.

"Do you not have the money?" I asked. "Is that the problem?"

"I don't mix my personal finances with the family finances," she sniffed.

"Well, your personal issues are affecting your family," I bit out. "Where do you go to gamble? Do you have a bookie?"

"Goodness, no. Nothing like that," she said, looking shocked. "There is a private casino in the Oakland hills that I sometimes visit."

"A private, *illegal* casino," I said.

"Well, yes, but it's very upscale," she said, sounding offended. "Lots of people from the club go. That's how I got invited."

"I don't give a shit if the President himself goes there. I bet those people from the club aren't twenty grand in the hole to a bunch of mobsters."

"Well..." she began.

"You will never, ever go back there again," I said, my eyes blazing. "If you do, I will know."

Her eyes narrowed. "I am grown woman, and I can go anywhere I please."

"Not anymore, you can't," I said. "If you do, I will tell Peter, and my parents. Peter loves you, but his kids' safety comes first. If he knows you are putting them in danger, he will ask for a divorce. Then, the loan from my parents will come due in full. And something makes me think you might have problems getting the caliber of clients you are used to once word spreads that you, an accountant with access to numerous private accounts, is an illegal gambling addict in debt to mobsters."

Sybil crossed her bony arms. "I always knew that you weren't normal. Maybe I will just tell Peter about this little scene, how you beat up a full-grown man in my office as easy as breathing."

I was around her desk with my hands on her before she was aware what was happening. I lifted her by the front of her silk suit and put her up against the wall so hard her pretty head slammed back and her teeth rattled.

I put my mouth right next to her ear, close enough to smell her expensive perfume, and whispered, "If you breath a word of this, I will kill you and make it look like a terrible accident. I never liked you, but I tolerated you because you seemed to be a decent mother, and because Peter loves you. But you have proven that you are selfish beyond measure, putting your kids in danger for your own dirty habits. The very second that I believe that they would be better off without you, something very, very tragic will happen to you."

I dropped her, and she hit the ground hard, a heap of thin limbs, expensive suit and heels. I left her there, undignified and on the ground.

On the way back to my office, it occurred to me that now there were two more people who knew I wasn't quite what I seemed, and one of them was too close to home for comfort.

This was getting out of hand.

"Well, if we're going public, maybe we should come up with a company name and a tagline," Howard said that evening.

I had just finished explaining the situation to everyone. We were gathered around the kitchen island, and Camilla had thrust a large glass of red wine into my hand three seconds after I first mentioned Sybil's name.

"How about, 'Miller Assassinations: When you need the best to kill the worst'," Hyde offered.

"No, I like, 'Miller's Killers: We'll whack 'em and stack 'em'," Howard said.

"I know how to set up an IPO on the stock exchange," Frankie said with a shrug. "If we are interested in taking on investors, that is."

"Fine, but I want input on the logo and which font we use," Camilla said, flipping the steaks she was cooking on the stovetop grill. "Absolutely no Comic Sans."

"Be serious, you guys," I said. "My sister-in-law knows that I'm not just an antiques dealer. My cover is blown."

"Your sister in law doesn't know shit," Howard said. "All she knows is that you lost your temper and were able to beat up a dude."

"He wasn't even a very big dude," Hyde said helpfully.

"I tore off his ears," I said dully.

"You maybe got a little theatrical and over-enthusiastic," Camilla said lightly. "Happens to the best of us."

"Do you still have them?" Howard asked. "Camilla, do we have any fava beans and a nice chianti?"

"Gross, Howard," I said.

"Plus, they are doing amazing things in reconstructive surgery with ears grown on the back of lab mice," Frankie suggested, ignoring Howard. "He'll be fine."

"I threatened to kill her and make it look like an accident," I grumbled.

"Anyone with siblings or in-laws won't hold that against you," Hyde said.

"Seriously," Frankie said. "If I spoke half the thoughts I had during the holidays, they'd lock me up for criminal threats."

"Your grandparents still asking when you will be married?" Camilla guessed.

"They are out of control," Frankie said. "Last time I saw them, my grandmother mentioned a professional matchmaker in Chicago."

"You could always introduce me to your family," Howard offered.

"That wouldn't help," Frankie said. "You're not Indian *or* a surgeon."

Hyde whistled. "Those are some narrow parameters."

"I make more money than a surgeon," Howard argued, his chin jutting out stubbornly.

"So do I, Howard," Frankie said. "But my grandparents still want to know when I'm going to apply to law school."

"Can we focus, please?" I snapped. Then added, "Sorry."

Hyde slung his arm around my shoulders. The weight of his arm was comforting.

"No worries, Layna," Howard said, backing away and covering his ears with a sly grin. "We all know you're stressed."

"Our point is that neither of these people actually know anything," Camilla said, topping off my wine. "Even if they suspected something, they aren't in any position to make accusations."

"Really," Frankie said. "Who would listen?"

"My parents?" I suggested. "The police?"

Howard snickered. "Neither of them are going to go to the police."

"And your parents would choose you over Sybil in a heartbeat," Camilla said, with confidence.

Her conviction surprised me. If what she said was true, it was news to me.

"Besides, what would she tell them?" Frankie said. "That you lost your temper and beat up the bookie that was threatening your niece and nephew? That's not really a *bad* thing."

"How do I explain my proficiency in doing so?" I asked.

"Maybe it's time for me to meet your family," Hyde suggested. "Camilla tells me your mother has been asking about the mystery man in your life."

I narrowed my eyes at Camilla. She had an innocent expression plastered on her face and studiously avoided my gaze as she put the steaks on a platter to rest.

"Yes, my mother's been asking," I said. "That's nothing new, and I don't see how introducing you to them would help my current problems with Sybil."

"We will tell them that we take jiu jitsu classes together," Hyde suggested. "That way, if Sybil does say something, it will explain your talent in violence. Plus, your family meeting me will take some mystery away from your whole situation."

"He has a point," Frankie said. "Knowing your mother, she will be so excited about Hyde being there that Sybil could lay out your whole dossier, with proof, and your mother wouldn't listen."

I frowned down at my wine. I wasn't quite sure how we had gone from my cover possibly being blown to introducing Hyde to my parents.

"Unless, of course, you don't want me to meet your family," Hyde said, lightly.

"No," I said quickly. "No, that's actually a good idea."

"Great," Hyde said. "Call your mother and set it up for tomorrow night."

I pretended not to see Frankie and Camilla smirking at each other.

"Hey," Howard said to Frankie. "How come Hyde gets to meet Elayna's family, and I don't get to meet yours?"

"You're cute," Frankie said, tousling his hair.

Chapter 21

I slept in the next morning. I figured that I would need extra fortitude if I was going to survive dinner with my parents this evening. Hyde and I were supposed to arrive at six. I wandered down the hall at ten to find the others. By this time, I had done a four mile run in the empty gym and showered without hearing a peep from anyone else.

I poured myself a mug of coffee in the kitchen and found them all holed up in the conference room. I watched them for a moment from behind the glass. Frankie was bent over her laptop, typing away. The printer in the corner was spitting out pages, and Camilla was organizing the sheets into packets, stapling the corners neatly. Hyde was studying one of the packets, his brow furrowed with concentration, a pen in hand. Howard was making careful notations beneath several pictures on the board.

I smiled and pushed the door open.

"Good morning, all," I said, grabbing a cranberry muffin from the sideboard.

"Welcome back to the land of the living," Howard said.

"Morning, babe," Hyde said.

Camilla looked up and smiled, but Frankie was too engrossed in her computer screen.

"What are we working on?" I asked.

"Sybil's case," Camilla said. "We are putting together who owns the casino in the Oakland hills. It's an interesting little group."

"Fill me in," I said, taking the seat next to Hyde.

"First up, your disfigured friend," Frankie said, rising to stand next to the white board.

I thought randomly about Vanna White when Frankie gestured elegantly to a DMV photo of a sneering white male.

"His name is Elroy Farley. Looks like he was hired as enforcement. Newly out of the Marines, dishonorable discharge for groping some female recruits. Works for this guy."

She tapped the DMV photo of an unsmiling man in his early sixties that was taped to the whiteboard.

"This is Anton Kuschov, your earless buddy's boss," Frankie said.

Howard interjected, "He defected from the Russian mob a couple of years ago."

"I didn't know you could do that," I said.

"He didn't defect," Frankie corrected. "It's more like he retired. He's still on friendly terms."

"Well, Mr. Kuschov here owns the illegal casino that Sybil owes money to," Howard continued. "Frankie got into his books, and Sybil does owe him the twenty grand."

"She's like the unluckiest person who has gambled there," Frankie said. "Most of the other customers are actually in the black."

"Any idea who all those customers are?" I asked.

"Yes, everything is recorded by social security number," Frankie said. "Sybil was telling the truth. I'm not finished yet, but everyone on the list so far is high class, lots of money. There's a judge, a bunch of lawyers, doctors. It seems like an uppity social club that happens to allow gambling."

"Sybil's the only one in debt?" I asked, my forehead wrinkling.

"No, not the only one," Frankie said. "She seems to be the only one who has allowed her debt to go past the ninety day grace period, though. The others all paid up."

"Is my brother's social security number in the books?" I asked, the thought not occurring to me before now.

"No," Frankie said to my immense relief. "I got into Sybil's email and texts, and it looks like your brother was home with the kids whenever Sybil was at the casino. He thought she was out to dinner with her friend Lucy."

"Who was she really with?" I asked, my hands curling into fists.

If Sybil was having an affair, I was going to tell my brother. I didn't care what she would say about me afterwards.

"Oh, she was with Lucy, but they were at the casino, not a long dinner," Frankie said. "Nothing to indicate that they are anything more than friends."

"Sybil's too concerned with appearances to become a lesbian. Even if she wanted to, she would be too worried about what people would think," I said. "Any idea how to get in and repay this debt?"

"Looks like there is a sort of texting tree with the password," Frankie said. "The casino is open three nights a week: Mondays, Wednesdays and Saturdays. Passwords are sent out the morning of that day. It changes every time."

"We could go in tomorrow, get a feel for the place," I suggested.

Frankie frowned. "I don't want you going in until I know where they are hiding the proceeds," she said. "I don't know where the money trail leads, yet. I would feel better if I found that out before you went in."

"Usually that's the first thing you find," I said.

"This casino is different. I can't find any outgoing proceed transfers," she said, entering a few more keystrokes on the computer. "There are some small cash withdrawals, but nothing that grabs my attention. With the amounts and regularity of the withdrawals it's more likely that those are just under the table payments to vendors and staff."

"So what does that mean?" Howard asked.

"It means that either they are doing a screaming good job at hiding their money trail, or that this casino isn't making any money," she answered. "I wouldn't run a coffee shop on margins this small."

"Maybe they are just getting off the ground?" Howard suggested. "Getting people hooked on the experience, and then they will start raking it in?"

"Usually, it's the opposite way around," I said. "With illegal operations like this, you have to rip people off right away. There is a certain number of people that will only try something like that once, since they are scared of getting caught. If you don't take their money the first time, there is no guarantee that you will ever get a second chance to do so."

"I need more time to find the money," Frankie said. "They're doing one hell of a job at hiding the transactions."

I looked back up at our whiteboard, and sighed. Now there were five cases on our whiteboard. Anton Kuschov's face was in the number one slot with Elroy Farley and Sybil below him. Fernando Almeida was in slot two, and next to that was a picture of our Kent Sulley, our whoring, murderous businessman in Los Angeles. The fourth section was dedicated to Mercer Fulton, the therapist who had been raping at-risk women and girls in San Diego, and Mikayla Johnson smiled innocently from slot five.

Then there was the small matter of not blowing my cover at dinner with my parents tonight. And I had to protect Hyde from my mother's judgemental questioning so he didn't decide I wasn't worth the effort and leave me.

I rested my forehead on the cool tabletop and closed my eyes. I needed to start clearing things off the board, instead of just adding more. I needed a plan.

"Ok," I said, raising my head. "Howard, I need you to take some cash and go buy Hyde a car for tonight. Remember his cover-- he's not the type to buy something in a neon color. Go for something fast and expensive, but in navy, dark green, black or grey."

"How much do I get to spend?" he asked, his eyes alight with excitement.

"I don't care," I said. "We need it for tonight, registered, insured, the whole bit. Tomorrow, Hyde and I are going to go clear up this Sybil issue," I continued. "I will pay off Anton Kuschov, and politely request that he doesn't allow Sybil into his casino again. Frankie, you have that GPS alert on her phone?"

"If she goes within ten miles of that place, I will get a notification," Frankie said.

"Perfect," I said. "Howard, after you are done buying the car, I want a little wearable insurance."

"Meaning?" Howard asked.

"If Anton has me killed, I want him to go 'boom' right then and there," I said.

"So you want a device hooked up to biometric monitoring?" he said. "That's cake, baby."

"Hey," Hyde said. "Watch who you're calling baby."

"Seriously," Frankie grumbled.

"Frankie, I want you to switch gears," I said, ignoring their comments. "I want you to do a quick analysis on Kent Sulley and Mercer Fulton, make sure they are both still single, no new relationships, no planned visitors or travel plans for the next week."

"That won't take me long," she said.

"I want us to be ready to head down to Southern California in a few days. This will be me, Howard, and Hyde. Frankie and Camilla, you will stay behind and work on the Almeida case. Camilla, tell Frankie every name you can think of during that time, and review all the information that Frankie finds. Above all, you are both to stay in the office the whole time."

"With all these cases, I'll probably be too busy to leave, anyways," Frankie grumbled.

"What are you thinking for our Southern California gentlemen?" Hyde asked.

"I don't want to take the time to do a personal touch on either of these," I said. "I want these scumbags off my board. I'm sick of looking at their faces. I was thinking 'robbery gone wrong' for Mercer Fulton. He's a coward, unlikely to be armed. For Kent Sulley, I was thinking an untimely gas line explosion."

"That works," Hyde said.

"Frankie, can you double-check that Sulley hasn't randomly cancelled his gas service? And Howard, can you prep whatever you need for it to look like that kind of an explosion?"

I felt better with a plan.

Chapter 22

When we pulled up at my parent's house, I could feel my mother hovering just on the other side of the door. The front walk was lit up like it was a runway expecting the arrival of Air Force One. I had worn my very favorite dress, an emerald green wrap dress from a New York designer who seemed to have my exact measurements in her studio. I had paired it with black heels and simple black diamond studs. My nails were buffed and polished; Frankie had taken creative license with my hair. I believed that dressing well was a form of armor, the closest thing I had found to kevlar for verbal bullets. Hyde turned off the ignition to the sleek sports car.

I went through our story in my head. We had agreed to say that Hyde was the man I had cut my family Christmas short for, the year prior. In reality, I had been called away to a case in Mexico, one that had gone horribly wrong. But Hyde had entered my life because of that case, so it was as close to the truth as we could come.

Hyde's cover career was that he worked in finance, something to do with technology. I was going to pretend to be ignorant about the particulars of his job, which was fine with me. We were supposed to have met when his art buyer introduced us last fall. Together, we enjoyed scuba diving, jiu jitsu, and wine tasting. Those were expensive hobbies, but unique enough to sound plausible.

I felt like this was the riskiest mission I had been on in over a year. Even though most of our story was fake, if Hyde and I broke up, my mother would continually be asking me about him, or hinting that I let a good one get away. That would hurt, since I was in a real relationship with him. This would be far less complicated if it all was fake, but this story was interwoven with threads of truth, strings of genuine feeling. Panic rose within me, and I gripped the leather armrest.

"What's wrong?" Hyde asked.

"Nothing," I said, managing a weak smile. "It's just that I feel impending doom."

Hyde laughed. "Afraid they won't like me?"

"On the contrary, I'm afraid I won't ever hear the end of it if we break up."

"There's you talking about the end of our relationship, again," he said with a light smile. "Should I be worried?"

"No. I just feel like my worlds are about to crash into each other. I have tried so hard to keep my family insulated from my professional life that this is all very strange."

"Was it your plan that I was only going to be a part of your professional life?" Hyde asked gently.

"No," I said. "That is why this is so odd. I've never had something start in my professional arena and leak over into my family life. I've never tried to have something that spans both areas of my life."

"Elayna, this isn't something that you can pigeon-hole. Our relationship isn't going to fit into one of your tidy niches. It will be alright." Hyde said, bringing my hand to his lips and brushing a kiss against my knuckles. "Worse comes to worse, I've got a .45 in the small of my back. If you want me to break us out at all costs, just give me the code phrase."

"What's that?"

"How about 'banana hammock'?" he said, opening the car door.

I laughed, but I still clenched Hyde's muscled arm as we made our way up the stone walk. Halfway up, I saw a rustle of curtains, and the front door was thrown open to reveal my grey silk pantsuit clad mother, fairly bouncing on the balls of her feet.

"Goodness sakes," I grumbled. "She can't even let us get to the door alone."

Hyde chuckled.

"Hello, Mother," I called.

"Elayna, you're almost late," she said, meeting us outside the door. "Jack has to get to bed on time, you know."

"Peter and Sybil are here?" I said, freezing mid-stride.

"Of course they are. Now introduce me to your friend," she said.

"I'm Hyde Garrison," he said, extending a large hand. "Very nice to meet you, Mrs. Miller."

I was still struck by the information that Hyde would be meeting my *entire* family that evening, not just my parents.

"Mother," I snapped, interrupting the syrupy greeting that my mother was giving Hyde. "Why did you invite them for dinner without telling me?"

"Why wouldn't that be alright? They're your family. They want to see you, too," she cajoled. "I didn't think that you would mind. Do you mind?"

As usual, my mother had caught me in a guilt trap.

"No, of course not," I mumbled.

"Besides, it's such an occasion, you bringing the man in your life home," she said.

She had a firm grip on Hyde's other arm and was pulling us towards the front door. I had the sudden image in my head of a kraken sucking a ship full of sailors down into its whirlpool.

"We haven't met anyone since I randomly bumped into Elayna and her boyfriend in college," she chirped. "What was his name again, dear? Raul? Ronald?"

"It was Rowan, mother," I said, sailors' screams echoing in my mind. "And you didn't run into us. You were waiting outside my Humanities class after you got my schedule from the Dean."

"You hadn't called," she said with a shrug for me and a sweet smile for Hyde. "I was worried."

"I actually met Rowan last fall through business," Hyde said, casually. "He was very polite, and had nothing but good things to say about the one who got away."

"I always had the impression that he was the one that dumped Elayna," my mother said with raised eyebrows. "Maybe he was just being polite when he told you that. What else was he going to say?"

We were inside the front door, now, and then the dining room. In my mind's eye, the sea covered the submerged ship, with only a few shreds of debris floating back to the surface.

"Everyone," my mother called before I could open my mouth. "This is Elayna's friend, Hyde."

"He's actually my boyfriend," I corrected.

"Elayna," my mother stage-whispered. "Not in front of the children."

"Mother, I'm a grown woman," I said.

"Definitely *old* enough," Sybil agreed, sidling over to size up Hyde.

She was wearing a shift of pale pink, with pearls at her ears and throat. She looked like she was about to try and sell us a tea set on the Home Shopping Network.

"Sybil Miller," she crooned, holding out a limp, delicate hand for Hyde to shake. "This is my husband, Peter, and my children, Jack and Isabel."

My mother was in a rush for us to sit down. She tried to seat Peter between me and Hyde, but my brother just rolled his eyes and traded places with me.

"Peter," my mother tsked. "How are we ever going to get to know Hyde if he sits right by Elayna?"

"I'm sure you'll still manage to get some answers," Peter replied.

"Not with Elayna sitting right next to him," my mother snapped.

"I'm an open book," Hyde said, unbuttoning his blazer and settling comfortably in his seat. "Ask away."

My mother looked embarrassed that Hyde hadn't pretended not to hear the exchange. I smiled at him.

I liked him even more, if possible, because he wasn't willing to play her little games.

My father seemed to think his input was needed.

"So Elayna tells us that you are in technology finance," he said. "What exactly does that mean?"

And they were off, through the salad, then the soup, trying to get to know this mythical figure who was my boyfriend. I pretended not to notice that Sybil's eyes were as often on me as on whomever was speaking, her fingers clenched around whatever utensil she was underusing at the time.

My father seemed satisfied early on in the conversation. It was enough for him that Hyde had a steady job, voted in every election, and seemed educated on the broad political strokes of the time. My brother was happy to find out that Hyde like sport fishing, but was disappointed that he didn't waterski. Peter enjoyed any sport where he could take his shirt off and work on his tan.

The preliminary rounds over, my mother and Sybil circled in on Hyde over the main course.

"Who does your taxes?" Sybil asked, batting her eyelashes.

As far as opening lines went, I thought it was time for Sybil to get a new one.

"I do them myself," Hyde said, taking a sip of wine.

"That must be very difficult for you," Sybile said, her eyebrows raised, a glob of mashed potatoes sliding off her fork.

"Not at all," Hyde said easily. "Taxes are just a bunch of rules, no imagination needed. It's rote paperwork. I do mine quarterly, and it takes me about an hour each time."

"Honey," I said in a gentle tone, "Sybil owns her own accounting business."

"What am I saying?" Hyde said, with a warm smile for Sybil. "If you're an accountant, you know exactly what I mean."

Sybil didn't seem to know what to say to that, so she pursed her lips and settled for looking vaguely irritated.

"Ever been divorced?" My mother asked in a high octave. "Any kids?"

"No, ma'am. I've never been married," he said.

"That's very rare, for a successful thirty-something," my mother said, with a sugary smile.

"It is?" I asked pointedly.

"No offense, dear," she said.

I poured myself a third glass of wine and thought of especially violent ways to end and dispose of my next target. Maybe I didn't want our Southern California cases to be quick and clean. Maybe I wanted to take them both to an abandoned warehouse and flay them alive. Maybe I would build cages for them and keep them for weeks.

"I think it's great that Elayna found someone so steady to date," my mother said. "We wanted her to become a doctor, but she did always have a problem coloring in the lines, following the rules. I'm just grateful that she found a way to make money that allows the freedom she likes."

"Oh, I agree," Hyde agreed seriously, giving a playful squeeze to my knee under the table. "I fully support her chosen profession."

"Yes, well," my mother continued. "When she dropped out of pre-med to pursue art history, it was very scary for us. We thought she was going to end up in a hippie commune, with dreadlocks, dancing under the moon."

"Then you don't know your daughter very well," I snapped. "I don't like living out of a tent, and I love deodorant."

"Yes, well," she said. "We're all just so relieved that your little art hobby turned into something that you can support yourself with."

I slid my hand to the small of Hyde's back and fondled his holster. He bit back a smile and squeezed my knee sharply in chastisement. I let my hand find it's way back to my wineglass and took another sip.

The wine was smoky on my palate and warm on its way down to my stomach.

"Maybe you could help her expand her business," my mother was saying to Hyde.

"My business is extremely successful," I argued. "I'm very well-known for what I do."

"It *is* easier to become well-known in a smaller field," Sybil purred. "The whole 'big fish in a small pond' phenomenon. It's much more difficult to gain notoriety in an established field, like accounting."

My mother nodded, her face solemn.

"What an interesting term you chose: 'notoriety'," I said, my eyes narrowed at Sybil.

She looked away, blinking rapidly, and took another sip of her Chardonnay.

"But to be a success in technology and finance!" My mother said, drawing the attention back to her inquisition of Hyde. "That's really something."

"You didn't get in trouble with the dot-com bust that happened awhile back, did you?" My father asked.

"Thankfully, we were pretty well insulated from that. It was going to happen, but the losses we did incur were minor," Hyde said.

Maybe it was because Hyde was playing his role so well, or maybe it was because I was on my fourth glass of wine, but I nearly opened my mouth to ask how his technology firm had forecasted the drop in the market so well. I realized my mistake before I uttered the words. I giggled into my Pinot Noir instead, sloshing some of the wine onto the tablecloth.

"Elayna," my mother tsked. "I think you've had enough wine. What will your friend think?"

"He's my *boyfriend*, mother," I snapped. "We're practically living together."

"Be *quiet*," she hissed.

Her mouth clamped into a thin line and her eyes snapped to Jack, but he was asleep, his head resting on the table inches from his plate.

"And if you think this is the most intoxicated Hyde has ever seen me, you're sorely mistaken," I continued, my volume increasing in proportion to my daring. "The first time we spent a night in a hotel together, we finished off a bottle of whiskey between the two of us. I was horribly hung over the next morning!"

My mother's perfectly-shaped eyebrows had migrated up behind her bangs. I didn't care. I couldn't have her approval, so I would settle for her shock instead.

"He loves me anyways! Imagine that! I finally have someone in my life who I can be myself with. I don't have to pretend, or make polite small talk, or act like I have better manners than I really do, all of which

I find *exhausting*. He likes me in dresses or sweats, and he doesn't find it scandalous that I like to eat cheap fried chicken and watch mixed martial arts. He doesn't mind that I'm not a doctor. He loves *me*. Me as I am, not me as you'd have me be. And mother, I've even *farted* in front of him."

My mother gasped, and I clamped my lips together. Sybil looked smug; my brother was grinning with raised eyebrows. I became aware of Hyde chuckling silently beside me.

"Then we're all very happy for you, dear," my father said, speaking with a serious tone into the stunned silence that punctuated the end of my slightly-inebriated rant. "People search their whole lives for someone to fart in front of. Who wants cake?"

Chapter 23

"That went well," Hyde said lightly, as he helped me to the car.

"I swear I'm not an alcoholic," I said, grasping his arm for moral and physical support.

"I know you aren't," he said. "Like you said, your worlds collided tonight."

"Was it as bad as I think it was?"

He kissed the tip of my nose and deposited me into my seat. "No. You did great."

I stewed in my embarrassment until he made it around to his side.

"My mother is never going to let me hear the end of it," I groaned as he started the car.

"Your mother doesn't fully understand you, but she does love you," Hyde said, pulling away from the curb. "You stood up to her tonight, in your own way. She wants you to be alright, but she has a very narrow viewpoint of what that means. The only reason she has been trying to get you to conform to her ideal life for you is that she thinks that is the only way for you to be happy. She doesn't realize that people can be happy in lots of different ways."

"How did you get to be so smart?" I asked, looking in my side mirror. "Was it all that technology finance schooling?"

"Hey, I own stock in Google and Amazon," Hyde argued. "That counts for something."

We slid into comfortable silence for a few minutes.

"Ugh, why do people always follow us when I've been drinking?" I asked.

Hyde's driving speed and physical stance didn't change, but his eyes came alive, darting between the rearview and side mirrors.

"Are you sure?" he asked.

"No. I'm tipsy," I said as he turned onto a different street. "But that blue sedan back there has been two behind and no closer since we pulled out of my parents' gate."

I fished my cell phone out of my purse and put it on speaker.

"Frankie," I said. "Hyde and I maybe picked up a tail at my parents' house. I need info on a license plate."

"Ready," she said.

I relayed the information and listened to the comforting sounds of precise, rapid keystrokes on the other end.

"Rental car. Origin point was at San Francisco airport," she said. "It was rented a week ago, under the name Daniel Thomas."

"Don't suppose that name tracks back to anything real?" I asked, my voice flat.

"Nope. It certainly does not," she said.

"Alright," I said. "I'll get back to you if we need anything else. Stay by your phone."

I ended the call and turned to Hyde.

"How do you want to handle this?" I asked.

"Well, we have two options: lose him or confront him," he said, his eyes stuck on the rear-view mirror. "If this is Fernando, I would love to have a chat with him."

"Who else would it be?" I asked.

"Just keeping our options open," he said, lightly. "In any case, this might not be the best time."

"Because I'm tipsy?" I said, pressing a hand to my mouth to stifle a burp.

"Because you're drunk," Hyde said. "The nice thing is, he has been quite persistent, and I think that we will get another chance to meet him."

He braked and changed lanes. The car behind us sped up, allowing me a glimpse of the driver.

"That's not our guy," I said, as Hyde accelerated again.

"No?"

"He's some white, young guy," I said. "Blonde hair, beard. Definitely not Fernando."

"Probably just a fan of the car, then," Hyde said. "That's the downside of driving something that costs more than the average house."

"No one's ever followed me just to look at Helga," I agreed.

"We don't want to disappoint our fans. Let's show him how fast this baby goes," he replied, reaching over to snug up my seatbelt.

I was up late again the next morning. Sleeping in was becoming a bad habit. I grabbed a cup of coffee and found my team hard at work in the conference room. Tonight, the Russian casino was going to be open. Hyde and I were going to make an appearance and pay off Sybil's debt.

Frankie was focusing on the first four cases on our board, as I had requested. But new newspaper clippings accumulated under the picture of Mikayla Johnson almost daily. As long as she finished all the work that I needed on Anton Kuschov, Elroy Farley, Kent Sulley, Mercer Fulton and Fernando Almeida, she could look into the gang murders as much as she liked.

"Elayna, your mother called. She wants to schedule a lunch date with you," Camilla said, by way of greeting.

"Now comes the part when I have to pay for my mistakes at dinner the other night," I grumbled, rubbing my forehead.

"Why, what happened at dinner?" Howard asked.

"Nothing," I snapped.

Hyde smirked over his cup of coffee, but didn't say anything.

"Tell her I will meet her tomorrow," I told Camilla begrudgingly.

"There was a new article this morning on the Oakland murders," Frankie said.

Howard rolled his eyes. I guessed that while Frankie was showing some restraint in bringing the case up to me, Howard had the pleasure of hearing all her thoughts about it when they were alone. I didn't mind the change in subject, however.

"What's it about?" Hyde had the kindness to ask.

"It's about one of the first victims," she said, her eyes sparkling. "This activist, Andrew Beck, wrote an editorial about Jerome Wallace, the fourth victim. He says that Jerome had left the gang life behind, and was really active in his community group, trying to get others out of gang activity."

"What's your point?" I asked bluntly.

I was feeling foggy and my coffee hadn't kicked in yet.

"The activist says that he doubts this was a gang hit, like the police are saying. Everyone on the street level knew that he was out. This community leader thinks that these killings need to be investigated as related," she said, shaking the paper. "The truth is going to come out!"

"And what truth is that?" Howard asked.

"That these killings aren't random gang violence. That they are all connected."

"It's one article," Howard groused. "Not even an article by a real reporter. Just an editorial."

"Thanks for your unquestioning support," Frankie snapped.

"I'm afraid my well of unquestioning support has recently run dry," he bit back.

Frankie looked away, not meeting his eyes. I rose my eyebrows and looked to Hyde. He just shrugged. It was clear that there was an undercurrent of something going on here that we weren't privy to.

"Where are we on the Russian casino?" I asked, changing the subject.

They could fight all they wanted, but I wasn't going to encourage or entertain it in the conference room.

"Fine. I did a profile on all the Russian casino's clients," Frankie said, recovering nicely. "I found something interesting. Turns out that most of the clients there are important, rich people. There are a few people that I can't figure out, mostly mid-level government employees, but there are some biggies here. There's a few lawyers who are big players, the head of the building development department, even a judge. The *really* interesting bit came up when I ran records of who is there, when."

"Ok, I'll bite," I said. "What did you get?"

"I noticed that there was this pattern," she said, taping up three pictures, two women and one man, to the whiteboard. "One of these three people is always there when the casino is open."

"I don't get it," Howard said.

"They work in shifts, almost perfectly," Frankie said, animatedly. "Usually, just the women are working. Then I noticed that the man would show up thirty minutes after Patricia Lewis, the head of the building department, arrived. It's like someone calls him whenever she shows up."

"Why?" I asked.

"Well, here's the kicker," she said. "They all were hired, six months ago, to the very same realty office."

I leaned forward and said, "That *is* strange."

"Right?" she said. "There's something else, although I'm not sure what it means, yet. A lot of the people who are winning all the time contributed heavily to the re-election campaign of the current mayor."

"Very odd," I said. "But why?"

Frankie gestured helplessly. "I don't know. That is what I have been trying to figure out for the last four hours. I do know that the metrics are way too precise to be coincidence."

"The realty company thing is weird," Hyde said. "What do they have to do with an illegal casino? Are all of these realtors wealthy?"

"Not one of them," Frankie said. "They only seem to have had a handful of clients over the past six months since they opened. I need to look into that more, though."

"Get on it," I said. "Hyde and I are going in tonight. Howard, where do we stand with that explosive vest?"

Chapter 24

The Russian casino was located in a huge house tucked back into a canyon. The city lights spread out below it like a moving, glittering carpet. Hyde and I walked up to the door ten minutes after it opened, and there was already a line. I was wearing nice jeans, designer flats that were perfect for running, huge diamond earrings, and a blazer that disguised the explosive vest I had on underneath my silk button-up. I carried a leather purse big enough to zip over the twenty thousand dollars inside. Hyde was dressed well, too, looking like he had just stepped out of an ad for expensive clothing for rugged men.

"You should take me on a date," I said, as we waited. "Like a nice one, where we get dressed up."

"This doesn't count?" he asked, chuckling.

I raised my eyebrows at him, but he was spared the sarcasm of my answer. It was our turn to show our phones to prove that the correct number had sent us the entry code. After that, we were ushered into a dimly lit foyer, where we received a very professional pat-down by a man in a dark suit. I noted his size, the communication piece in his ear, and the tell-tale bulges at his right side and ankle.

"I'd like to speak to Mr. Kuschov, please," I told him quietly, as he slid his hands lightly over my hips.

"I don't know who that is," he replied.

"Please let him know that I am here regarding Sybil Miller. I am here to pay her debt."

"I'm afraid you have made a mistake. There is no one here by that name," he said with a frown.

"My friend and I will be at the blackjack table, so whenever is convenient for him to meet with me..." I said.

But he had moved on to the next person.

"Let's get some chips," I said to Hyde.

It didn't take long. Twenty minutes later, Hyde was up two hundred dollars, and I was down fifty and disgruntled. A young blonde woman appeared at my side. She was dressed in a black sheath dress that looked expensive but was cut an inch too low at the bust, and her hair and makeup were flawless. If I had searched for images of expensive prostitutes on the internet, I wouldn't have been surprised to see her face come up.

"Please follow me," she said, touching my elbow.

I slid the rest of my chips over the felt surface to Hyde, kissed him on the cheek, and followed her.

A dark hall led to a well-lit office. There were three men there, and to my great surprise, I recognized two of them. Anton Kuschov sat behind a glass desk. He was a little grayer and a few pounds thinner than the picture on my office whiteboard. He was flanked on the left by the man who had performed my pat-down in the foyer.

On Kuschov's right was a man that I had never expected to see again, a blonde mercenary I knew only as 'Smith'. It had been almost a year since we had met, since I turned down his application and hired Hyde instead. I had grown out my hair since then, and he hadn't known my name. He hadn't struck me as smart then, so I prayed his memory was not as sharp as mine.

I studied Smith surreptitiously as I approached the desk and sat. He was massive through the chest and in the arms, and I wondered where they had found a suit big enough for him. His dull blue eyes rested on me, but they didn't show a flicker of recognition or interest. He didn't strike me as the type to hide his emotions well, so I hoped this meant that he didn't recognize me at all.

"I hear that you have something for me," Anton Kuschov said in lieu of a greeting.

I let the large purse slide from my shoulder and handed it over to the woman beside me. She opened it and nodded.

"Your sister's debt will be erased from our books," Anton said.

"I don't want her coming here anymore," I said flatly, my eyes flicking back and forth between the two guards.

Smith's hand was too close to the inside of his pocket for my comfort, and I couldn't relax.

"You," Kuschov said to Smith. "Get out. You are making her nervous, and I need her attention."

Without a pause, Smith left the room.

"He can be twitchy, that one. But he listens well, and he is very large."

I waited for him to say more. Now that Smith was gone, I had the opportunity to study Anton closely. His nose was large, but there were no tell-tale broken blood vessels that spelled out a lifetime of hard drinking. His eyes were clear and intelligent and were taking in my face and mannerisms in the same way I was watching him.

"After my associate told me what you had done, I asked about you," he said. "I know a little bit about who you are, and what you do."

I nodded once, and raised my eyebrows, waiting.

"My question is whether you are looking to interfere with my business or not."

I took a deep breath, and answered carefully. "I would not be here at all, if your man hadn't come to my home and threatened me and my family."

"I am sorry for that," Anton said, with a grimace. "I would give you one of his ears as a proof of the sincerity of my apology, but he has none left to give."

I didn't even try and look apologetic, because I wasn't.

"He will not bother your family again," he continued. "I have taken care of it. It was overzealous and foolish of him to come to your home without the proper knowledge and deference. He has too much pride, that one. I gave him a very small promotion, and it went right to his head. Started collecting debts on his own, began ordering people around, telling them that he was going to run this group someday. *Fool.*"

"Doesn't sound like the kind of employee you need," I said. "You want people around you who know how to be discreet."

"Oh, he is no longer an employee of mine," Anton said, frowning deeply. "The things he said to me! It was very lucky for him that he did not say these things to me in person. He demanded that I kill you, as payment for his ears. When I told him I would not, he threatened to kill me, instead."

"Then I will feel free to shoot him if I see him again," I said seriously.

"Why *did* you take his ears?" Anton asked. "Of all the things..."

"I told him to listen," I said with a shrug. "When he didn't, it occurred to me that if he wasn't going to *use* his ears, maybe he didn't really want to have them anymore."

Anton threw his head back and laughed. It was a surprisingly pleasant noise for a Russian mobster.

"I do not want my family involved with your establishment, at all," I said, drawing the conversation back to the central point.

"Your sister will be removed from our phone list, and her debt has been paid. If she comes to the casino, she will not be allowed in."

"Thank you," I said. "You said that you know who I am?"

"Yes."

"Then you know that it would be best if we never saw each other again," I said.

"Are you threatening me?" Anton asked, his voice level.

"I'm simply stating a fact," I said. "I have no interest in interfering with what you have going here, as long as my family is left out of it."

"Then I hope this is a final goodbye."

Chapter 25

I called Luis on the way back to the office. Luis was the premier liaison for high-quality soldiers of fortune. He was the one who had found Camilla for me, and Howard, and Hyde. I knew that he would be able to answer my questions about Smith working for Anton Kuschov. I got a voicemail, which was odd. Usually he or an assistant would answer.

I left a message asking him to contact me as soon as possible. It was past midnight when we got back to the office. I found Frankie alone in the conference room, two laptops open in front of her. A stack of newspapers sat to the side, the top one was folded to an interior page that displayed a picture of Mikayla Johnson. Despite our full caseload, Frankie didn't seem to be able to let that one go. I suppressed a flicker of annoyance.

"Hey, did you ever find out anything more about the Russian casino's finances?" I asked her.

"I thought we were moving on to other cases," she said, brushing back strands of hair that had escaped her messy ponytail.

"We are, mostly," I said. "But I saw one of Luis' men at the casino tonight."

"Why does that change anything?" she asked, pushing a stack of paperwork to the side and scrounging for a pen.

"I know how much he costs," I said. "A casino that isn't making much money shouldn't be able to afford him. I wondered if you ever found out how they are hiding their transactions."

"No," Frankie said. "I moved on to other things. I thought this case was going to be closed tonight."

"Well, it is," I said, glancing at the board.

Frankie had already cleared the casino from the number two slot. Kent Sulley frowned at me from that position, and Mercer Fulton was right behind him.

"So, when do you want me to look into this guy?" she said sharply, after I gave her the information.

I frowned at her tone, and said, "Whenever."

"Oh, ok. Whenever," she snapped. "I hope you know that with my current case load, 'whenever' means 'never'."

"I know you're busy, Frankie..." I began.

"I'm not busy. I'm swamped," Frankie interrupted, gesturing wildly at the mounds of paperwork on the table. "You have me profiling an entire Brazilian cartel. I'm monitoring the movements and communications of your bitch of a sister-in-law, Kent Sulley, and Mercer Fulton, all at once. I'm watching the investigations in the Kollins case, and the Werther case. I'm hacking into Penelope Givens' computer periodically to make sure she isn't trying to hunt you down. You want me trying to break complex computer algorithms to track a casino's hidden payments, just because you're curious. And now I get the pleasure of trying to find a blonde, large mercenary with a fake name, from a case that is currently marked as 'closed'."

I blinked at her.

"And no one cares about the case that I think is important, so I don't know how Mikayla Johnson is going to ever have justice," she said, her voice trembling.

"We've been over this, Frankie," I said gently.

"Yeah, yeah. Acceptable losses, and all that bullshit. I think it's crap. Some thug threatens to remove your nephew's toes, and you go ape-shit. But this little girl?" she said, poking the newspaper violently, a tear slipping from her eye. "Someone shot her in the head, Elayna. While she was baking plastic muffins in her play kitchen. So, yeah. I'll get right on that Smith background. You know. *Whenever.*"

She was up and out of the room while I thought of, and instantly discarded, four things to say back to her.

"I think Frankie's stressed," I finally said to Hyde, who had stood silent in the corner during the entire exchange.

"You have been asking a lot from her, lately," he replied. "But I think it's the Oakland shootings that are really eating at her."

I sank into a leather armchair and sighed. "If we can just get through these next few cases, get our board cleared enough to take a breath..."

I trailed off, and Hyde was kind enough not to say what we were both thinking. There would always be more cases than would fit on our board. At times like this, it felt like the flow of evil was a gushing artery and we were a band-aid.

"Do you think I should be giving this Oakland thing more consideration?" I asked.

Hyde took the chair next to me and stared at the board.

"Not right now," he said. "You can number things however you want, but to Frankie, the Oakland case has been number one since Mikayla Johnson was killed. If she had found actionable intelligence, she would have told you."

I gave a weary smile. "That's an understatement. If Frankie knew who was behind that little girl's death, we wouldn't hear the end of it."

"Exactly," Hyde said. "We can't do anything until we know who did it. And Frankie's obviously been looking."

"I don't know that the pattern supports action, even if we find out who did it," I said reluctantly. "Whoever pulled that trigger isn't in the business of going after innocents. What if I choose not to act, even if we find out who did it?"

"That is going to be really difficult for Frankie to overcome," Hyde said. "I don't know if she will be able to let this one go."

"I guess we all have cases like that, cases that jab you right in the heart," I said.

"Yes."

Hyde and I spent several moments with our own separate files of regret before he pointed at a security monitor and winced.

"Someone followed us back here," he said.

My head snapped up; my eyes searched the feeds. "Who? Fernando?"

"The white guy that liked my car," Hyde said darkly. "Guess he's not just a fan of incredible automobiles."

"Where is he?"

"Across the street, biding his time," Hyde said.

I moved to the security console, typed in a few keystrokes, enlarged the security footage in question.

"I see him. So what the heck does he want?"

"Don't know," Hyde said, "He doesn't look like one of Kuschov's men."

"You know what?" I said, pulling a gun from my waistband. "I think I'm gonna go ask him."

Moments later, I strode out of the office, Hyde at my back. I held my gun by my side until the shitbag across the street spotted me and started his car. I drew up and shot his windshield out. He screamed and held up both of his hands, trembling.

Definitely not one of Anton Kuschov's men.

I approached his open driver's window and pressed the warm muzzle of my gun to his temple.

"What's your name?" I chirped with a false smile.

"Kevin Dart," he said. He was starting to shake already.

"Why are you following me and my people around?" I asked sweetly.

He wasn't even going to pretend to be tough. I glanced down and saw a spreading wet spot on the front of his pants.

"Elroy Farley told me to do it," he said. "He says that you are an antiques dealer who owes him twenty thousand."

"I don't owe him shit," I said, caressing his temple and cheek with the tip of my pistol.

"I'm sorry," he said. "I'm sorry. Please don't hurt me. Please let me go."

"That depends on your answers to the next couple of questions."

"Anything, anything," he panted, his eyes screwed shut.

"What happened to your windshield?"

"A rock," he said, latching onto the idea after a few moments. "A rock on the freeway."

"Did you ever follow anyone here?" I asked.

"No," he said.

"Would you be able to find this place again, or tell anyone else where to find it?" I slid the barrel of my gun to press against his throat.

"Never. I wouldn't even know how to begin," he sobbed.

"Good," I said, holstering my pistol. "Go back to Elroy and tell him that you're not interested in being in his fake little gang anymore. Better yet, just stop answering his phone calls. And change your pants."

I turned and strode away, hearing the sound of a car peeling out before I was even back across the street.

Hyde was laughing at my side. "Feel better?"

"A little," I said with a small smile.

I slept well that night, even though I woke with memories of strange dreams of being tied to giant roulette wheel and being spun round and round.

I met my mother for lunch the next day. I followed her lead and ordered a salad, figuring that was almost as good as any verbal apology. She nodded her approval, and we made circular small talk until our plates arrived, never getting to what we both knew was the point of this meeting.

"I feel badly about how things went the other night," she said, spearing a chunk of lettuce with her fork.

"I do, too," I said, honestly. "I didn't mean to drink too much and make a scene. I was just nervous enough with the prospect of introducing you and Dad to Hyde-- I wasn't expecting Peter and Sybil to be there, too."

"What is your problem with Sybil, anyhow?" she asked. "She's never done anything against you."

"We are just very different people."

"I know that you've never been close to her, but *we* used to be close. Lately, I feel like you are so busy with work and your friend that I never get to see you."

"Lunch is a start," I said, smiling, trying to keep things light.

"It is," she said. "I wanted to talk to you about what you said at dinner."

I sighed. "I shouldn't have had that much to drink, and I shouldn't have yelled like that."

"Yes, that was unfortunate," my mother agreed, nodding over her chardonnay. "But what bothered me most was *what* you said, not how you said it."

"What do you mean?" I frowned down at my Ceasar salad and wondered if they had forgotten to add the cheese.

"Do you really feel like I wish you were different?" she asked, sounding perplexed.

"Mother, all you go on about is how I'm not a doctor. How disappointed and frightened you were when I changed my major," I said.

"It's a funny story, dear," she said. "People always laugh."

I waved at a passing waiter. "Can I get some parmesan cheese over here, please?"

"Besides," she continued, "it's only funny because it has a happy ending. You're very successful, and we're very proud of you."

"Maybe you should begin and end with that, and just leave out the funny story altogether," I suggested.

"That's not what I wanted to talk about," she said. "I was thinking that it might be nice if we spent some more time together. I don't know all that much about your work."

"It's pretty straightforward," I said, eye-stalking a thin waiter as he grated cheese over a diner's soup across the room. "Just buying and selling."

"Yes, dear," she said. "But how do you find all the wonderful items?"

"Bazaars, estate sales, things like that," I said, tracking the waiter's progress to our table. "Sourcing items is often the easiest part."

"Cheese?" he offered.

"Yes, please," I said.

"Because I was interested in finding some new furniture for the living room and the dining room."

"Mm-hmm," I said, as the waiter swiped his grater against the block of cheese in an ineffectual movement.

"More?" he asked.

"Please," I said.

"All of the furniture that I like has a classic style," she continued.

"Yes, you have good taste," I said.

"Thank you, dear," my mother said, smiling.

"Is that good?" the waiter simpered.

"More, please," I said.

"I don't want to pay so much money for reproductions if I don't have to," my mother said. "Not when I have a daughter in the antiques department, who can help find me the real thing."

"That makes sense," I said, watching a single translucent shaving fall from the grater onto my plate.

"I'd rather have authentic pieces," my mother was saying.

"Absolutely," I said.

"Which is why I think I should come on your next buying trip with you," she concluded.

"How about now?" the waiter asked.

"No," I said, snatching the cheese and the grater from his hands.

I drug the block of cheese over the grater three times with considerable pressure, and handed them back to the alarmed waiter.

"*That* is how you grate cheese," I said, then turned back to my mother with raised eyebrows. "What, now?"

"I think I should come with you on your next buying trip," she said, her cheeks flushed with excitement. "It would be fun, like an international girls' shopping trip."

"I don't have any trips planned for the near future," I said quickly. "I'll let you know if I plan one that sounds like a good fit."

I couldn't tell her the truth, that I was too busy killing people to take a shopping trip, that most of the antiques I had in my shop and my home were sourced from an auction house in New York City. It weighed heavily on me in that moment that my parents were proud of a complete lie.

Chapter 26

The next morning, I took Hyde's car and drove out to the building site. The contractor and interior designer needed final approval on flooring, cabinet finishes, tile, faucets, and knobs. I had argued that I didn't care, that whatever they chose was fine, but since it was such a huge custom order, they needed my signature on the dotted line. The interior designer told me to plan on the meeting taking two hours. I thought twenty minutes would be plenty.

The sports car's engine was pure power; every acceleration felt as smooth and easy as water drawn from an endless well. The interior was luxurious, the leather seats conforming to my body like the hug of a long lost friend. I enjoyed the drive. It had been a long time since I had enjoyed driving anywhere. Most of the time I was too impatient to get wherever I was going. Or I was being followed by people who wanted to kill me.

Though the car got me to the building site twenty minutes early, I was met by John Trammel, wearing his customary jeans and pressed button-down plaid shirt. Next to him was a slight brunette wearing a black pencil skirt, white button-down shirt, and black wedges. She smiled at me brightly, and came forward with an outstretched hand.

"Ms. Miller? I'm Amy Buckwith, from Buckwith Designs," she said, smiling with even, bleached teeth.

"You look quite young to own your own design firm," I said, shaking her hand.

"I'm very good at what I do, but I inherited the company from my mother," she said. "Family business. I grew up playing with carpet samples."

She led me into the house, where sheetrock was up. I could really envision what things were going to look like now. I smiled.

"I know," Amy said, with an answering smile. "Don't you just *love* that smell? This is when things start to get exciting."

She must have been at the site for awhile, because she had tacked up a board in every room, showing the specs of her designs. We started in the foyer, where she had chosen a large chandelier, sconces to match, dark grey paint, and deep ebony flooring in a herringbone pattern.

"Love the lighting and the floor pattern, but I want the paint and the floor lighter," I said, tapping the board. "I want the whole house to feel airy, serene. I'm not trying to make a grand statement or impress anyone. This house is for me."

Amy bent down and shuffled through a large leather tote.

"How about we go with the same tone of grey, but just go a few shades lighter? For the flooring, how about this?" she suggested, holding out a paint chip fan, and a chunk of wood in a light tone. "It's still hardwood, but it's a lighter walnut color."

"Perfect," I said, moving into the living room while she made furious notes in a leather-bound binder.

We continued on, room after room. I knew why the architect had contracted with Amy Buckwith by the time we were through the kitchen. She had an amazing vision for the space, and she was able to translate my very few criticisms into tangible options that satisfied us both.

"Do you work with furnishing design as well?" I asked her after I had approved tile choices for the bathroom.

"Yes, but I was under the impression that you already had a finishing designer."

"I usually choose my own furnishings, but I'd be curious to see what ideas you came up with."

"Will do."

I lingered at the site after Amy Buckwith and John Trammel left. I promised Trammel that I would drop the keys in the door slot of the trailer that he was using as an office when I was done. I explored the house at my leisure. It was far larger and grander than the one that had stood here before. I smirked at the unobtrusive sprinkler system that had been installed in the ceilings. Sprinklers wouldn't stop one of Howard's bombs, but it was building code and made the architect feel better that he wouldn't have to rebuild this house in another couple of years. Maybe.

I was walking through the front hallway, admiring the custom windows and the view, when a car squealed onto the driveway. I slunk back into the shadow of the wall and drew my pistol from my ankle holster in one fluid movement. It was a silver sedan. I watched as the car lurched to a stop by the front walkway. A blonde woman emerged from the driver's side. Her eye was swollen and red, her lip was bloodied.

"Elayna!" Sybil screamed, running towards the front door.

I holstered my pistol and went out to meet her. She latched onto me, crying hysterically.

"Is there anyone with you? Is anyone following you?" I asked tersely.

"No," she sobbed, sagging against me.

"What happened?" I demanded, guiding her to sit on the stone step of the porch.

"He...he came back to my office, when my assistant was gone," she said, clutching the front of my shirt. "Told me that I owed him twenty thousand dollars. Said that it was my fault his ears were gone."

"Elroy Farley did this?" I said, taking in her swollen eye, her bloody lip, the bruises forming on the side of her face.

"He said that he didn't care that you had paid my debt at the casino. Said that I owed *him*, not the casino," she said, her voice cracking. "Elayna, he said that he is going to give me a week, then he is going to pay my family a visit. He gave me these."

She produced four sheets of computer paper. They were black and white, grainy images, no doubt printed off a low-resolution digital camera. There was Peter smiling down at Isabella as he pushed a cart out of a grocery store, Jack biting his lip in concentration as he played soccer, Peter carrying a briefcase in a parking lot, the front of Isabella's private day care center... He was stalking them. He was stalking my family, threatening them.

"What am I going to do?" Sybil blubbered. "I need twenty thousand dollars. Elayna, can I borrow twenty thousand dollars? I'll pay you back, I promise."

She must be terrified to humiliate herself enough to ask for a loan.

"Elayna," she continued. "Please..."

"I need a minute, Sybil," I said, coldly.

I was still staring at the photos, a hot rage roaring in my blood. From practice, I took some time, trying to catalog my thoughts, separate my reckless impulses from my logic. I inhaled slowly and expelled the air through my nose, as my teeth were clenched.

"First things first," I said evenly. "You will need a way to explain your face."

"My face? What about the pictures? The money?"

"I will take care of the money, and I will take care of that asshole."

"How?" she whined, tearing up again.

"The less you know, the better," I said lightly. "Suffice it to say that I know someone who will help me handle this situation."

"Is it your boyfriend?" she sniffed.

"Stop asking questions," I said. "The easiest way to explain away your injuries is a car accident."

"A car..."

"Yes, a car accident," I snapped. "On your way home, you are going to buckle up, and drive into a tree. You'll want to be going about twenty-five miles per hour when you hit it. There needs to be significant damage to your car to explain your face, but you don't really want to hurt yourself."

"Alright," she said, sounding uncertain.

"And don't tell anyone that you were here, that you spoke to me."

"Fine."

"I'll take care of the rest," I said firmly. "Off you go."

"Now?" she asked.

"You'll be heading home late as it is," I said.

I stood, helped her up, and gave her a little push towards her car.

"Alright," she repeated, looking a little dazed.

I didn't spare much worry for her. My concern was on the pictures clutched in my hand, on my niece, nephew, and brother.

Sybil slipped into her car, and I heard the engine purr to life. I watched her pull around the circular drive, then looked on in horror as she pulled her car off the pavement.

"Not here, you idiot!" I cried, just as her car listed off the road and came to stop after bumping into a pine tree.

I ran over to her car, my feet giving flight to my frustration. By the time I reached the car, I could hear her voice through the open window.

"I've been in a terrible accident," Sybil was saying. "I'm at Elayna's house. Come quickly."

I snatched the phone from her hand and hit the disconnect button on the screen, noting that she had been speaking to Peter.

"Are you the biggest moron on the entire planet?" I yelled. "How are you going to explain why you were over here?"

"I don't know," she sniffled. "Maybe we had lunch plans?"

"You are having lunch with someone you despise at three in the afternoon?" I shouted.

"Don't yell at me," she said, her face screwing up in genuine tears. "It's been a very hard day."

"You didn't even wreck the car properly. No one is going to believe you got *those* injuries from *this* weenie car accident."

"I didn't know what to do," she sobbed.

She was full-on ugly crying now. Her perfect features were twisted and leaking, but I had no time to enjoy how terrible she looked. I had no time for sympathy, either. Peter's office was only thirty minutes away.

"What are you doing?" she shrieked as I wrenched open her car door and yanked her from the driver's seat.

"Go sit over there," I demanded.

I slid into the driver's seat, buckled up, put the car in reverse, and backed up in a cloud of dust. Then I put the car in drive, and floored the accelerator. At the last possible instant, I released the steering wheel to throw my arms up in front of my face. The impact into the tree was rough. I was thrown against the seat belt, and the force of the airbag deployment jarred the air from my lungs.

I turned off the ignition and exited the car, shaking the after-effects of the wreck from my head. I was a little woozy, and I would definitely have bruises tomorrow. But the front of the car was molded around the tree trunk and the windshield had exploded. It was convincing.

I loaded Sybil into my car and called my brother.

"Hello?" he answered, his voice sounding frantic.

"I'm taking Sybil to Mercy General," I said, starting the car. "You should meet us there."

"What happened? Is she ok?"

"Just some bumps and bruises," I said. "I think she will be fine."

"I'll meet you there," he said, disconnecting the call.

Chapter 27

"Oh, look," I grumbled. "The whole hee-haw gang is here."

Sure enough, my mother, father and brother were gathered outside the entrance to the emergency room when we pulled up.

"Remember," I said to Sybil. "If you don't know what to say, let me do the talking."

The time spent in the waiting room was aggravating, to say the least. The nurses took one look at Sybil and directed us to some chairs in the back. This infuriated my brother, who thought that the damage to his wife's face merited a declaration of emergency. My mother wrung her hands, over and over, and wondered what was taking so long.

I wondered if I could leave without being rude, and by the look on my father's face, he was pondering the same thing. But I didn't trust Sybil to come up with a convincing story. Finally, finally, Sybil and my brother were escorted back to a curtained room.

It was an hour later when we were able to go back and see her.

"I just don't understand how your face could be so banged up from a tiny car accident," my brother was saying. "Was your airbag defective? Should we sue?"

Sybil looked at me desperately, and I realized that she had no idea if the airbag had deployed or not. I slid over beside Sybil's slight quivering frame and took her tiny hand.

"Sybil," I said, injecting gentleness into every word. "It's time to tell the truth."

"It is?" she said, trying to blink back the moisture in her blue eyes, a tremor in her voice.

"Tell us the truth," I repeated in a low tone. "You weren't really wearing your seatbelt, were you?"

Sybil looked back and forth between the questioning faces around her bed.

"You're right," she said, breaking down into tears again. "I wasn't."

"Sybil!" Peter exclaimed. "How stupid! As it is, Dr. Berath says that you will have bruising for a couple weeks, but this could have been so much worse. You could have been really hurt. Or even scarred!"

"I know. I'm sorry, Peter," Sybil said thickly. "It won't happen again."

"I certainly hope that you always strap the children in," Peter accused, standing straighter, his eyes wide.

"Of course, I do," Sybil said, sounding offended. "I wouldn't ever be reckless with their safety."

I raised an eyebrow and looked pointedly at her. She met my eyes briefly then ducked her head.

"I'm glad to hear that," Peter said.

"It was a stupid thing," Sybil said.

"I still don't understand why you were at Elayna's," my mother insisted, as if this were the most important part of the equation.

"I suppose we are going to have to come clean about that, too," I said, ducking my head and avoiding my mother's eyes.

Sybil looked alarmed, but thankfully no one was watching her at the moment.

"Peter's birthday is coming up," I said, trying to sound regretful. "Sybil asked for my help planning something for him."

"You were planning me a surprise party?" Peter asked with a small, pleased smile.

"Without me?" My mother demanded, to me. "You never said anything at lunch."

"It was just in the beginning stages," Sybil said to my mother. "I was headed to your house to get your input on the color scheme and the menu when I hit the tree."

"Oh, well..." my mother trailed off, waving her hands and sounding a bit mollified.

"Where is it going to be?" my brother asked.

Sybil looked at me again, her mouth opening and closing like a fish out of water.

"My house," I said, then regretted the words the moment they were out of my mouth. "We thought it would be fun to decorate the big empty space."

"Oh, that *will* be fun," my mother exclaimed, clasping her hands together.

By the time I left the hospital, my mother and Sybil had decided on the theme, colors, and menu of the surprise party that we had never planned on having. It was going to be in two weeks, and I had agreed to ask Camilla to make all the food for a fiesta-themed bash. Peter solemnly promised to act surprised.

I wondered how I was going to get my family clear of the Elroy Farley danger, kill everyone who needed killing, and host a party, too.

I explained the new development to my team when I got back to the office.

"Elroy Farley needs to die," I said, slapping the printed photos of my family on the conference room table. "I want to do it before we head down south. I don't feel comfortable leaving the area with this one pending."

"So now we have another case on our board," Frankie grumbled.

"Do you have a problem with that?" I asked, raising my eyebrows.

"Oh, no. Not at all," Frankie said, in a tone that contradicted her words.

I let it go. I didn't have the energy to address her attitude at the moment.

"Super," I snapped. "Get me an address. Howard, get another gas line bomb ready."

"Don't you think this case deserves a more up-close-and-personal treatment?" Howard asked, his forehead creased.

"I just want to blow him to kingdom come," I said, pushing my hair back from my face.

"I get trying to send a message, but..." Howard said.

I cut him off. "I just want it done, Howard. Ok? I have two Southern California assholes calling my name, a Brazilian gangster following us around, not to mention Luis hasn't gotten back to me about Smith. And now I have a surprise party to plan."

"Elroy Farley, twenty-three," Frankie said. "American father, deceased. Russian mother, which must be how he got in with Kuschov. From what we can tell, he was a very low-ranking member of the organization, more like someone trying to earn his way in. Kuschov kicked him out, and now he's gone a bit rogue with his collections."

Frankie continued, "From what I can tell, he lives alone. Or at least, he's the only one paying the bills."

"That makes that easy," I said.

"I have no way of knowing if he really lives alone," Frankie cautioned. "You know how these houses are. Someone is paying the bills, but there could be six dudes crashing there."

"We'll do it late at night," I said, waving my hand to clear the air of her arguments. "If there's more than one guy there, we will hold off on the whole thing."

Chapter 28

E lroy Farley lived in a single-family home deep in the bowels of Oakland. The paint was peeling in large strips and chunks, giving the house the appearance of a large snake in the midst of shedding its skin. The front patch of yard had been filled in with lava rock years ago, but much of it was gone now, exposing mounds of sun-blanched earth. It looked like the scalp of a pale redhead who was going bald.

Hyde's thermal imager told me that there was only one occupant in the house. That heat signature was prone, about six inches off the ground, the height of a mattress tossed on the floor. I opened the car door to the relative quiet of the night. It was well past midnight, in the magic time where the bars have closed but it isn't time for the early commuters to be up yet.

The constant whoosh of traffic from the nearby freeway muted other noises--a barking dog in the distance, someone's television left on. It's owner was most likely in a self-medicated stupor to be able to sleep through that. The fog of the early morning was just now overtaking the heat of the day. The smell of warm asphalt was still present, but car windows were being laced with moisture, and my breath left a faint impression in the air.

Howard slunk beside me, a small device in his right hand. We were going in together and Hyde was going to be our driver on the way out. I moved to the back of the house, Howard right behind me. We were both wearing black, and I thought we looked like the world's shortest funeral procession. The thought saddened me, then I rolled my eyes at the emotion.

Elroy Farley's funeral would show no such pomp and circumstance. There would be no somber, silent procession of mourners dressed in black. Instead, friends, relatives and acquaintances would crawl from every crack in his life, determined to be the one who knew him best, the one who talked to him last, the one who had a feeling that something wasn't right the night he died.

If a local news camera appeared after the explosion, they would jostle for position in front of it, wailing their loss while privately wondering who was going to get his car. There might be a makeshift shrine erected in front of the scorch that used to be his home. He would be toasted again and again, and at the end of it, his name would be inserted into slurred attempts to get laid. Elroy Farley would be far better and more popular in death than he ever was in life.

We were at the back door, and Hyde's voice was in our ears. "He's still sleeping. No movement."

I had the door open in seconds, the cheap brass knob a pitiful barrier to my lock-picking skills.

"Still no movement," Hyde said as Howard and I entered the house.

The light in the hall was on, and I watched my feet on the worn-through linoleum, stepping over a pair of scuffed leather lace-up boots and around an over-stuffed bag of trash. The house stank of unwashed males and unopened windows. The faint smell of old Chinese take-out or flatulence mingled with the distinct odor of shoes worn too long with too little drying time. I crept up the stairs towards the bedroom as Howard made his way to the kitchen.

The carpet on the stairs was oily and matted in the middle. I focused on keeping my steps to the outside of every tread to minimize squeaks. From behind me, I heard the very slow groan of an oven being opened cautiously. I paused, until Hyde reassured me once more that Elroy had not woken.

At the top of the stairs was a tiny landing, not large enough for two adults to stand comfortably. The door to my right was closed, but it was the room directly ahead that was my concern. That door was open, and I could see my target. The blonde hair was a contrast to the darkness of the grubby pillow beneath it. His frame was the right size and shape. It was enough to satisfy me.

I began to back down the stairs, placing each foot carefully and easing my weight onto it before lifting the other. Howard was waiting for me in the hallway.

"We good?" he whispered.

I nodded. "It's a go."

The explosion wasn't as satisfying for me as it usually was. My mind was already on the next case.

The next morning found me uncomfortable, holding my to-go coffee cup because Hyde's stupid sports car didn't have a cup holder in the miniscule backseat.

"If I'm the leader of this group, how come I got stuck in the backseat?" I grumbled, trying to stretch my legs out one at a time over the center console.

"It's cause you're the woman," Howard said, goading me.

"Nah," Hyde said, practically. "It's cause you're the shortest."

"Well, I don't like it," I said. "The engine is so loud back here. When you accelerate, we can't even hear each other."

"You mean like when I do this?" Hyde said, accelerating.

The engine roared, my sullen eyes met his amused ones in the rearview, and I stuck my tongue out at him.

"Fine," I said when he let his foot off the gas pedal. "But the next time we stop for fuel, someone has to switch with me."

Hyde pressed his foot on the accelerator again, and Howard yelled back at me, "Sorry! We can't hear you!"

"Sorry, babe," Hyde said, when he let off the accelerator. "It's this car. Makes me feel immature."

"Yeah, yeah. Blame the inanimate object for your shenanigans," I grumbled.

He caught my eye in the rearview, giving me a smile and a wink.

"You guys are really going to make this work, aren't you?" Howard said in a serious tone.

"What do you mean?" I asked.

"Like, the two of you, together," he said waving his hand to encompass the space between me and Hyde. "Your *relationship*."

"Yeah," Hyde said, his eyes flicking to Howard's face, and then back to the road. "Why do you ask?"

"It's just... I don't know if Frankie and I are as solid as I thought," he said, a frown marring his features.

"Why would you say that?" Hyde asked. "I thought you guys love each other."

"We do," Howard said. "Well, I do, at least. The past couple weeks, Frankie has been really preoccupied with something. The other day, I answered her cell phone when it rang because she was in the bathroom, and it was another guy. He asked for Frankie, and when I said she was busy, he wouldn't give me his name, and just hung up."

I was struck dumb by this information, my eyes round.

"Did you ask Frankie about it?" Hyde asked, calmly.

"That's the worst part. I'm sure there could be a million plausible reasons for that call, but it was her reaction that made me worried," Howard said sadly. "She got completely weird about it, stuttering and denying. She even argued at one point that it must have been a wrong number. When I reminded her that the guy asked for her by name, she got really flustered and she wouldn't even talk about it anymore."

"Did you check the number through the system?" I asked.

"It was a blocked number," Howard said, sounding defeated.

"If everything else is going well, I wouldn't worry too much about it," Hyde said confidently.

"You think?" Howard asked, sounding hopeful.

"Anyone who spends time with Frankie can tell a few things right off the bat," Hyde said. "One, she loves you. Two, she is a terrible liar. And three, she has a strict moral code. So if she is keeping something from you, it's probably not something that will end your relationship. It's more likely she is planning some sort of surprise."

"Yeah?" Howard said.

"Frankie isn't the kind of girl that cheats. I've known a few of those, and she isn't like that," Hyde said. "Believe me."

"Still doesn't feel good," Howard said. "Not knowing everything, her keeping something from me, lying to me like that."

"Nope," Hyde said. "Can't imagine that it does. But I bet there is a good reason, and I bet she will tell you before long."

"I hope so," Howard said, turning to look out the window.

I waited for a few moments, until I was sure that Howard wanted the conversation to move on to new things.

"I would like to go back to the part of this conversation where you mentioned that you knew a few girls who cheated," I said to Hyde, leaning forward over the console with my eyebrows raised. "Were you the victim of, or a willing perpetrator in this cheating behavior?"

Hyde looked forward and pressed the accelerator so hard that I was pushed back into my seat with the momentum.

"Oh, very funny!" I shouted over the roar of the motor. "Hilarious!"

We reached Los Angeles right as the beginning throes of rush hour gripped the city. We had switched drivers at a gas station on the way, but I was still in the backseat. Hyde had attempted to get back there, but the only way he could fit was if he pulled his knees up to his chest. Since I needed him to be able to walk when we got to L.A., I conceded defeat.

"What good is all this horsepower if we are stuck in traffic?" Howard grumbled, jerking us to a stop again.

"What I don't understand is why you keep getting right up behind people and then slamming on the brakes," I snapped.

Four hours in the backseat had done little for my mood.

"*This* is why I hate Los Angeles," Howard said, slamming on the brakes again. "All the traffic."

"I thought it was all the smog," Hyde said, with a smirk.

"I thought it was all the dirty hippies," I said.

We had spent the last five miles with Howard playing his own very cranky version of 'I Spy'. Howard narrowed his eyes and continued to put first gear and the brakes through the ringer.

By the time we reached the hotel, we were all ready for some space. Thankfully, Frankie had reserved us an enormous suite toward the top of the Los Angeles Ritz Carlton. The room was lovely, and I sighed as I shrugged off my leather jacket and took in the views of the city, mountains, and ocean.

"I've never asked you this before, but why do you spend so much money on hotels?" Hyde asked.

"Security and service," I answered. "Expensive hotels have the best of both. And they are used to odd requests. I once was able to have a spot of blood removed from an overcoat at three in the morning so I didn't blow my cover the next day."

"Plus, room service is way better than a vending machine," Howard said, seriously.

I laughed and added, "The high thread count sheets don't hurt, either."

Chapter 29

Kent Sulley lived in a tidy neighborhood with neatly trimmed squares of green in front of every stucco house. This was the kind of neighborhood with high homeowner's association fees, a roving security service, where people knew their neighbors and made note of strangers. We drove through once in the non-descript rental car that we had picked up near our hotel, then parked down the block from Sulley's house.

"Frankie says that he's home," Howard said after a brief phone call.

"How's Frankie doing?" I asked. I hadn't spoken to her since our difficult conversation the night before.

"She's still there," Howard said in a clipped tone.

I didn't ask any more questions.

"We all clear on the plan? I asked.

Howard pointed to me, then Hyde, then himself, in quick succession and said, "Distract. Infiltrate. Explode."

"That's it in a nutshell," I said. "Contact me once you're in position."

I waited while Hyde and Howard exited the car. I tried to focus on the case. Kent Sulley was a successful Human Resources executive who killed prostitutes on his lunch break. He liked hiring pretty young women and then killing a hooker that bore a resemblance to them. He would tell the prostitutes to bring drugs along, enough for two, then would inject them with all of it.

It was a difficult one for the police to pursue, even if they had caught on to the mere existence of a pattern. Sulley wasn't an aggressively-paced killer. One woman every six months or so was enough to keep him satisfied. In all of the deaths, the police had deemed them as accidental overdoses. After all, the hookers were the ones buying the murder weapon.

Frankie had only found out about the murders by running a statistical analysis on deaths in Los Angeles. These were too regular, too perfectly spaced to be random. Frankie had identified the killer by hacking a drugstore's security video. She had found Kent Sulley on the video, buying the gift credit card that he later used to pay for the room. He had also bought a tube of lipstick. Frankie went back through all the prostitute autopsy photos and realized they all had freshly-applied lipstick.

So we were here. My earpiece came to life with a muffled crackle.

"We're in position at the back door," Hyde said. "We will need about two minutes once you knock."

I shut the car door quietly behind me. The fewer people who noticed someone speaking to Kent Sulley before his house blew up, the better. I strode up to his door, my heels clicking a confident rhythm. I knocked on his door, my face in a friendly smile, my lips painted the same color as his last victim, anything to keep his attention as long as possible.

"Kent Sulley?" I asked when he cracked open the door.

His pinched expression relaxed a bit as he took me in from head to toe, but he didn't open the door further.

"I'm Sara Trent," I said, smiling broadly. "Tara Moore gave me your address, told me to stop by if I was interested in a job."

Tara Moore was one of his most recent hires, the one who his latest victim most resembled. He opened the door further, raked his eyes over me again. I had dressed like I was going to a job interview, if hookers went on job interviews: black blazer, black mini skirt, black hose, six inch heels.

"She didn't mention it," he said.

I pasted a look of concern and confusion on my face. "She didn't mention me? Sara Trent? She said there was an opening in her department that I would be perfect for, Assistant to the Human Resource Director?"

He nodded, "We have an opening, but I'm sorry, interviews are already scheduled for next week."

I winced. "I'm really sorry. I thought that she had let you know that I was coming by."

"Her giving out my home address is highly irregular," he said, looking me head to toe again, and frowning.

"I guess she thought it would make me stand out as an applicant," I said, pressing my lips together and looking up like I was blinking away tears. "Shit, this is just my luck. I've been out of work for months. Much longer, and I'm going to be out on the streets."

That got his attention. I saw his pupils dilate slightly. So that was his thing? He liked the women who were down on their luck, not the successful ones he hired?

"Do you have a resume?" he asked.

"Yes," I said, rummaging through my purse handing over a single sheet of paper.

It was a sad resume, with misspellings and no relevant work experience. His pupils seemed to dilate more as he looked at it. He reached down and adjusted his crotch slightly. I had to work hard to keep my face vulnerable, hopeful. Then I thought of how happy I was to be here, and my smile grew a little bigger and a lot more genuine.

Hyde's tense voice came, unexpectedly, over my earpiece, "We need more time. Ran into an unexpected problem. We need another minute."

I slumped my shoulders, leaned against the doorway, into Kent Sulley's space.

"Who am I kidding?" I said, letting the smile slide off my face, working my bottom lip into a tremble. "I know that my resume isn't that good. I just hoped... I mean, I thought there might be something I could do to get an interview."

I looked up through my fluttering lashes, and I knew I had him. He was a predator at heart, no matter how well he kept it covered from day to day. Like a wolf who had unexpectedly spotted an injured doe, I was on his doorstep, unplanned but irresistible.

How much of the minute was left? I pressed my luck, licking my lips and reaching my hand out to press it against Sulley's chest. His breathing hitched, his heart beat wildly, and I looked up.

"Isn't there anything?" I almost whispered, sliding my hand slowly in the direction of his belt. "Anything I can do to get an interview?"

"Yes," he grunted. "But not here. Not now."

"Where?" I said, leaning in. "When?"

"Tomorrow, the hotel on Wentworth and Broadway," he said, watching closely to see if I balked.

I leered at him. "What time?"

"Noon," he said, firmly. "Bring some special refreshments. You know what I mean?"

"Yeah, baby," I said, my fingers scratching a circular pattern on his lower stomach. "I like to party that way, too."

"We're out," Hyde's voice said in my ear.

"See you then," I said, turning away.

He grabbed my arm roughly, spun and pulled me to him. I forced myself to stay loose, compliant.

"You better be willing to make this worth my while," he hissed. "You wouldn't like what I do to women who tease me."

"If you will get me an interview, I'll do anything tomorrow," I said, pressing my body against his as his hand clenched my rear viciously. "Anything."

I pulled away, blew him a kiss, and sashayed down the walk. I felt his eyes on me nearly as plainly as I had felt his hands a moment ago. I turned the corner, out of his view, and strode the rest of the way to the car.

Hyde was already in the driver's seat, a stony expression on his face, his eyes straight ahead.

"What was the hold up?" I asked as I slid into the front passenger seat.

Then I turned, and came face to face with the issue.

Howard was holding a hissing, massive white cat.

"What is *that*?" I asked.

"It's a cat," Hyde snapped. "Howard wouldn't leave it behind."

"I got groped for a *cat*?" I asked.

"He groped you?" Hyde asked. His jaw clenched, and he gripped the steering wheel until his knuckles blanched.

"I couldn't just leave him there," Howard said, his voice almost a whine.

I was speechless for a moment, trying to absorb the situation. Then I noticed that Hyde and Howard were bleeding from numerous scratches on their forearms, but Howard also wore those same marks on his face. He was holding the angry cat out from his person like it was a hot potato that he longed to hand off to someone else.

I laughed until I bent at the waist, tears streaming from my eyes. Neither Hyde nor Howard joined in my amusement.

"It's not funny," Hyde said, after my laughter subsided for a moment.

"Oh, yes it is," I said. "I mean, *look* at Howard."

"We put you in danger for a *cat*," Hyde said, staunchly. "You could have been killed."

"By that guy?" I scoffed, raising my eyebrows. "Part of me just wanted to snap his neck in the doorway and be done with it. Speaking of... Howard, isn't it time to flip the switch?"

"I...I can't," Howard said, bewildered. "If I put the cat down, he claws me half to death."

"Hyde, pop the trunk," I said, matter-of-fact.

Howard looked horrified. "The trunk? He can't ride in the trunk."

"Oh, that cat's going in the trunk," I said. "The only thing up for debate is whether you go in there with him."

Hyde finally cracked a small smile, and pressed the button. I opened my door, slid the seat forward, and Howard slid-shuffled out, the open-mouthed, hissing cat held in front of him. He tried to gently place the cat in the trunk, but it turned and clamped down around his arms, digging its claws into Howard's flesh. Howard gingerly tried to pry the cat loose, with no success.

"Oh, come *on*, Howard!" I said.

I grabbed the cat around the midsection with both hands, yanked it off Howard's arm, tossed it towards the back of the trunk, and slammed the lid.

"Elayna!" Howard gasped. "Do you think you hurt him?"

The continued yowling from the trunk let me know that the cat was not hurt. It was, however, extremely pissed.

"Can we get back to the task at hand, please?" I said, once we were back in the car.

I texted Frankie and had her make the call. She texted back a moment later.

"We're a go. Frankie's got him on the line, asking if he wants a discount on his phone service."

Howard pulled out his cell phone, entered a few keystrokes, and an explosion rocked the neighborhood.

"Yeah, there's an app for that," he said.

We drove by the remains of the house on our way out of the neighborhood. I had to give Howard kudos. Kent Sulley's house was nearly flattened and engulfed in flames, but the neighboring houses were unscathed. Neighbors were gathering at the fringe of the destruction, several with phones up to their ears, several more recording the footage.

"As always, excellent job, Howard," I said.

The cat was still yowling in the trunk, which made me think of a potential problem. I called Frankie back and put her on speaker.

"Frankie, can you check and see if Kent Sulley had a tracking chip implanted in his cat?" I asked.

A couple minutes later, she replied, "Yes, the cat is chipped. Why?"

"Can you turn off the tracking chip?"

"Do I want to know why?" Frankie asked.

"Howard got himself a new pet," I said.

"Can you inform my *darling* boyfriend that I am allergic to cats?" she snapped.

"You just did," I said. "You're on speaker."

There was a silence on the other end of the line for a moment.

"You guys are never going to believe what this cat's name is," Frankie said, sounding horrified.

"What is it?" I asked.

"Kent Sulley named his cat Sir Darcy Langston McWigglesbottom the third."

Hyde and I looked at each other with wide eyes while Howard made an indignant choking noise from the backseat.

"That makes me feel even better about that kill," I said, finally. "Sulley was definitely a sociopath."

"Completely," Frankie agreed.

"Can you find us a store where we can buy a cat crate, and some food?" I asked Frankie.

"There's a Walmart a couple miles from your location," she said.

"We're going to a Walmart in Los Angeles?" Howard said anxiously. "Do you think we have enough ordinance?"

I rolled my eyes at him. "Thanks, Frankie."

Chapter 30

Howard bought several of everything at the store. He argued that he didn't know what the cat was used to, so he should try different options. Then he rode back to the hotel with it all crammed in the backseat with him, since he didn't dare open the trunk.

When we got back to the hotel, however, there was nothing for it. Howard brought the new crate around to the back of the car and opened the trunk. Howling and spitting, Sir Darcy Langston McWigglesbottom the third leapt out and attached himself to Howard's head.

"Come on, Davy Crockett! Get a move on," I snapped, as Howard tried to pry the cat off his forehead.

When the cat was finally stored in the carrier, courtesy mainly of Hyde, we were able to get back to our room. I was looking forward to a long, hot shower. I couldn't wait to scrub Kent Sulley's touch off my skin. I sighed when my phone rang, but put it up to my ear and kicked off my heels.

"Hi, Camilla," I said. "How are things?"

"Your case went well?" I could hear clattering in the background, like she was emptying the dishwasher while we spoke.

"The prostitutes of Los Angeles can sleep easy tonight. Well, they can sleep easy whenever they sleep, at least. We head out to San Diego tomorrow morning."

"Luis called back. He wanted to set up a meeting with you, wondered if you would be willing to stop by his house while you're down there."

"He's never invited me to his home, before," I said, confusion seeping into my voice. "Why now?"

"He just said that he wanted to talk to you," Camilla said.

I noticed for the first time that her voice sounded tense.

"There's something else," Camilla continued. "I don't want you to worry, but Frankie left the office. She said that her old friend was in town, tonight only, and she needed to go see her."

"An old friend?" I said, lowering my voice and turning away from Howard.

"That's what she said, but I overheard her on the phone, and I don't think it sounded like a casual conversation."

"How so?"

"She kept saying no. It sounded like she was arguing with someone, and when she saw me walking by, she stopped talking until she had closed the door."

"Huh," I said, not wanting to say more in front of Howard.

"She was dressed funny when she left," Camilla said. "Like she was in a bad spy movie."

"A spy movie," I repeated dully.

Howard and Hyde both looked up at me with curious expressions on their faces.

"Yeah, like big black glasses and a scarf over her head," Camilla said. "It looked ridiculous, but that's not the point. For one thing, it's late at night. Also, that's not what you wear to see an old female friend."

"Yeah, you want to look extra cute when you see an old friend," I said.

"Exactly."

"Well," I said, keeping my voice light for the benefit of the men who were eavesdropping on my end, "we will figure it out when I get back."

I ended the call.

"What was that about?" Howard asked. "Something about a spy movie, and looking good for an old friend?"

"They are watching old movies tonight," I said. "And Frankie is giving Camilla a new haircut. Camilla's thinking something shorter, maybe with more layers. She might get bangs. Or highlights, maybe do a deep conditioning treatment..."

"Nevermind," Howard said. "Sorry I asked."

I told Hyde the truth once we were alone in our bedroom. I sat on the edge of the bed and looked at my feet.

"You don't think she's cheating on Howard, do you?" I asked him, my eyebrows drawn together in concern.

"No, I don't," he said. "But that would be the safest thing she could be doing, so saying that isn't much of a relief."

"I bet that's not what Howard would say."

"What is she doing? She's meeting with someone, and she wants to keep it a secret," he said.

"Based on the phone call that Howard intercepted, we can assume that she is meeting with a male."

"That narrows it down," Hyde said, running a hand through his hair and sitting next to me.

"Also, Luis wants to meet with me while we are down in San Diego."

"Have you met with him before?"

"Never at his home," I said.

"When people invite you into their home, it's usually either a gesture of goodwill or they are going to kill you," he said bluntly.

"Luis has no reason to kill me," I said, yawning. "We have a wonderful professional relationship. One of the reasons he is so successful is because he refuses to betray his clients. He stays neutral. Killing me would really break that streak for him."

"Be that as it may, I wouldn't mind going with you," he said.

"Fine with me," I said, shrugging.

"Now, enough shop talk. I want to have a conversation about this skirt," Hyde said, skimming his fingers along the hemline.

I laughed and let him kiss me.

I had brunch sent up around noon the next morning. I skimmed the *Los Angeles Times* and *The San Francisco Chronicle* while Howard tried to chase down his cat.

"There are too many hiding places in this damn place," Howard said, stopping by the dining table long enough to snag a piece of bacon.

"Well, we can't leave him," I said.

"This is good tactical practice," Hyde added, sipping his coffee. "Clear room by room. Try and think like your target."

"Shouldn't be too hard," I said. "You're already an angry white man. All you have to do is think like an angry white cat."

Howard wiped some sweat from his brow and left the room.

"Look at this," I said, sliding the *San Francisco Chronicle* over to Hyde. "It's a story about the shootings in Oakland."

Hyde skimmed the article, his eyebrows rising higher with every paragraph.

"That reporter has big testes, I'll give him that,' Hyde said.

"What's his name?" I asked.

"Samuel Edwards."

"Yeah," I said, thinking. "I'm not sure I would publicly lob accusations at this group without knowing who they are."

"He really goes after the police, too," Hyde added. "Says that they are half-assing these investigations because of who the victims are."

"That headline isn't a new one," I said. "What really caught my attention is the ballistic information that he lays out."

"Yeah, that isn't exactly public information, now is it?"

"It isn't," I said. "The Detectives on the case haven't ever connected and laid the evidence out like this, even in internal memos. I wonder who is going to be more pissed, the police or the group responsible. And how did this reporter get this information?"

Hyde raised his eyebrow at me, and I knew we had the same suspicion.

There was a thump from the other room.

"I got him!" Howard crowed. "He was under the sofa, but I got him!"

"Yaaaaay," I said, sarcastically.

Hyde kicked me lightly under the table, and I winked back.

Chapter 31

Hyde and I met Luis for lunch two days later at his sprawling La Jolla estate. Mercer Fulton was dead as of the night before. We had served up a tidy case to the investigating police officers. It looked like a classic home-invasion robbery gone wrong, complete with a struggle in the hallway and two sloppy shots to Fulton's chest.

I was wearing a high-necked top. In the struggle the night before, when Hyde had intentionally knocked over a vase in the living room and I had met a stumbling Mercer Fulton in the hallway, he had gotten one good punch in before I ended his life. His wild strike had landed on my upper chest. It hurt like hell and had left a huge bruise above my left breast.

Oddly enough, Hyde had insisted on thoroughly inspecting my injury once we were alone in our hotel room. I smirked at the memory, and Hyde smiled slow and gave me a wink, like he could read my mind.

Luis' house was beige stucco and sat heavily on a point that jutted into the ocean. The effect was spectacular; no other houses crowded the panoramic ocean views. An infinity pool seemed to drop into the ocean itself, and large palm trees swayed in the breeze. I wondered if any of his neighbors had figured out that the large cupola at the top of the building was a functioning sniper tower.

While Luis provided mercenaries for hire, he had picked and chosen along the years, and his own private group was legendary. Depending on how Luis felt about an individual, this compound was either the world's safest or most dangerous place to be. Luis was Cuban, and had come over with his parents on an aluminum fishing boat. He had developed his business with a keen mind for business and a sharp eye for dangerous talent. After fostering an impeccable reputation in the business, he had eliminated every competitor, either by buying them out or by giving literal meaning to the term 'hostile takeover'.

"Not bad for a first-generation immigrant, right?" Luis said after he had welcomed us, and gestured toward our surroundings. But his mouth was turned down at the corners, and his cheeks seemed hollow compared to my memory of him.

He was a short man, just meeting my eye level, which is why I was wearing flat sandals. His tan skin and pleasant face had made many people underestimate him. I knew that under that smile and grandfatherly paunch was a dangerous foe or a strong ally.

He wore white linen pants, a loose hawaiian print shirt, sandals, and sunglasses. But his gait and manner were tense, and I found myself scanning our surroundings and feeling grateful that Hyde had come with me. Luis led us to a table set under a billowing white cloth cabana. The sides expanded and contracted in the breeze, giving the impression that we would be dining in the lungs of some giant beast.

Lunch was already spread on the table, fresh-cut fruits in the center, plates of salad and sandwiches at each spot. Again, I wasn't sure if the offered meal was an honor, or a distraction from danger. I scanned for snipers. Luis caught my glance at the roofline, and smiled wearily.

"I understand that you might be wondering why I invited you to my home, when I never have before," he said. "There are two reasons for it, and they have more to do with each other than you might think."

I smiled politely, waiting.

"I had a client call me, asking if I knew about you. The same evening, you called, asking if I had any information about him. This puts me in a difficult position, one that I have been very careful to avoid until now."

"You are talking about Anton Kuschov," I stated.

"Of course," Luis said. "I have run into a... *difficulty* with this man."

He pursed his lips and looked out over the ocean. I waited for him to continue.

"About five months ago, Kuschov hired six of my men on a monthly-payment basis," he said.

I was familiar with the contract option that Luis offered, but I never liked it. I preferred to pay Luis' hefty finder's fee and then pay my employees directly. Luis offered the monthly payment plan to individuals who weren't sure how long they would need the employees that he offered. I had used it several times, when I needed back-up for an evening, or required an extraction team. The biggest problem I had with this "rental" method was the question of loyalty. If you were paying Luis, who was then paying the men, how could you know if the men were really ever yours?

"The initial period was for three months," Luis said. "At the end of that period, he renewed five of my men for three more months."

"Why are you telling me this?" I asked, sitting up straighter.

One of Luis' business tenets was strict confidentiality. It was written into his contracts, and he swore to keep his client's confidence, even if that led him to death or to prison.

"I am free to do so, since he first broke his contract with me," Luis said, frowning. "The sixth man, the one that he didn't renew the contract for, that is the man you know as 'Smith'."

I raised my eyebrows. "I saw Smith working for Kuschov a couple nights ago."

"The men still under contract have reported the same thing," Luis said, his hands clenched in his lap. "When I contacted Kuschov to correct the issue, he refused to pay the monthly fee, and refused to pay a finder's fee. He said that Smith has been converted to his cause, and is working for him directly, now."

I raised my eyebrows. If this were true, Kuschov might as well walk up to the devil himself and give him the middle finger. Luis had access to the best mercenaries on the planet, he had black teams with helicopters on standby up and down both seaboards, and his contract enforcement was legendary.

"I still don't understand why you are telling me this," I said.

"When Kuschov called me the other evening, we didn't end the phone call on excellent terms. Apparently, he had just had a meeting with you."

I nodded in confirmation, and Luis continued.

"He seems to think that you pose some potential threat to his business. He wanted me to give him personal details about you, and became infuriated when

I wouldn't. He asked if you would be a problem to him, started asking questions about your family."

My back clenched, and my fingers became rigid around my glass.

"This is against what I stand for," Luis said, quietly. "When I informed him of this, he became enraged. He then threatened me and my family."

I was stunned. The audacity of it took my breath away. Even more shocking, if possible, was the fact that Luis was here lunching with us instead of introducing Anton Kuschov to his own intestines.

"I am still unclear how I come into the picture," I finally said.

"Like I said, Anton Kuschov hired six of my men," Luis said, a deep frown marring his features once more. "What I have withheld until now is that one of those men is my wife's nephew."

"Kuschov threatened to kill him," I guessed.

"Normally, that wouldn't concern me. A sterling reputation is worth more than five living nephews," he said, glancing back toward his house with concern on his face. "But my wife is ill. The doctors say that they have done all they can do and they need her to get stronger before they start the next treatment. This situation with Marcos has been difficult for her. We never had children, and he is the closest thing to a son that she has. I am afraid that if Kuschov kills him, she will not recover."

"I am sorry to hear about your wife," I said, sincerely.

I had met her once. She was pretty, with lively eyes and a teasing laugh.

"She is the sunshine to my darkness," Luis said, his eyes on the house once more.

"What do you want me to do?" I asked.

"I want you to draw his attention and anger to you," Luis said, simply.

"Why?" I asked.

"If I mount a rescue attempt, Marcos will be killed. But if Kuschov is fighting someone else, Marcos will have time to escape," Luis said. "Also, Kuschov told me that the full weight and support of the Russian mob was behind him. I cannot have that pressure right now. I do not want to move my wife from her home."

"My house was blown up once this year, already," I said. "I only just have standing walls again."

Luis slid a folder across the table. "This might help you with your decision."

"I don't like to be manipulated into things," I said to Luis, not touching the folder.

"This isn't manipulation, Elayna," Luis said with a sigh. "I want to hire you for a case. I want to pay you for a case. I know your code. I hope that what's in that folder will give you sufficient motivation to take my money."

I picked up the thick file and flipped through the paperwork. The first few pages were things I knew, pictures of Anton Kuschov, the casino and the realty office, the same ones that Frankie had up on our board at home. I glanced a few pages past that, and my head snapped up.

"What is this?" I asked, my eyes blazing.

"He asked for snipers," Luis said, simply. "I gave him six."

Chapter 32

We took Luis' private jet home. He was having one of his men drive the car back for us. Once we were in the air, I called Camilla.

"We'll be home in about an hour," I said. "We are going to need something to eat, and we will eat in the conference room, so we can debrief at the same time."

"Alright," she said, her voice hesitant. "We have a new case?"

"Something like that," I said. "We are moving on it soon. Tonight or tomorrow. Can you jot down two addresses and get them to Frankie? I want her to crack into the video surveillance at each site."

"Frankie's not here," Camilla said.

"Where is she?" I snapped.

"Same thing as the other night..." Camilla began.

"Call her on her cell phone," I snapped. "Tell her to get her butt back to the office, now."

I hung up, and found Howard staring at me.

"Frankie's not at the office?" he asked, his eyes wide. "Where did she go?"

"Camilla doesn't know," I said, looking out the window.

"Is this the first time this has happened, while we've been gone?" he asked, his voice low and serious.

I reluctantly met his eyes. "No."

Howard leaned back in his seat, closed his eyes, and expelled a controlled breath.

"Why didn't you tell me, Elayna?" he finally said, his forehead wrinkled.

"I am trying to navigate being your boss, and her boss, and frankly, staying out of your relationship."

"That's bullshit!" Howard said, his face growing red. "You better believe that if Hyde was screwing someone behind your back, I wouldn't keep his secret!"

"She's not cheating on you, Howard," I soothed. "There's no way..."

"You know, after all the shit you've seen, you think you wouldn't be this naive," he snapped. "She's beautiful, and smart, and better than me. She's getting calls from some handsome guy, late at night, and now she's meeting him in secret."

"How do you know he was handsome?" I asked, my eyebrow raised.

"He sounded very handsome!" Howard shouted, belligerently. "And the part that hurts the worst is that you are doing the same thing that she is doing."

"What?" I said, genuinely confused.

"You both are lying to me to try and keep the team together!" he yelled. "She's stringing me along, lying about our relationship because she doesn't know how to tell me that it's over. She's afraid it would destroy the team. You aren't any better! You are trying to spare my feelings, not telling me the truth, for the same exact reason!"

"Howard," I said. "Frankie wouldn't do that to you."

"Maybe you really believe that," he said, his chin starting to tremble. "But facts are facts. And right now, she's out with some man. And she lied about it."

My eyes widened. I didn't know what I would say if he started to cry.

"I'm going to go take a nap," he said, standing. "Call me when we land."

He retreated to the bedroom in the back of the plane.

"That could have gone better," I murmured to Hyde.

"Is there any good way to find out that the one you love has been lying and might be sleeping with someone behind your back?" he asked.

"She's not cheating on him," I demanded.

"It doesn't look good," Hyde said, gently. "Howard apparently has some insecurities when it comes to their relationship. Secrets have a way of amplifying those."

When we got back to the office, Frankie still wasn't back.

Howard was now giving all of us the silent treatment, and he kept shooting Camilla nasty looks, like she should have kept Frankie at the office by force if necessary.

"Let's start without her, I guess," I said with a sigh.

We had called Frankie four times, left four messages.

"These cases," I said, pointing to the Russian casino case, which had been crossed out, and Mikayla Johnson's case. "They are one and the same."

"What?" Camilla said.

Howard looked vaguely interested, but mainly he just looked mad.

"Anton Kuschov hired snipers from Luis," I began.

The door slammed inward, and Frankie stumbled in. She was sobbing and covered in blood.

"Frankie?" I shouted, running towards her.

She fell into me as my arms wrapped around her slick torso. My heart was pounding, my adrenaline spiked. Hyde drew his weapon and went out to check the hall. Howard and Camilla were frozen to their chairs, their mouths gaping.

"Are you hurt? Frankie, are you hurt?" I asked. "Were you attacked?"

"It's not my blood," she managed between sobs.

I led her to a chair and helped her sit.

"What happened?" I asked.

"He killed them," she sobbed. "We were just sitting there, and he just... *killed* them. Shot them both in the head."

"Who, Frankie?" I asked. I noticed Camilla slip from the room.

"Andrew Beck and Samuel Edwards, the activist and the reporter," she said. "We were having lunch at Bistro P, you know, that place with the cute little patio, and the great tomato soup, with the, with the croutons on top?"

"Focus, Frankie," I said, giving a little squeeze to her arm. "Why were you there?"

"I'm so sorry," she sobbed. "I couldn't let it go. I was helping them look into the Oakland shootings, the deaths."

"It's alright, Frankie," I said. "Whatever happened isn't your fault."

"Yes it is!" she yelled. "They stood up because I encouraged them to. Edwards only wrote that article after I put him in contact with Beck. I gave them information, stuff that only the police had."

I nodded. I had guessed that the anonymous source was Frankie after I read the article while I was in Los Angeles.

"They wanted them to shut up," Frankie cried. "So they shot them."

"Who shot them?" I said. "Howard, grab a pen. Frankie, can you give us a description?"

"I don't need to describe him. I know his name," she sobbed. "It was that big blonde one. Smith."

Camilla came back into the room carrying what looked like a hot chocolate, but I could smell the alcohol from where I was sitting.

"Come on, Frankie," Camilla said, lifting her gently from the seat. "The shower's hot. Let's get you cleaned up. You can answer the rest of their questions later."

I turned Frankie over to Camilla's care, let her lead Frankie out the door. I turned to Howard. He looked like he might be more in shock than Frankie was.

I gripped his shoulder hard. "Howard, are you alright?"

"She was covered in blood. I thought for a second that it was hers. That she was going to die."

"Howard, I need you to focus. I know you want to go be with Frankie, but I want to take these fuckers out, tonight. I need two structure devices. Can you focus enough to do that for me?"

His eyes finally met mine, and a dangerous smile spread over his face.

"I'm going to enjoy this more than the first time I killed," he said.

He left the conference room and turned down the hall, away from the bedrooms, away from Frankie, towards his workroom.

Hyde found me standing in the conference room, clenching and unclenching a fist that was covered in someone else's blood.

"You ok?" he asked, leaning in the doorway.

"Yes," I said. "I'm just getting my mind right for what's to come."

"Frankie left her car running, so I parked it properly," he said.

"Thank you," I said idly, focusing on the feel of the sticky blood between my fingers.

Sir Darcy came streaking around the hallway corner, followed closely by Bruno. They ran down the hall, then Sir Darcy flicked around the next corner, a streak of white fur. Bruno struggled to get enough grip on the hardwood floor, and he hit the far wall with a meaty thud, falling to the ground in a heap of wagging tail, waving paws and lolling tongue. He scrambled up, gave a little shake, and was off again. He, at least, seemed to think this cavorting chase was all in good fun. I didn't really care how Darcy felt about it, as long as Bruno was enjoying himself.

"I understand now why you love that dog so much," Hyde said, chuckling. "He brings a little levity in when it's needed most."

I nodded. Hyde stepped in front of me and gripped my upper arms gently.

"Hey," he said in a low voice. "Look at me."

I raised my blue eyes to meet Hyde's chocolate brown ones. His brow furrowed at whatever he saw in my face, and he wrapped me up in a solid hug.

"We'll get them, Elayna," he murmured against my hair. "You're not alone in this. We'll get them together. Just tell me what you need."

I thought for long moments, and finally said, "I need this. For just a few more minutes, while I figure something out."

He didn't laugh at me, like I was scared he might. He just tightened the hug, until I was breathing in his scent, breathing in the security of his embrace and the strange feeling of being alright with being cared for. When I finally broke the hug, Hyde told me he loved me, and I almost, almost said it back.

But it wasn't the right time.

Chapter 33

Frankie was sitting cross-legged on her bed, sipping another mug of warmed alcohol by the time I found her. She was swathed in a big cashmere sweater and yoga pants, her hair wet but pulled back into a ponytail. I had changed my clothes and had been careful to wash all traces of blood from my hands before I went to see her. I thought she might be done with blood today.

"How are you doing?" I asked, crossing the room to sprawl on the bed beside her.

"Fine," she said.

It was a lie, but at least her hands had stopped shaking. Her eyes and nose were red and puffy. I let the silence fill the space between us, as soft and comforting as a cotton ball.

"Where's Howard?" she finally asked.

"I have him building a couple packages," I said. "Has he been in to see you yet?"

"No."

"I'm keeping him busy," I offered.

"That's not it. He's mad because I didn't tell him what I was doing, who I was meeting with." Her voice was soft, tremulous.

"Wouldn't you be?"

"I guess so. I just didn't want him to have to choose," she said.

"Between what?"

"Me, and the team. I know that I betrayed you, going to the press like that." She sniffed, a fresh tear sliding down her face.

"We will have to talk about that later," I conceded. "Right now, it's enough for me that you are safe."

"If it makes you feel any better, I really regret it," she said, her face crumpling into tears. "Without me, Beck and Edwards would still be alive."

"They were grown men who knew what they were choosing," I said. "Without you, how many more Mikaylas would have to die before we paid attention?"

"So it's the Russians," she said, her chin lifting. "They killed Mikayla."

"And now we're going to stop them," I said.

"I don't understand why, though," she said. "The casino isn't in downtown Oakland. Those gang members didn't pose a threat to their organization."

"It was never about the casino," I said. "You know those realtors, the ones at the casino?"

She nodded.

"They may not have been wealthy individually, but their clients were. They were buying huge amounts of Oakland real estate, only in the worst, most gang-infested parts of town."

"They were speculating real estate?" Frankie asked, her grip tightening around her mug.

"Then they were cleaning house, getting rid of the gangs."

"Gang activities decrease, real estate values go up. They make a huge profit," she said.

"Exactly," I said.

"Then what was the casino even for?" she asked, her brow crinkling. "Why open themselves up to vulnerability with that operation? It wasn't even making money."

"It was very clever, really," I said, threading my fingers together behind my head. "The casino was where they made their contacts for *after* the neighborhoods had been cleaned up."

"Building department employees," Frankie breathed. "I always wondered how they were included in the clientele."

"And a bunch of rich people, who could afford to buy or invest in the new developments," I concluded.

She exhaled. "They are playing the long game."

"They were," I said. "Now they're done."

"For Mikayla?" she asked, tearing up again.

"For Mikayla, and Andrew Beck, and Samuel Edwards, and for Luis. And for you."

"When are you going to do it?"

"Tonight," I said simply. "We're briefing in a few minutes."

"I want to help," she said, her chin lifting.

"Are you sure?"

"I'm absolutely sure," she said. "I wouldn't miss this case for anything."

We let a few more moments of silence build between us.

"If you don't want to talk about it, I understand, but I am wondering how you got out unscathed," I said.

It wasn't like a trained professional to leave an up-close witness alive.

"There was a police officer on the corner," Frankie sniffed. "It was a good part of town. He got a shot off at Smith, and Smith ran. I ran the other direction, didn't even wait to be questioned. I owe that officer my life."

I held her hand while tears drizzled down her face once more.

We met in the conference room as soon as Howard was finished with his work. He looked like he had aged in the hours he had been building his bombs. His face seemed to have lines on it that weren't there before, but the set of his chin was stubborn, determined.

"Why didn't you tell me what you were doing, who you were meeting with?" Howard demanded of Frankie.

"Yes," I murmured. "Fantastic timing, Howard."

Everyone ignored me.

"I didn't want to make you choose," Frankie said, her eyes filling with moisture again. "I thought it would be easier this way."

I would be really glad when all this crying was over.

"Remember what we said, Frankie?" he said. "*We* come first. It's us. I may not agree with all of your choices, but I'm sure as hell not going to choose Elayna over you."

Hyde and Camilla were looking at me, watching my reaction.

I laughed. "How stupid do you people think I am? You think I would ever ask Howard to choose me over Frankie? I only fight battles I know I can win. Now if you guys can focus, I need to work on picking a fight with the Russian mob."

At least Hyde and Camilla were amused. Howard and Frankie were too involved in their own emotions to get the joke. Howard sat with his hands clenched together, his lips a pressed line. Frankie was dabbing furiously at her eyes, as if she believed that as long as the tears didn't mark her cheeks, they didn't count.

"Howard," I said, trying valiantly to get us back on track. "I'm going to plant these bombs myself. You will still be the one to pull the trigger when the time comes, but I want Kuschov to be furious with me, not anyone else."

Howard nodded.

"Frankie, I need to know which security cameras are up and operational."

"You want them disabled?" she asked, her voice still thick with tears.

"No," I said. "I need to know where they are so my face is loud and proud on the footage."

"Why would you do that?" she asked.

"Luis is paying us to take the heat on this one," I said. "Don't worry. There's a plan."

We hit the realty office at midnight. I took both my guys along with me: Hyde to man the thermal imaging device, Howard to flip the switch when it was time. The neighborhood was still and cool as I hefted the black duffel bag onto my shoulder. It amused me how easy it was to walk up to a building, place a bomb, and walk away if you didn't care about being seen.

The explosion rent the new morning's stillness. Flames unfurled towards the sky like the arms of a great conductor. Smoke billowed, car alarms began wailing and beeping, and local dogs joined their barks and howls to the symphony of destruction.

"Hot damn, that was a good boom," Howard said.

"It's the simple things," I said.

"It really is."

We drove away.

Chapter 34

"This is definitely not in my job description," Howard said as he wrangled the multi-colored party lights from the box.

"Do any of us actually *have* job descriptions?" Hyde asked.

Frankie answered from where she was watching the monitors. "I can write some up, if you want, but you should know that I am going to include 'party set-up' in each of them."

"Don't bother," Hyde answered.

I was unspooling ruffled paper streamers from one of the hundreds of rolls that Camilla had ordered. We were all trying our best to pretend that we weren't nervous, but it was showing in the tension of Frankie's shoulders, in Howard's lack of banter, in the tightness around Camilla's mouth. Luis had gotten word to us that Kuschov was going to retaliate today.

We wanted to draw them here to my house, where there wasn't anyone around to be caught in the crossfire. Though if our plans held, there wouldn't be any firefight at all. Howard had placed charges up the driveway, specially-designed to blow the vehicles up without damaging my freshly-resurfaced driveway. I had spoken with the contractor, telling him sternly that no one was to come to the building site today, as we were prepping it for a party.

"Here we go," Frankie said, finally.

A moment later, from down the hill, we heard the resounding booms.

"Call in the clean-up team," I told Frankie.

"They only blew the three charges," Howard said, wonderingly. "I thought they would bring more men."

"Guys!" Frankie yelled. "I think we're in trouble. The men, the dead men, the one who blew the charges... those weren't the Russians."

"What do you mean?" I asked.

I had sudden, horrific images of an innocent subcontractor being blown to bits. My heart clenched in my chest, and I grabbed my throat.

"I'm rewinding the footage, and it looks like it was Elroy Farley," Frankie said quickly. "He was in the lead car, and is now very, very dead."

"If Elroy was still alive, then who did we blow up in his house?" I asked, looking around to my team members for an answer.

Hyde shrugged.

"Howard, how many charges did you place again?" I said.

"Five," he said.

As if on cue, we heard two more resounding booms from down the hill.

"Frankie?" I yelled.

"One black SUV took out both of those," she said, her face blanching. "We've got two more SUVs incoming. Moving fast."

"Frankie go hide in the basement," I yelled, as two black SUVs crested the hill. "Tell Luis' team that we need them here, *now*, and not just for clean-up."

Frankie ran, crushing her still-open laptops to her chest. She was out of the room by the time the first bullets hit the front windows. The noise made my ears ring. It sounded like someone was drumming on the glass with hammers. There was still no door on the basement, otherwise we could have all gone, shut the door, and waited for Luis' black team to arrive. But without a door, the steel room would be far more fatal for us than the proverbial fish in a barrel scenario.

"Fifty caliber?" I screamed to Hyde, as I flattened myself against the floor.

The windows and walls I had specced for my house could withstand anything but a high-caliber round.

"No," he yelled back.

Hyde was already up and moving, pulling out the metal case from beneath the table. This was our insurance policy, but we hadn't thought we would need it. For a second, I watched Hyde set up the Browning 50 caliber machine gun with quick, practiced movements. The sight of it made my guts clench with anxiety. This was proof that our day had gone seriously sideways.

Camilla, Howard, and I pulled long guns from another case. I strapped on an armored vest and handed the others out. Howard slung a bag of molotovs over his shoulder. I hadn't even noticed him bringing those into the house today, but I wasn't complaining. The only group sport Howard ever played in school had been baseball, and he still had amazing throwing aim. The gunfire ceased from the front of the house, as if the Russians finally realized that they were just wasting bullets.

Hyde was kneeling in front of the 50 caliber. He turned to me and pulled one ear of his high-grade earplugs up. "Are you sure?"

"Do it," I said. "The rest of us are going to flank. We need to keep them out in the open, so Luis' team can pick them off when they arrive."

Hyde repositioned his ear protection, then lit the Russians up with the 50 caliber from inside the house. Each shot was deafening, and the front windows exploded in a shower of glass. I rolled my eyes and briefly wondered how long of a setback this would cause with the construction crews. Then I snapped to my senses and remembered that it wouldn't matter if we didn't survive the day. As Hyde's bullets tore through the front of the house, Howard and Camilla went left out the back door. I went right.

I sprinted through the backyard around to the front and took cover behind one of the cement construction barriers, just as Howard threw his first molotov cocktail. It erupted in a shower of fire and glass right on target, it's victim screaming. I used the momentary distraction to pop up from behind cover and take out two men. I counted ten more, and they were all wearing bulletproof vests. If I was going to kill these guys, it would have to be a headshot every time.

The men recovered from the sudden onslaught faster than I would have liked. They ran with controlled steps, rifles up, dividing and regrouping around obstacles and fallen comrades like water flows around rocks. These were professionals. They regrouped in formation, splitting into two teams of five, even as Hyde targeted the team moving towards where Camilla and Howard were hunkered down. Hyde took out one, and Howard threw another molotov, taking out another.

Three for them, five for me, I thought. I didn't like those odds, for either of us.

I popped out from behind the cement barrier again, took aim, and fired twice. I hit one in the forehead, and removed the ear of another. It would have been a clean shot, but a whistle past my head forced me to duck. I heard the distant whomp-whomp of helicopter blades reverberating in the canyon behind the house.

Thank you, Frankie, I thought.

We only had to survive for another minute or two, but that might be too long to hope for.

I army-crawled over to another section of the barrier, and gunfire erupted from where Howard and Camilla were hiding. I stuck my head around the block to look how they were faring. A chunk of cement exploded near my head, but before cement dust clouded my vision, I saw that Howard and Camilla were being flanked.

I threw myself up over the cement block, and took a shot to the chest. My ballistic vest held strong, but my shot at the man sneaking up behind Camilla went wide. She was focused in the wrong direction. I kept running, trying to get another shot, and felt pure horror grip my heart as the mercenary took aim at her back. Then his head exploded into a fine pink mist, his body slumping over close enough to make her jump.

I couldn't tell where the friendly shot came from, but I didn't have time to ponder it. I rolled and sprinted, and came up behind the blade of the earthmover parked in the driveway. There were answering pings of bullets hitting the metal as I ducked for cover.

"Well, fancy meeting you here, behind the blade of an earthmover," Hyde said in my ear. "Want to make out?"

"How many are left?" I gasped, trying to get my heart rate under control.

"I took out two on the way over. You started running and jumping around like a spider monkey, and I didn't want to accidentally hit you with the 50 caliber."

"So there's two left for them, and four left for us?"

"I took out two that were coming after you," Hyde said, ducking as a new storm of bullets pelted the metal behind us. "I didn't take anyone out in their group."

"Then who..." I began. "Nevermind. Two left for us, two left for them."

I heard the unmistakable sound of glass breaking, and a blood-curdling scream.

"Check another one to Howard's molotovs," I said. "One for them, two for us."

But we had stayed in one place for too long. One man came from the right, one crept in from the left. They had flanked us. In the span of an inhale, I pulled up, aimed, and pulled the trigger.

And heard an unmistakable, grinding click.

A misfire.

I could have sworn that I saw the man smile in the breath before he pulled the trigger. In the same moment, I registered that the man who had me in his sights was huge, with blonde hair. *Smith.* Hyde swung around and changed his aim from the man who was targeting him, to Smith, who was targeting me.

My hand went to the pistol at my belt. Two shots rang out at the same time. One bullet went between the eyes of Smith, who was trying to kill me.

The other went through Hyde's shoulder, right where his vest ended and his undefended flesh began. I heard the thunk of the impact a half-second before Hyde gasped in response.

I had drawn my pistol. I had my aim, and I shot the mercenary twice in the face as he swung around to put me in his sights.

The percussion of the helicopter blades was deafening now. Wisps of my hair were being tugged free from my ponytail.

Blood was pooling around Hyde.

"No. No, Hyde, no," I screamed.

"It's ok, baby," he said dully. "I got him."

"You've been shot," I said, pressing hard against the gushing wound.

It had to be arterial. It was bleeding too fast.

"I know. It's ok," he repeated.

"Luis' men will be here in a second. Hold on," I said, my hands clamping down, as if I could push the spilled blood back into his body.

"S'ok. I love you," Hyde said, his words slurring, his blinks lasting too long.

"I love you, too," I said, tears running unchecked down my cheeks as I desperately tried to staunch the flow of blood. "Oh, Hyde, I'm so sorry I didn't tell you before."

"S'ok," he repeated, sounding lazy. "I knew before you did."

"How can I help?" I asked stupidly, keeping pressure on his wound.

"There is one thing," Hyde mumbled.

"Yes, anything," I said desperately.

"Just one kiss..." he said with a limp grin, his eyes closed.

I laughed, a bark of inappropriate, panicked mirth.

Somebody pulled me back, and several pairs of gloved hands worked over Hyde, while others pulled him onto a lowered stretcher. They raised it and ran him over to the waiting helicopter. In an abrupt lift-off and a cloud of dust, they were gone.

Chapter 35

"What?" I asked the empty air, my bloody hands, my skinned knees.

Then Camilla had one arm around my shoulders, and Howard was tugging me to my feet by my waist.

"Let's go, Layna," Howard said. "Come on. We gotta go. We need to be with Hyde."

I willed my limbs to move. Camilla joined me in the backseat of the car, keeping one arm wrapped around me. Frankie was on the phone already, talking about blood loss and surgeons and hospital rankings. Howard drove us down the hill at a reckless speed that felt far too slow for me. I pressed my palms to my eyes to try and clear my thoughts, but they felt sticky on my face.

I pulled my hands back, looked at the blood that was drying there, and felt a tremor of fear. Behind that, I felt a small flame of anger. I pushed back the fear, and yanked the anger to the forefront of my mind. Fear did nothing for me. Hyde was in the hands of trained personnel. They would do all they could for him. It was my job to do the same, and I could use the anger.

Focus. What is next? I thought for long moments, came up with a plan.

"Howard, drop Frankie and Camilla off at the hospital," I said, sounding more tired than I would have liked. "Then head to the office. I want to finish this tonight."

"You don't want to go wait at the hospital?" Frankie asked.

"I wouldn't be doing Hyde any good, sitting there. And there is something practical I can do for him. I can make sure that the man who sent those assholes is dead. Make sure there isn't anything hanging over his head once..." My voice broke, and I cleared my throat and swallowed with difficulty. "Once he is out of the hospital. Camilla, since Frankie's busy, can you call Luis, and see if the diversion was enough?"

I lapsed into silence, hearing but not listening to Frankie and Camilla as they worked, not noticing the ebb and roar of the motor as Howard pushed the car to it's limits. I focused instead on refining the violent plans that were taking shape in my imagination.

"Elayna," Camilla said.

From her tone, I could tell it wasn't the first time she had tried to get my attention.

"Yes."

"Luis says that Kuschov believes this is all you. Doesn't suspect Luis' involvement at all. His nephew should be safe," she said.

"Great," I said with a sigh. "Did you tell him about the men sent to our house?"

"None were his," she said. "They are waiting and marked."

"Perfect," I said.

"Are you sure that you are up for this? Anton Kuschov isn't going anywhere. He will be there after a night of sleep."

"He won't be expecting us to regroup so quickly," I said. "Especially once he hears that his men took one of us out."

"They didn't take Hyde out," Frankie snapped. "He's in the hospital, not dead."

"He's off of the playing field, for now," I said calmly. "I haven't given up on him. I'm just doing my best to keep a level head right now."

"Sorry," she mumbled. "I didn't mean..."

"This is a high-stress situation for everyone, but try and keep your thoughts clear. I'm going to need you all at your best so no one else gets hurt today."

"Luis wants me to text him, let him know if your plans have changed at all," Camilla said.

"Tell him we are going forward exactly according to plan," I said.

She frowned, but nodded.

We rode the rest of the way to the hospital in grim silence. When we pulled up to the curb, I could barely look at the large white building. I knew that Hyde was in there, somewhere, and I couldn't do a damn thing to help him survive. Still, it was all I could do to get out of the back seat and then get back into the front seat. Despite all my training, a surprisingly large part of me wanted to dissolve into hysterics, to curl into a ball and weep, or to run through the halls like a madwoman until I found him.

But I forced the rational part of myself to bring the other parts of my psyche to heel. I stiffened my spine and turned my face cold, and made sure that Frankie and Camilla were both carrying loaded guns in their handbags. Then I asked Howard to drive us back to the office.

Hyde was in surgery. I tried very hard not to think about it as I went into the bathroom we shared and washed my arms up to the elbows in scalding water. I splashed water on my face and watched the dirt and blood swirl away into the drain. I wondered if I had touched his face for the last time. I wondered if I would ever see his slow, easy smile again. I fought back the urge to weep.

Instead, I suited up for the task at hand. Howard helped me and watched me when he thought I wasn't looking. Frankie and Camilla sent a steady stream of texts and phone calls with all the information except what I wanted to know.

I was already planning the deaths of the surgeons if something went wrong and I found evidence of wrongdoing.

"So help me!" I snapped at Howard as I loaded full magazines into a black duffel bag during the first hour of Hyde's surgery. "If one of them was drinking the night before..."

"They aren't airline pilots," Howard said, trying to soothe me. "They know they have to have their shit together when they go to work. Plus, Frankie called in some favors. They know it's a VIP patient. These surgeons are supposedly the best."

I just growled at him, at his futile attempts to calm me, and triple-checked the cleanliness of my guns. It was one stupid misfire that had placed us in this situation. One clean shot was all I had needed. One clean shot, and we would have walked away, free and clear. I heard that grinding click over and over in my mind as Howard and I got ready.

Click.

Click.

Click.

I shook my head free of the morbid soundtrack as Howard's cell phone rang. He had it up to his ear before one ring had completed.

"Yes?" He asked, his face tight with tension.

I watched his features, trying to read what the voice on the other end of the line was saying through his expression. I wondered what it meant that they had called Howard instead of me. Would he have the task of breaking the terrible news to me?

But his face slackened in relief and his eyes closed tightly in gratitude. I found myself suddenly shaky, tears clouding my eyes. I would allow myself this emotion, for a moment. But only for a moment.

Howard stowed his phone in his back pocket. "He's out of surgery, and it went really, really well. He is definitely going to pull through, and the surgeons are confident that with rehabilitation, there won't be many permanent effects, if any at all."

"Thank you," I said, steadying my breath, my heart rate.

I imprisoned my trembling lower lip with my teeth, swiped the escaped tears from my cheeks, and stood.

"Elayna," Howard started, his voice gentle. "You can go be with him, that's ok. This can wait."

"No, Howard, it can't. I need to clear this from my periphery before I can really focus on Hyde," I said.

"I need to be able to look him in the eye when I see him and tell him that this is taken care of."

"Can't you just buy him flowers like a normal person?" Howard said.

I raised an eyebrow, but realized that Howard was joking, that he understood on some level.

"This bung-hole Kuschov covered Frankie and Hyde with blood," I said. "It's past time to return the favor."

"Bung-hole?" Howard asked, with a raised eyebrow.

"I'm trying to keep things light," I said, jamming a full magazine into a long rifle and pulling the slide back with a deadly snick.

The trip back into the canyon seemed long. We hit traffic on the freeway. Despite the tinted windows, weapons and body armor, I felt oddly exposed as we inched along behind tail lights, flanked on either side by disgruntled commuters.

The casino was closed today, but lights were on. Howard and I wore special glass visors over our eyes. I had twenty pounds of firearms strapped to my body, and I was in the mood for bloodshed. The snipers on the roof saw us approaching, but they both glowed green in my visor. They let us pass, and I thought I saw one give us a half-salute as they began breaking down their firearms.

Our first opposition met us at the front door, his gun up, his face curled into a snarl. His first shot whizzed wide of my head, and without breaking stride, I gave him a lesson in how to complete a head-shot. He crumpled in the doorway, conveniently propping the steel door open. We stepped over his still-twitching limbs, over the syrupy pool of blood collecting around his ruined head.

Two more men glowed green in the entryway, and they pressed against the wall to let us pass without meeting our eyes. They exited the same way Howard and I had come in. Two heat signatures were present in the dark expanse of the main casino room. There was no glow of green around either one.

"Left is yours," I told Howard, even as I raised my pistol to aim at the one on the right.

Howard ducked behind a roulette table as gunshots filled the air to bursting with noise. I took one in the chest, but I could tell by the impact it was a small caliber round, and nothing to be anything more than pissed about. I returned fire and my quarry ducked behind a thick board that tracked the current leaders in a running poker tournament.

I switched pistols and aimed as though there was nothing standing between me and the man trying to kill me. With a Desert Eagle .50, that might as well be true. I fired, and the bullet plowed through the board like it was paper. I heard the scream that let me know the shot hadn't been as clean as I would have liked. I was here for death, after all, but I'm not overly fond of pain. I ducked around the board and ended my target's misery just as Howard lobbed a fiery projectile at his target on the left.

The thermal readout through my visor seared my vision for a moment, so I dropped behind a poker table to recover my sight. I blinked rapidly, trying to clear the latent outline of the explosion from my view. I heard a gunshot and sprang to my feet in case Howard had missed his target, and was now under fire.

Howard was standing over a burning corpse, looking like he was considering whether a molotov cocktail and a bullet to the brain was enough damage for his opponent.

"Howard," I said, gripping his arm. "You keeping it together?"

He shook me off, but finally said, "yes."

"I need you to keep a focused mind, Howard," I said.

I wasn't the only one who'd had their significant other threatened by these people.

Howard took a deep breath, met my eyes. "No worries, Elayna. I'm with you."

The hallway leading up to Kuschov's office could have been a fatal funnel, but there was only one man guarding the expanse. I took him out with an easy double-tap to the skull before he got a focused aim at either one of us. He slumped against the wall, leaving a messy streak of blood down the wallpaper as he fell. Kuschov's office door was unlocked.

Anton Kuschov was seated behind a huge glass desk. His face was set in grave lines, with a hint of curiosity around his mouth. He hadn't expected us to make it to him alive. Two large men flanked him, their automatic rifles trained on me and Howard. I approached the desk, and Howard took a position in back of me, on my right.

I flicked my visor up and then released the tension from my arm, letting my gun point toward the ground.

"That is not very wise," Anton said, color high in his cheeks, "considering how many of my men you just killed."

"I know what I'm doing," I said.

"I thought you did, the first time you came to see me," he said. "But then you blew up my realty office. As if that weren't enough, it seems that the realty bank accounts were drained."

"Unfortunate," I said, my voice clipped.

"You give me the money back, promise to leave me be, and *maybe* I will let you live," he said.

He was gaining confidence now, smirking, whereas I was having problems restraining my temper. This was the man who was responsible for covering Frankie in the blood of two innocent men. This was the man who caused the drying puddle of blood on my driveway, the pallid hue of Hyde's skin, the beeping machines that watched over him like sentinels. I took a deep breath and honed my focus.

"I think we are past that point," I said.

"You're right," he said airily. "I'm going to kill you either way. But if you give me my money back, I won't take so much time and pleasure in the act."

"I don't understand," I said. "Before you killed Andrew Beck and Samuel Edwards, I actually thought that I could live with whoever was taking out the gang leadership."

"Ah, yes. I have heard about your code. Believe as you will, but I too have a code."

"So why kill them? Why draw attention to what you were doing?"

"It was those men who were drawing the attention. Couldn't they just leave well enough alone?"

"You killed a reporter and an activist. It's in their job description to not 'leave things alone'."

He smiled. "I am from Mislov, a small city outside of Yekaterinburg. You have heard of Milslov?"

"No," I said.

"It was an engorged tick on the back of the country, a town full of gangs. These gangs were all made up of young men, angry at each other, angry at the government. They claimed to be for their town, claimed to have city pride. But all they did was destroy the good, and drag the city down."

He watched me for a moment, and then continued, "When I made a name for myself with my colleagues in Moscow, the first and only thing I asked for was to return to Mislov. You see, I had an idea, a theory. These individuals, who were beating and pillaging and raping the good people of Mislov, they could be controlled, and spurred to new purpose."

"What purpose was that?" I asked.

"Instead of drowning the city, they could be used to prop it up, to protect it," he said, leaning forward in his chair. "The police in Mislov were useless. I wanted to scrape away the old, and replace it with a group that did have pride in Mislov."

I waited. I wanted to shoot him in the head and get it over with, but if Kuschov wanted to fulfill every movie mastermind stereotype and explain his entire operation to me, I felt I should listen. I might learn something that would help me deal with the extremely dangerous loose end in this situation.

"I thought it would take longer than it did," he said. "But with a year of good direction and constant pressure, the efforts of the young men of Mislov were redirected."

"And you made money from it," I said.

"Not as much as I could have," Anton said, raising a finger. "Not as much as I *should* have, that first time. But the experiment worked. I had proven a theory that I had held for many years, ever since I was a small child."

"So the businesses pay protection money, and in exchange, the community stays safe," I said.

"See? You have heard of this system, as well," Anton said. "It has worked, many times, in history. Your country used to have this same idea. In New York City, there was the Italian mob. In Chicago, they had this system as well, for a time."

"That is the problem, isn't it? It only works for a time," I said. "Until the gang becomes too unfocused or unorganized or greedy to be effective."

"I have never been accused of being any of those things," he said. "I have done this many times over, in my country. This will be my finest experiment, I think. We have been running the analysis for years, you know, whether we should bring our model to the suburbs of Los Angeles, or New York, or Chicago, or San Francisco."

He was bragging here, but he was giving me tidbits I didn't know. He didn't think I was going to leave alive. "So why Oakland?"

"We have found for this to work, you must have two conditions present," he said, leaning forward and ticking off his fingers. "One, you must have a wealthier population waiting to move in. In Oakland, that is the case. The area is ripe for gentrification."

I nodded. "Other firms have tried and failed already."

"Exactly," he said, smiling. "But as you know, sometimes one must use methods outside of the law to get the desired results."

"What is the second condition?" I asked.

"The public must be tired of the current situation," he said. "Public opinion must be against the status quo. If the majority of the people are fond of the gangs, we have no chance of succeeding. However, if we start to act, and the average person and the average police officer think that we are doing the community a favor? Well, half the battle is won, right there."

He opened a desk drawer, and I tensed for a moment until I saw that he was pulling out a stack of newspapers.

"Look at the headlines," he said, shuffling the newspapers. "*'Gang Murders Down by Twenty Percent', 'Murders up; All Other Crime in Sharp Decline'.*"

I nodded. I had copies of the same articles posted on the whiteboard in my conference room.

"This is today's newspaper!" Anton exclaimed with a barking laugh, sliding a newspaper across the desk. "The Police Chief is getting a commendation from the Mayor for the reduction in gang activity! They are congratulating each other for our work. They do not want to stop us. Why should they? Their statistics don't even tell the whole story. They can only count the reduction in crimes that are reported, after all. The change is even greater than they know."

I didn't respond.

"Gang members are hiding out in their homes like frightened little bunnies, and the children are coming out to play in the parks again," he said. "It is as it should be."

"Not for Mikayla Johnson," I said. "Not for Andrew Beck and Samuel Edwards."

"Mikayla Johnson was a mistake. The other two? They wouldn't have left it alone. People would have started paying attention."

"Then you truly don't understand the American public," I said. "The average citizen can choose to ignore almost anything that they don't want to see. Those newspaper articles would have meant nothing in a week. But add a murder or two? Now you've given the people a mystery, a conspiracy. If there's one thing we value as a society, it's the right to figure things out, the right to know the sordid truth. We are all too curious for our own good."

"You know what curiosity did to the cat, right?"

I felt Howard stir beside me, a restless shifting of his feet. I turned my head slightly, saw him frown and press a finger to his ear. He grew pale, and his wide eyes met mine. I saw terror there.

"Elayna, we have to go, *now*," he snapped. He sprinted for the door.

There was only one reason Howard would abandon me.

There was only one person on the planet that he loved more than me.

Frankie was in danger.

And Frankie was with Hyde.

I turned, lifted my pistol, and put a 45-caliber bullet between Anton Kuschov's eyes.

"Clean it up," I yelled to Luis' men.

Then I turned and ran.

Chapter 36

We got the story from Frankie on our way over to the hospital. Howard was driving and I listened to Frankie's strained play by play of what was happening. Traffic had cleared, so the drive took us twenty-two of the longest minutes of my existence. All we knew was what Frankie could see through the glass door of Hyde's hospital room.

When we rounded the corner in the postoperative wing, Fernando Almeida was still in Hyde's hospital room with Camilla. No one else seemed alarmed. Nurses and doctors bustled about their tasks in a business-like fashion. Only the straightness of Frankie's back and the alertness of her gaze cued me in to her emotions. She was sitting across the hall from the room, her eyes locked onto the tense scene playing out over an unconscious Hyde.

"Howard, get Frankie around the corner," I said, giving him a little push in her direction. "Then watch the door."

"What are you going to do?" he asked, his fingers already closing around Frankie's upper arm.

"I really don't know."

My dark, tangled thoughts contrasted with the crisp, clean halls, the bright overhead lighting. The roaring in my ears stood starkly against the hospital soundtrack of professional conversation and clinical beeping from the machines. The past few weeks, things had been coming from my blind side, one after another. The most exhausting part was that I thought every single one was something I should have seen coming. Every single one was something that I should have prevented. Including this.

I watched the situation in the hospital room for a moment. Camilla was perched in a metal chair against the wall facing Hyde's bed. She looked grave, and met my eyes through the window, then she turned back to look at Fernando. Fernando was facing Camilla, his back to the far wall. He was on the other side of Hyde's bed. Fernando was talking to Camilla, but I couldn't hear the words through the glass.

Hyde's eyes were closed, his thick lashes like two fans across his cheeks. His dark hair was flopped over his forehead, and I had to smother a searing instinct to go to him and smooth it back out of his eyes. He looked surprisingly whole considering the gravity of the wound he had sustained. His jaw was still strong, his full lips were parted slightly in breath. His skin was still that perfect shade of golden brown, albeit a little pale. Except for the IV line, the oxygen monitor on his finger, and the edge of a white bandage peeking out from under his powder blue hospital gown, he could have been sleeping.

Fernando Almeida was exactly as I remembered him. His tan skin and dark eyes were nearly the same shade as Camilla's. The family resemblance was strong, and as I watched, he shrugged and gestured with his left hand, a move that struck a deep chord of recognition within me. It was a move I had seen Camilla make a hundred times.

I felt a surge of fury as my view narrowed on Fernando's right hand, which was resting lightly on Hyde's pillow. I knew that hand probably held a gun. There was no way to sneak up on him, and even as I looked on, he turned towards me. Fernando saw me, and nodded. I drew my gun, pushed open the door and entered.

"Do I need to kill him?" I asked Camilla. I was so tense with rage I could barely get the words past my lips.

"I am here to explain to my dear cousin..." Fernando began.

I held my hand up, my eyes sparking with anger as I met his gaze. "I didn't ask you a damn thing. Camilla?"

"No," she said, her voice quiet.

Camilla's face looked vulnerable, sad, the creases around her mouth looking less like laugh lines and more like wrinkles.

"So one vote for sparing you," I bit out. "But then, there's still *my* vote. And you are holding a pistol to the temple of the man I love. So I really don't know how this is going to end for you."

Fernando winced as he took the gun off of Hyde's pillow and let it drop at his side.

"Better," I snapped.

"I'm sorry. I needed her to listen," he said.

I took the chair next to Camilla, and rested my pistol lightly on my lap, pointing it in Fernando's general direction.

"Start at the beginning," I said. "Talk."

Fernando's mouth took on a rigid set. "This is family business."

"I'm Camilla's family. I sure as hell don't like it, but that means I'm in your extended family. Talk."

He sighed. "What do you know about our family business?"

"Probably more than you do at this point," I said.

"Fair enough," he said, shrugging. "When Thiago passed, God rest his soul, the only instruction that he left was that his will was in a safe, and that Camilla is the only one with the code."

"I don't have a code," Camilla said, turning to me, her palms up as if to show that they were empty. "I don't know what he is talking about."

"Your brother Alex has gone half-mad with the idea that you have been planning this for years. That you want to take over. I'm sure that the only reason that he hasn't had you killed is because of the safe combination. He tortured one of the servants, Rosalia, because you had been close to her. He thought that she might know about it."

"Rosalia?" Camilla's hands fluttered up to rest on her bosom like lost birds coming home to roost. "But she has to be an old woman by now."

"She did not survive," Fernando confirmed, nodding solemnly.

"Alex did this evil thing?" Camilla asked. "He was always the one to preach peace and caution."

"It seems Alex has been biding his time and that his goal was always uncontested leadership. His motive in dealing with the businesses was to control the money. For if you control the money, you control the men. Or so he believes."

"What do you hope to achieve here?" I asked brusquely. "What do you want from Camilla?"

I didn't like the way he was yanking her emotional chains with stories of tortured old women and a family dynasty in chaos.

"I want Camilla to come home, back to Brazil. We need her to open the safe and read the will," he said, his eyes still pleading and on Camilla.

"What do you hope the outcome of that will be?" I snapped. "What if the will doesn't leave everything to Caio, as you obviously hope? Are you going to take it out on her?"

"Of course not," he said, sounding appalled. "I came to her to offer my protection."

"Then why were you following me all over Italy?" I asked.

"We couldn't find her. The only thing we knew was that she worked for you. Trust me, I didn't enjoy watching you play sucky-face with this one here," he said, jerking his head toward Hyde.

I realized that Fernando didn't fear or respect me as much as he should have, which made me happy. I could always use a measure of surprise in a fight.

I also realized that Hyde was awake, and watching the proceedings from lowered eyelashes. His breathing was low, measured, but the tendons were standing out in the one forearm that wasn't in a sling.

"Camilla doesn't want us to kill him, Hyde," I said with a smirk. "At least not yet."

I saw him relax, a half-smile flitting over his lips.

"You," I said, nodding to Fernando. "Get out, and leave your contact information with the guy in the hall."

He frowned, and his chest expanded. He was definitely not used to taking orders from a woman.

"Out!" I snapped, before he could open his mouth and make a huge mistake. "We will get back to you. Stop following Camilla around."

"It worked out in her favor this afternoon," he grumbled as he slipped out the door, shutting it firmly behind him.

I turned my questioning eyes to Camilla.

"He was on the roof. He took out two of the men trying to kill me and Howard with his rifle." She looked tired.

"Are you alright?" I asked.

"I just need time to think. Sweet Rosalia... I cannot believe that Alex would do such a thing."

"If Fernando is lying, we will find that out. And if Alex did that..." I trailed off.

"It has been many years since I worked with my brother," she said. "People change."

"We will figure it out," I said. "Go back to the office to rest. Take Howard and Frankie with you."

She stood, touching me on the shoulder and then Hyde on the foot as she exited. "Hyde, I'm so glad you are awake."

I watched her leave, watched Howard and Frankie follow her.

Then my attention was on Hyde, and I smiled wearily. "Hey."

"Hey," he croaked. "We made it."

He shuffled over on the bed and patted the spot beside him. I didn't argue, and I pretended not to see him wince when I jostled the bed. I snuggled carefully against his good side, his arm around me, and he played with my hair absent-mindedly.

"Kuschov is dead," I murmured.

I hadn't really felt the ache in my bones until I lay upon a soft bed.

"You had fun without me?" Hyde asked lightly.

"It was a get-well present for this guy I'm sleeping with."

Hyde poked me in the ribs and huffed indignantly. "You mean the stud you're madly in love with?"

"That's the one." I smiled against his chest.

"How did it go?"

I opened my mouth to answer, tried to collect my thoughts and feelings. Before I could muster a syllable, I fell asleep.

I woke up the next morning next to Hyde, wooly-mouthed, with crusties at the corner of my eyes.

"Hey, gorgeous," Hyde said.

I stretched, noticed that we weren't alone, and sat up.

"Sorry," I mumbled to Hyde, to the pretty Indian nurse checking his IV.

"Don't be," she stated firmly. "It's good for Mr. Garrison to have loved ones near while he heals. Plus, all the baked goods and flowers at the nurses station have earned you an overnight stay."

"Oh, thank you," I said. Frankie and Camilla must have worked quickly to have won over the entire staff overnight.

"You're welcome. Those brownies alone make up for all the snoring," she said, slipping out the door.

I turned to Hyde, my mouth open, my eyes round, as he burst into great guffaws of laughter.

Chapter 37

Hyde was discharged two days later, once the doctor was convinced that he had no fever or other signs of infection. Privately, I thought that Hyde was down-playing his position on the pain scale, but I could not blame him wanting to get out of the hospital. We could feed and house him more comfortably at the office, and he wanted updates on everything, from the status of my house damage, to how Frankie and Howard were getting along. I told him that I didn't know, didn't care, that all I was worried about was him getting well. I told him things were going great, that everything was well under control.

This was a huge, fat, farting lie.

Howard had decided that the emergency-induced truce between him and Frankie was over. He was now taking the mature, high-road option of giving her the silent treatment. She had apologized more times than I could count, in a variety of different ways.

The last attempt had been disastrous. She had filled Howard's workroom full of balloons with "I'm sorry" written on each one. She apparently pushed too many balloons into the room, because the next morning when Howard opened his door, he was greeted with a succession of loud bangs. This is not what an explosives expert considers funny, and he unleashed such a tide of verbal malfeasance that Bruno started to bark and howl in response.

To Howard's infuriation, Sir Darcy McWigglesbottom had decided that although he hated Howard, he *adored* Frankie, who was the only person not willing to pet him, due to allergies. Apparently, living with a sociopath produces some unhealthy relationship parameters. Sir Darcy would not accept attention from anyone, but stalked Frankie around the office relentlessly. I caught Howard trying to hold the cat down and *make* Sir Darcy take affection from him, with predictable results. That night, Howard wore band aids to dinner.

Camilla was avoiding everyone, and when I managed to catch her unawares, she swiped tears from her cheeks, pasted on a false smile, and talked to me in a cheery, almost sing-song voice that freaked me out. She hadn't made any decision about Fernando, and she hadn't contacted him again, but she was producing baked goods at an alarming rate. Muffins, cookies, cakes, and brownies decorated the conference table, littered the kitchen counters, and were sprinkled on our bedside tables. Hoping to avoid baked good critical mass in the office, Frankie, Howard and I regularly delivered sweet treats to the nurse's station on Hyde's floor. On the second day at the hospital, I witnessed a stream of nurses arrive from other units to share the burden and spirit away some of the bounty.

Bruno was the only one who sought me out when I was at the office. He seemed to be picking up on the odd emotional dynamic of the people around him, and he was super needy. Every chance he got, he leaned against my legs, bumped his head into me to get my attention, or shoved his muzzle under my hand, demanding to have his fur rumpled. The other pet of the office, Sir Darcy, seemed to thrive on the discord, and took to jumping out of strange places to hiss at whoever disturbed him.

Although Luis' team had removed the bodies and scrubbed the bloodshed from my home, I received a panicked call from my contractor, John Trammel. He seemed to think that someone had vandalized my property while it was vacant. This wasn't an uncommon problem at construction sites, although I wondered how many vandals used a Browning .50 caliber in their crimes.

John needed to know if maybe I forgot to lock the gate at the bottom of the hill. If I had, I was liable for the repairs. He sounded so frightened to tell me this that I had Frankie call him back immediately and tell him that darn it, yes, I forgot to close the gate, and that I would pay for everything. Then I had her tell him I needed it all repaired by this Friday, as I would be hosting a surprise party for my brother on Saturday.

None of us were up for planning a party. Camilla could be entrusted with the baking of a cake, maybe, but there was a chance we would end up getting five dozen brownies instead. And I currently didn't give a shit about whether orange and pink "worked," or if we should go with a "less ethnic" color scheme for the fiesta, which was the exact question that Sybil had sent me via email. She was concerned that the Mexican-fiesta-themed party not be "too Mexican," whatever that meant.

If I had to field another reminder from my vapid sister-in-law that nothing be "too homemade," or "too spicy," and "no yellow tortilla chips," I was going to have six taco trucks park on the front lawn, roll out a couple of kegs of cheap beer, hire the cheesiest mariachi band I could find, and call the party done. Hell, maybe I'd even spring for a bounce house and have the whole party on the front lawn. It was very tempting... but no. I decided to pass off that particular bag of crazy to someone who could be paid to deal with it. I told Frankie to get me the best party-planner and the best caterer available on such short notice. No budget, I said.

Despite Hyde's hospitalization and the rapid degeneration of the mental state of the rest of my team members, my biggest concern was that I was in the cross-hairs of the Russian mob. After all, I had just imploded (literally) the business operation that they had heavily invested in. I had killed a man who was in good standing with their organization.

It was possible that they would forgive the murder of Anton Kuschov, but what really concerned me was the four million dollars in one of my off-shore accounts that we had pilfered from Kuschov's real estate company's bank accounts. Frankie had finally traced it back to it's origin, and it was very bad news, indeed. Two million was Anton Kuschov's private investment, but the other two million was traced back to the Moscow bank account of Nestor Pankrati, a high-ranking member of the Russian council.

A killing might be forgiven, but theft was never overlooked.

I asked Luis to reach out to someone in the organization, asked him to let them know I just needed to know where to send the money. Then I crossed my fingers and prayed that the Russian mob didn't blow up my house when my whole family was inside on Saturday night.

I tried to keep all of this under control and out of sight while Hyde was in the hospital. I wanted him to have a break from thinking about problems that he couldn't solve. But I caught him watching me with narrowed eyes when I texted and made phone calls. I saw him take note of the sheer number of baked goods flooding the nurse's station. He saw Frankie and Howard come in to visit him, never together, and Camilla not at all.

"How bad is it, really?" he asked me finally, as I drove him back to the office.

His arm was in a sling, and he grimaced when we drove over the speed bumps in the parking lot.

"Bruno actually started barking, at one point," I muttered, conceding that I hadn't done a very good job of covering up the state of chaos that had descended on the team.

"Why?" Hyde asked, aghast.

So I told him the story of Howard's bitter silence, Frankie's increasingly desperate attempts at reconciliation, and the exploding balloons in Howard's work room. I only stopped when Hyde was laughing so hard that he had to swipe tears from the corners of his eyes.

"Please tell me that we have footage of that," he finally gasped.

"It happened in the hallway, so we should, yeah," I said.

"Poor Bruno!" he added.

"Oh, it was the saddest sound you ever heard," I said. "He was *so* upset."

"Did you yell at Howard?"

"Hells yes, I did," I said, my forehead wrinkling. "Frankie and Howard are going to have to deal with this problem between them. But they can figure it out without upsetting my dog."

"Damn straight," Hyde said stoutly. "It's important to have priorities."

I stuck my tongue out at him.

When the door swung open to the office, Camilla stood holding a plate of cookies, flanked by Frankie and Howard.

"Hyde, so happy you are back with us," Camilla said, an oddly bright smile on her face.

"Yeah, good to see you up and about," Howard said, stepping forward to hit Hyde on the shoulder. At the last moment, he thought better of it and let his hand drop awkwardly to his side.

"Hi, Hyde," Frankie said.

She looked close to tears, and I wondered if Howard had rebuffed her again.

"Camilla," I said, taking the cookies and handing her Hyde's bag. "Could you please help Hyde get settled in? Frankie, Howard, in the conference room."

Hyde followed Camilla down the hall one direction, while Frankie and Howard tried to avoid each other while they slumped and followed me to the conference room. Bruno was so close on my heels, he nearly tripped me. Howard and Frankie looked like a couple of junior high kids who had just been summoned to the principal's office. They took chairs on opposite side and ends of the large table, looking determinedly at me, and not at each other. I shoved a cookie in my mouth as a stall tactic, and thought about what I was going to say.

"Goodness sakes," I said with my mouth full. "What is in these cookies? Crack?"

"Butter," Frankie grumbled. "She's buying it in bricks now."

"Ok," I said, brushing crumbs off my front. "Howard, you are mad at Frankie, because she went behind your back and lied to you about what she was doing. Also, your feelings are hurt, because she didn't trust you enough to tell you what she was going to do."

"I..." Frankie began, holding up a finger.

"*So* not your turn to talk," I said, cutting her off. "Howard, is that about right?"

"It's not just that," Howard said, looking only at me. "I am mad on two levels. I'm mad as a boyfriend, and I'm mad as a member of this team."

"Fair enough," I said, nodding and taking another cookie. "I'm kinda pissed, too."

"You are?" Frankie said, going white.

"You released private case details to a reporter without running it past me," I said. "Of course I'm ticked. You had no way of knowing if that would come back to the team in a bad way. At the very least, you put yourself in terrible danger. What if that danger had followed you back here? If you were new to the team, I would boot you in a heartbeat."

"I...I'm sorry," Frankie said, her eyes watery and downcast.

"I know," I said, matter-of-factly. "Here's the thing. You guys can be together, in a relationship, or not. That is none of my business, and I am not a therapist. But I am telling you, not asking you, that this not talking to each other bullshit stops tonight. So you two are going to sit here with this plate of crack cookies, until one of three things happens."

I took a bite of cookie and continued with my mouth full, "One, you break up, and decide to act like mature adults who can work together. Two, you stay together, and decide to act like mature adults who can work together. Or three, one or both of you leaves the team."

They both looked up at my last statement, shock evident on their faces.

"Hey, this may be the best workplace in the world, but it is still a workplace," I said with a shrug. "I'm your boss. And I'm telling you to square your shit away, right now."

I grabbed a handful of cookies on the way out and shut the door behind me.

Hyde was reclining on the bed when I found him in our room.

"Where's Camilla?" I asked, kicking off my boots.

"She kept fussing over me. It was making me nervous. So I told her I was really craving a rum cake," Hyde said, a wicked grin tugging at the corners of his mouth.

"You did not." I chuckled.

"It was the only thing I didn't see on the counter when we walked past the kitchen," he said, holding out his good arm for me to snuggle under as I crawled over to him. "She seemed excited, like she wished she had thought of a rum cake earlier."

"I'm worried about her," I said, wiggling to get comfortable and inhaling his familiar scent.

"I think she just needs some time. I think baking might be something she can do to keep her mind busy, feel like she is accomplishing something."

"Hence the rum cake?"

"Exactly."

"Have you tried these cookies?" I asked, waving one in front of his face until he obliged me by opening his mouth wide.

I shoved it in as Frankie ran past the open door. She was sobbing.

I sat up straight. "Oh, shit."

Hyde's mouth was set in a grim line and he mumbled around the cookie, "Yeah, that doesn't look good."

"I brought them in there, told them to figure it out, one way or another."

"Not. Your. Fault." Hyde said, poking me to enunciate every word.

"I better go see how she is," I said, sliding off the bed. "Can you call Camilla and tell her we need booze and brownies in Frankie's room, stat?"

"Nice medical terminology, you got there," he said, picking up his cell phone.

"I've recently been hanging out at a hospital, waiting for some bum to stop lazing about and get back to work."

"A bum?" Hyde asked, skeptical.

"A bum!" I shouted, biting into the last cookie with relish as I stepped into the hall.

I found Frankie sitting up against her headboard, a pillow clutched to her chest.

"I'm so sorry, Frankie." I shut the door behind me.

"It's my own fault," she said, shuddering a little.

"What did he say?" I sat on the edge of her bed.

"He said that I had broken the trust between us." She paused a moment, trying to collect her composure. "I honestly thought that no one would ever know."

"Would that have been better? To keep a secret from the man you love?"

"I don't know. I thought I could."

"Why would you want to?" I asked.

"I thought it would be easier."

"Maybe in the short term," I agreed. "But secrets are like termites. Even if you don't see them, they're doing damage."

"I just want to go back," she said.

"He still loves you, Frankie," I said. "But he's hurting. You may have to give him some time."

"What about you?" she said. "Are you going to need some time to trust me again, too?"

I sighed. I didn't want to pile on additional stress when she was already going through pain, but I wasn't going to lie to her, either. Her actions had consequences.

"You have to be able to follow, even if you don't like the direction I'm leading," I said. "I can't be wondering if you are going to go behind my back every time you don't like my decisions."

"I would never..." she began.

"But you *did*," I said, as gently as possible. "I love you Frankie, and you're amazing on my team, but you need to spend some time thinking whether that is going to work for you."

"Do you still want me on the team?"

"Of course I do. But you need to figure out if that is something that *you* want. Can you follow orders that you don't agree with? Can you work alongside Howard, even if you guys aren't together anymore? I don't want an answer right now. I need you to spend a day or two really thinking about it."

I patted her leg and left her alone.

Howard was in his workroom, and he looked worse than Frankie. Tears dripped down from his eyes and nested in his goatee. I didn't say anything. I just pulled up a stool, sat right next to him, and slung an arm around his shoulders.

"She could have been cheating on me," he said finally.

"She wasn't."

"But she could have been," he argued.

"That is a risk you would have to take," I said. "So the question is, is the risk of her possibly breaking your heart worth the reward of being in a relationship with her?"

I let the question hang in the air for many moments. Then I added, "I'm all for pre-emptive strikes, Howard, but this seems like a lose-lose."

"I want to be alone," he mumbled, wiping his nose on the sleeve of his flannel shirt.

"Alright," I said, giving his shoulders a quick squeeze and sliding off the stool. "Whatever you decide, I'm here for you."

He nodded in acknowledgement and I closed the door behind me.

"How did that go?" Hyde asked me, when I slunk back into our room.

"Not well," I said. "They are both hurting, but I can't do anything about it. I can't fix it. I can't control it."

"No, you can't," Hyde agreed.

Chapter 38

I gave it two days, then called a meeting in the conference room. Things had not improved, but we had no choice but to move forward, even as crippled as we seemed to be. We were all seated around the conference table when I made my first announcement.

"Ok, first off, the baked goods have got to stop," I said, looking at Camilla. "Even my forgiving jeans are getting tight."

"You think that's bad?" Howard asked. "Yesterday, I did a twosie that had the exact appearance and consistency of a brownie."

"TMI, Howard," Hyde said, wincing.

Frankie smiled tentatively at Howard, but when he didn't look in her direction, her eyes slid down towards her lap and began to fill with tears.

"You don't have to stop baking," I added quickly, seeing Camilla's forehead begin to crinkle. "But can we find some places who would like to take them? An old folk's home, maybe? Or a daycare center?"

Camilla nodded, not meeting my eyes, and I felt instantly chagrined.

"Hyde is healing up well," I said, to change the subject.

"The doctor says that it will be a couple months before I can return to normal activities, but I will be getting my strength back the whole time."

I nodded gratefully at him. I knew that he was elaborating on the subject to try and keep the meeting from slipping into awkward silence.

"So we are just waiting to hear back from Luis on the Russians," I began.

"You didn't get my note?" Camilla asked, her eyebrows drawing together.

"What note?"

"I left it next to the plate of cookies on your bedside table, yesterday, or the day before," she said.

I vaguely remembered sweeping a plate of cookies into the trash a day or so ago. The now too-familiar smell was making me sick.

"What did the note say?" I asked, my tone cold, my eyebrows raised.

"Luis called, and said that someone wanted a meeting. Hestor something?" she said. "I wrote it down."

"It wasn't Nestor Pankrati, by any chance?" I said, my tone deceptively light.

"Yes, that was it."

I gripped the edge of the table until my knuckles were white. I looked around the table, at Hyde's serious frown, at Howard's drawn features, at Frankie's downcast, teary face, at Camilla, who rarely let me down.

"You people need to get your shit together. I love you all, but this is getting ridiculous. We cannot function with these mistakes."

"What about *your* mistakes, Elayna?" Frankie snapped.

"Excuse me?"

"Has it ever occurred to you that the reason your team is in shreds is because of *your* mistakes?" Her eyes dripped tears, but they latched onto mine with a sudden cold confidence, her lip curling.

I leaned back, folded my arms in front of my chest. "Enlighten me."

"If you had listened to me about the Oakland shootings, I wouldn't have felt like I needed to go behind your back, explore other options."

"Oh, so now your lies are my fault. That's convenient," I said, rolling my eyes.

"That's not the worst part," she continued. "If you had listened to your team members when you went after Elroy Farley, maybe you would have actually killed him, instead of his friend. Then Hyde wouldn't have gotten shot."

My heart constricted, I gave a small gasp, and my wide eyes flew to Hyde's arm in a sling.

"Frankie, shut your mouth," Hyde bit out. He leaned forward, and his tense body seemed to be radiating heat. "Don't you dare and try to make her feel like me getting shot is her fault."

"Don't you tell her to shut up!" Howard bellowed, leaning across the table and jabbing a finger towards Hyde.

"We aren't together anymore, Howard," Frankie snapped. "I don't need you to defend me."

I stood and stepped back from the table, my eyes flitting from the belligerent set of Frankie's jaw, to Howard's red face, to Hyde's menacing stance, to Camilla's downcast face.

"Frankie, pack up your personal items and get out," I said, quietly.

"Wh- what?" Frankie stammered.

"You're fired," I said, feeling numb. "At the end of one week, if you would like to rejoin the team, you can give me a call, and I will meet with you. Use this time to really think about whether you want to be on this team. I am going to take the same amount of time to consider if I want you back."

Frankie's face was blanched white. "Because I told the *truth*?"

"Because you are still trying to justify your actions!" I roared. "You lied! You went behind my back, and Howard's back, and the team's back, and left us open and vulnerable by sharing case secrets with civilians! And you *still* aren't taking responsibility for it."

"But..." she argued, her eyes landing on each face around the table in desperation.

"Get out. Now," I said.

She pushed her chair back from the table violently and ran from the room. I noticed that Howard's eyes followed her every movement. He began to push back from the table.

"We're not done," I said, sounding as exhausted as I felt. "Howard, Camilla... I know that this last week has been brutal. I need you guys to decide where you stand as well. Take the same amount of time to re-evaluate what you want, in terms of your future with this team."

"You're firing us, too?" Howard said, his voice trembling.

Camilla looked up at me with the same question on her face, tears in her eyes.

"No," I said, firmly. "Absolutely not. But I want you both to take a week-long paid leave of absence to rest and reconsider your future with this team. Pack a bag, get a hotel room somewhere nice on your company credit cards. Really think about it. This isn't a profession that you can do without your mind and heart being fully in it."

I wouldn't meet their eyes as they pushed back from the table and filed out of the conference room. I was afraid they would see the moisture gathering in my eyes. When they were gone, I sunk back into my chair and pulled my legs up to my chest, resting my forehead on my knees. A moment later, I felt the comforting weight of Hyde's hand on my shoulder.

"How bad did I mess that up?" I asked. I felt numb, like the only heat in my body was the warmth leaching in from Hyde's hand.

"You did a hard thing," he said. "You did what needed to be done, not what they wanted. That's being a leader."

"Being a leader feels really shitty right now," I said. "I don't want Frankie to leave. But I can't have her out of line like that, either."

"No, you can't."

"Do you think it's my fault, what happened to you?" I said. "What Frankie said was true. If I had been more careful about Farley, there would have been enough charges on the driveway to take out all the Russians. There wouldn't have been a fire-fight at all."

He squeezed my shoulder. "Stop it. My shoulder is absolutely not your fault."

"Even you agreed that I should have been more cautious about that kill."

"You made an executive decision," he murmured. "What happened afterwards was not your doing."

"Could you stop being so supportive?"

"Alright, alright. Frankie's lies and the subsequent demise of her relationship with Howard is completely your fault. Also, the fact that a Russian conglomerate set up shop and started off-ing gang members is something that you should have seen coming. And you should have known that Luis was going to hire us to piss them off, and that Howard didn't set enough charges on the driveway, and that your gun was going to jam at an inopportune moment..."

"Ok, ok," I chuckled, relenting.

"We are in a dangerous line of work, Elayna. You can't protect us from everything."

"Maybe we should quit, then," I said with a sigh. "Would you still love me if I didn't kill the bad guys?"

"I would love you if you flipped burgers or if you took up knitting organic pashminas from the wool of Irish sheep."

"That's oddly specific," I said. "Are those my only options?"

He ignored my sarcasm and said, "The real question is, if you didn't take out the bad guys, would you still love you?"

We sat there with that thought and listened to the intermittent beeps from the security feeds that told me three people had left the office. From the spaces between the beeps, I knew that they left one at a time, alone.

Chapter 39

The party at my unfinished house was lovlier than I had expected. The caterer and the party planner had done a fantastic job. I noticed that they were both avoiding Sybil like they were cats who had recently been pulled into a full bathtub by her, the toddler. Sybil thanked the guests when they complimented the tiny appetizer pork tacos with cabbage slaw on top, when they admired the paper fringes of muted pink and orange that fell in gracious swags from every doorway. Sybil hadn't done any of the work herself, but she was thankful for the credit just the same.

After I told Sybil that I had hired a caterer and a party planner and that I would be footing the bill for the entire affair, the guest list had swollen from thirty-five to a hundred and twelve. It looked like a wedding instead of a faux-surprise birthday party. Sybil absorbed the accolades without deferring any attention to the caterer who was running to and fro with sweat glistening on her brow, or to the party planner

who had seamlessly produced four more place set-
tings for the guests that Sybil had invited at the
last minute. Sybil certainly didn't spare a comment
for me, who had paid for everything. Sybil was like
a black hole for compliments: they went in with no
reflected light to others, and with no hint that she
would ever receive enough attention to satisfy her.

Hyde and I had been there since noon, watching
over the set-up and the logistics. We had dressed for
the party only a half an hour before the first guests
arrived. I greeted many of the guests myself until
my mother pulled me away from the door and into
the throngs of the cocktail hour. I was sharing inane
conversation about the possibility of rising interest
rates with several of my brother's friends when Hyde
appeared at my side and gave a hard squeeze to my
elbow. I glanced up at his face and read the concealed
tension there.

"The caterer has a question," he said for the benefit of those watching us.

"Probably a problem with the tacos, again," I said
with a sigh. "If you all will excuse me..."

We stepped away into the crowd and I scanned
over the people in the room.

"Russians," Hyde murmured.

"Where?"

"By the door," he said.

We moved that direction while my mind worked at a furious pace to think of a way to get all of these innocent people out of harm's reach. My eyes flicked from my nephew, who was hosting his own one-man miniature taco eating competition at the appetizer table, to my niece, who had swathed herself in a spare fringed garland and was wearing it like a feather boa. Sybil and Peter were holding court at the far edge of the room, and my father was chatting with the bartender. They were all too far apart, too exposed, not to spare a mention for the hundred or so other people milling about.

The two men were standing at the edge of the crowd near the door, watching. They wore suits and dark shirts, like they were trying to blend in. They were both shorter and smaller than Hyde, but I could see the wicked scar that marred the younger one's face. It ran from his earlobe to the corner of his mouth. Hyde and I strove to cover our lethal natures, but these two men wore theirs proudly. I thought I saw a flicker of relief across one of their faces when they saw me and Hyde approaching.

"Good evening," I said, holding out my hand.

Neither one made a move to shake my hand, so I let it drop smoothly by my side.

"Why are you here?" I asked bluntly.

"Mr. Pankrati wants a meeting with you," the older one said.

His eyes were such a deep brown they looked almost black. They reminded me of obsidian. His accent was heavy, but he didn't stumble over the English language.

"I've already agreed to that," I said. "So why are you *here*?"

"He wanted to be very clear that you should come to this meeting, and that you should be prepared to return his property," the younger, scarred one said.

"If I had any intention of keeping his property, I wouldn't have contacted him in the first place," I said, my patience wearing thin. I was all too aware of my family milling about behind me. "You didn't answer my question. Why are you here, tonight?"

"We have no ill intentions," the older one said, smirking. "But Mr. Pankrati wanted us to show you that if you refuse to meet with him and return his property, that he has ways of taking away things that belong to you."

I stiffened, but forced my words and tone to remain polite. "I will attend a meeting with Mr. Pankrati, but I would prefer that it occur in a well-lit, public place."

"He would prefer the same conditions," the younger one said with a slight wince.

I let a small smile dust my lips. Then Nestor Pankrati knew not to underestimate me. That was a good thing. I felt Hyde stiffen beside me.

"Elayna, introduce me to your friends," my mother said, inserting herself between me and the older Russian. She smoothed her perfectly-coiffed hair demurely.

"These are some business associates of Hyde," I said. "I was just being introduced to them, myself. Unfortunately, they aren't able to stay for dinner."

"Whyever not, if they came all this way?" My mother asked, looking both of the Russian men up and down. She was pleasantly flushed with alcohol and the success of the party.

"Allergic to pork," Hyde said smoothly.

My brain was running a sprint, trying to get ahead of the situation, trying to get my mother away before the Russians figured out that she was my mother.

"I'm Elayna's mother," she said, killing my hopes of an easy extraction. "Blythe Miller. We have chicken and shrimp and beef, as well. Not just pork. I'm sure that you didn't drive all the way out here just to turn around and leave."

"We have another meeting," the older one said awkwardly.

I was pleased to see that he looked uncertain. I let out the breath that I had been holding in a careful exhale. It didn't seem like these men had planned on having any actual contact with my family. The threat was supposed to be implied and not acted out.

"At this hour?" My mother put her hand in the crook of his arm and latched on.

My eyebrows flew up right along with his, like they were controlled by the same marionette string.

"Nonsense," my mother said, pulling the older Russian along with her, back towards the party. "Let's get you a drink. You sound Russian. Do you like vodka martinis? What's your name, anyways?"

I heard him stutter that his name was Mikael as she hauled him bodily over towards the bar. The younger Russian and I wore identical expressions of shock, our eyes wide, our mouths open.

"How long are you planning on staying?" I asked him, after I had recovered from my momentary surprise. "Did Pankrati put you up to harassing us for the entire evening?"

"We were just to tell you about the meeting," he said, his eyes searching behind me for his partner. He looked oddly lost and small without him.

"So tell me about it," I said. "And what's your name?"

His eyes returned to mine. "Sasha. Mr. Pankrati wants to meet you Friday in San Francisco."

"I'll be there," I said. "Tell him that next time, I would prefer a phone call. These threatening tactics just make me angry."

"That wasn't his intention," Sasha said, his eyes scanning the crowd once again for Mikael. "He simply wanted to stress the importance of the meeting. It wasn't.... we weren't supposed to talk with anyone but you."

I could see the truth of his statement on his face. His forehead was wrinkled in concern and he seemed flustered. These men had been instructed to deliver a message, but they were not here to harm anyone. I smirked when I wondered how much trouble they would be in once they reported to Pankrati that they had spoken with my mother.

"You can assure your boss that I will attend any meeting that he sets, as long as it meets my conditions. Now, you better go and rescue your friend," I told him.

He nodded solemnly, and moved away through the crowd, in the general direction of the bar.

"Watch him," I said to Hyde. "But I don't think that they are going to be a problem."

He nodded and followed Sasha.

Sybil appeared at my elbow. "Did you invite more people without checking with me?"

"Yes," I said, snagging a frosty margarita from the tray held aloft by a passing waiter.

"This was supposed to be my party, Elayna. Not yours."

"I thought it was Peter's party. Silly me," I murmured, keeping my eyes on the revelry so I wouldn't have to look at her.

"You know what I mean. The caterer already was upset when she heard I invited the Thompsons and the VonGelphons. I don't know if there will be room at the table for those two."

"Don't worry, Sybil. They aren't staying for dinner."

She pursed her lips and ducked back into the crowds without answering me.

As it turned out, I was wrong. When the crowd began to sit for dinner, my mother absolutely insisted, in terms so vocal that Mikael and Sasha looked nervous as the interaction began to attract attention. So the two Russians ended up seated next to me and Hyde at the table. Sasha sat directly next to me, and Mikael and Hyde were across from us.

Mikael had taken advantage of the cocktail hour to it's fullest extent, and he was drunk when we sat down to eat. His breath reeked of vodka and he swayed a bit where he sat. As he talked with Hyde, he would often lapse into Russian and then back to English, with no sign that he realized what he was doing. I was surprised to learn that Hyde was fluent in Russian, so it made no difference to him.

Sasha looked tense, like he was liable to stand up and bolt at any moment. He and I made attempts at polite conversation a couple of times, but it was awkward. Hyde and Mikael seemed to be getting along well. Mikael was regaling Hyde with stories from the motherland.

"...and then I just gutted him, like this!" Mikael said, with an upward, thrusting motion of his hand that nearly overturned his plate.

Hyde laughed, the rich sound helping to ease my stress. My brother's lawyer leaned over towards me with questions in his eyes.

"They're talking about hunting," I said, batting my eyelashes. "Hyde and Mikael both enjoy hunting wild boar."

He looked vaguely repulsed, but he turned his attention back to the ongoing debate about wealth diversification occurring next to us.

Sasha helped a stumbling Mikael out the door somewhere between dinner and dessert. He tried to regain some of the intimidating composure that they had arrived with by frowning at me and reminding me of the upcoming meeting in stern tones. But just then Mikael broke into a traditional Russian drinking song at the top of his lungs, and I smiled and waved as I saw them off.

"That went well," Hyde said at my elbow.

I smiled up at him. "I enjoyed the power shift, myself. Though I do need to get things lined up for that meeting."

"This is when it would be nice to have Frankie to do background checks and recon," Hyde said.

My eyes narrowed as I looked at him. "I thought you agreed with my decision when it came to Frankie."

"I do. I just don't want you to forget that you will need someone with her skills moving forward."

"Believe me, I'm aware."

Chapter 40

I walked into the San Francisco restaurant promptly at ten Friday night. Heavy burgundy curtains
hung from the twelve foot ceilings, and the walls
were upholstered with the same fabric. The overhead
lights were dim, but the large bar was backlit and
filled to the ceiling with glass bottles of every shape
and color. The bottles glowed and cast colored re-
flections against the walls and ceiling. The effect was
like walking into a giant, velvet-lined jewelry box.

I had dressed well for the occasion. I decided that
if I couldn't carry a gun anyways, I was going to wear
a dress that was usually out of the running because
it left no place to hide a holster. I had chosen an egg-
plant-colored sheath dress with a front slit. It was off
the shoulder and tight enough to highlight the assets
that heavy squats had given me. I paired it with black
high heels and an intricately jeweled clutch.

Nestor Pankrati sat in a corner booth. A slight
man with just a bit of red remaining among the grey
in his thick hair, he looked like he had dressed for a

formal board meeting: three pieces in his navy silk suit, red tie, crisp white shirt. I couldn't see his shoes, but I bet they were polished to show a reflection. He studied me with grave eyes as I approached.

He was flanked by the required two large men that every high-ranking mobster seemed to tote along. Sasha and Mikael were nowhere to be seen. I wondered if they had been in trouble after the debacle at Peter's party. I was patted down so thoroughly by one of the bodyguards that the second time he slid his hands over my buttocks, I raised an eyebrow at Nestor.

"If your man's going to touch me like that, the least he could do is pay me a compliment and buy me a drink," I said.

"Rolan, enough," Nestor said in curt tones. His voice was a pleasant tenor.

"I'm unarmed," I said. "At a meeting with one such as yourself, carrying a gun is an insult, and does no good."

He nodded and gestured gracefully for me to take a seat. His movements were cultured, languid, and his fingernails had recently been buffed. He didn't possess the kind of power that puts bullets between eyes, that pummels someone into submission. Nestor Pankrati possessed the kind of power that killed with a sideways glance, a frown, a shake of the head. He was the brain that controlled the muscle. I wondered how many people had been eliminated with just a motion from one of those manicured hands.

I slid into the plush leather booth and waited for him to speak. He seemed to be waiting for the same thing from me. We sat there and the silence that stretched between us was obvious but not uncomfortable, like smoke blown from an expensive cigar. I didn't shy from his gaze as his light blue eyes wandered over my face, my hair, my neck, my chest.

Eventually, he tapped his chin with the fingers of his left hand, regarded me intently, and said, "You killed Anton Kuschov."

"Yes."

"You blew up his business," he pressed, his eyes locked onto mine. I was reminded of a snake charmer I had seen in India once. I wondered if he thought I could be controlled like that, mesmerized by just his gaze. Probably. There wasn't much this man couldn't do.

I shrugged and said, "I will admit that I lost my temper a bit. He killed an acquaintance, and then one of my people took a bullet. It made me angry."

"Some people would call that excessive," he said.

"I call it thorough."

"Why did you reach out to my organization?"

"I wanted to make sure that there are no...residual misunderstandings, moving forward from this," I said, choosing my words carefully.

"Anton Kuschov was a valued member of our organization," he began. "However, this American venture was completely of his making."

"It was my understanding that your organization had a financial interest in his operation."

"An intelligent investor knows that for every successful endeavor, there will be multiple failures. If he had succeeded here, it would have been a very profitable thing."

"So you are not going to try and revive his attempt?" I asked.

This was hugely important to me, one of two questions that I wanted answered.

"No," he said, bluntly. "Anton knew that he was on his own here. I tried, many times, to encourage him to be content with what he had built in our homeland. We tried to explain to Anton that although the American field looks ripe for picking, the very soil is different. "

"How so?"

"Americans lack one particular element that is necessary for Anton's model to work. You have been raised on a culture of righting wrongs. Revolt and rebellion is your mother's milk. You lack a proper fear, the fear that has been bred into the blood of us Russians. There are only some Russians willing to stand against things inflicted upon them. They are the exception, not the rule. Most of my countrymen are willing to keep their heads down, accept that things are what they are and cannot be changed."

I raised my eyebrows and said, "But not here?"

"Americans? Every little wrong grates on you," he said, sounding frustrated. "You are like that fairy tale, the one with the princess who cannot sleep because of the tiny pea?"

I chuckled.

"I knew, as Anton did not, that he would incur opposition from every angle. He thought that because he was able to please the police, there would be no additional problems."

He paused, swirled his drink, and continued, "He told me about you, about your meeting, after you came to visit. I knew then that his project was dead. That even if you let it sit, someone else would root it out."

"Someone else did," I said, the corners of my mouth tight, turned down.

"Yes," he agreed. "Someone did. Even in killing those reporters and in coming after you, Anton showed his ignorance of the landscape here. He still believed that in eradicating individual problems, he could insulate himself from opposition. But I know that things are different here. For every opponent you remove, more will rise up against you. My organization has no interest in playing whack-a-mole."

"You have whack-a-mole in Russia?" I asked lightly.

"It transcends all cultures," he said with a charming smile.

"If you have no interest in resuming his operation in Oakland, why did you come to meet with me?"

"I looked into you, after Anton told me about your meeting," Nestor said. "When you came to see him the final time, he admitted everything to convince you of the viability and benefits of his plans. Anton always did have a problem with bragging."

"You had cameras in his office?"

"No, but our personnel is as talented at hacking as yours."

Everything clicked soundly into place.

"You are concerned that I will try and interfere with your operations in your homeland," I said.

He replied, "Like I said, I looked into you after you met with him. My organization has no interest in developing enemies because of Anton's mess. We hope that you have better things to do than engage in the suicidal attempt to pick apart our business operations in Russia."

"Of all the countries I've visited, yours is my least favorite," I said. "I have no interest in returning any time soon."

"Good. Because you would fail. This meeting is a show of good faith," he said, spreading his hands. "I could kill you right here, right now."

I smiled sweetly and replied, "You could, but you wouldn't leave the room alive."

"Ah," he said, his eyes scanning the room. "Yes. I thought that the waiters were unusually large, here."

"Oh, it's not just the waiters you need to watch out for," I said casually. "The diners and the bartender are in on it, too."

"Fascinating," Nestor murmured, leaning back in the booth to get a better view of the room. If I didn't know any better, I would have thought he seemed impressed. I thought I glimpsed a smile at the corners of his mouth.

"I guess that brings us to our next topic of conversation," I said.

"You want to know if there will be retaliation for Anton's death," he said.

"Yes."

"When Anton persisted in trying his experiment here, we made sure that all of his operations in Russia were self-sufficient. We have structured it so that we feel no personal loss in his passing. As long as you return the money we had invested in the realty venture."

"Give me the account number, and it will be done."

"Two million," he said, sliding a thick card across the table. "The rest was Anton's personal money. Consider it payment for the excellent clean-up job you did."

"Then it sounds like we are both done here," I said.

He slid out from the booth, stood, and buttoned his suit coat.

"It was a pleasure doing business with someone as reasonable and lovely as you, Miss Miller," he said. "I sincerely hope we never speak about Anton Kuschov again."

"Likewise," I said.

"However, if you ever change your mind and come to my homeland on other business, I would love to change your opinion about Russia. After all, my country has many pleasures you have yet to experience. I could show you." Then, to my surprise, he leaned over and kissed me briskly on the lips.

I watched him leave with eyes rounded in shock. I sat there long after he had left, clutching the card he had given me and wondering if there would be a time when I wouldn't have to shake hands with monsters to keep them from roosting underneath my bed.

Hyde was propped against the tufted headboard when I got back to the hotel room, his computer open on his lap.

"How do you think it went?" he asked.

"Well, there was no bloodshed, which is the Russian mob's equivalent of bringing roses," I said, exhausted.

I kicked my heels off and sat on the bed next to him.

"I'm glad you're back," he said, pecking me on the cheek.

"I'm surprised you were so reasonable with me going to the meeting without you," I said, tousling his hair. "I did miss you, if you were wondering."

"I told Luis that if his men let something happen to you, I was coming after him personally," Hyde replied. "Plus, he let me watch."

"How?" I asked.

He held out his laptop, which showed a view of the restaurant.

"I had visual *and* audio."

"Sneaky."

"I almost blew a gasket when Nestor's man was patting you down," he growled. "I'm glad you said something."

"It was either that or lean into it," I said with a wink. "My boyfriend was recently shot. It has been a mighty long time."

He snapped his laptop shut and tossed it aside with a slow grin. He ran his hand up my back and began to fiddle with the zipper on my dress.

Hyde affected a thick Russian accent and said, "Russia may have many pleasures, but allow me to show you why the best country is still the good ole U.S. of A."

Chapter 41

On Monday afternoon, Camilla found me in the office kitchen. Howard was already back in his workroom. He showed up that morning, still looking sad but more rested than before. He told me that he wanted to get back to work as soon as possible.

"Are you back?" I asked Camilla.

"Yes."

"Good. I cannot cook and I missed you," I said, giving her a hug.

She returned my hug fiercely. Her scent was sweet, familiar. She smelled like home to me.

"I need to talk to you about something," Camilla said.

She reached for a bottle of wine, and opened the drawer that held the corkscrew.

"This conversation is going to require that you ply me with wine?" I asked. "How worried should I be?"

"I have to go back to Brazil," she said.

"For how long?"

"Just long enough to open that safe, read the will, and wrap up any loose ends. I'm hoping two weeks, tops."

"When?" I accepted the glass of wine she slid over to me.

"I was hoping to leave soon, get it over with."

"Well, I'm not booked. Want me to come with you?" I offered.

She let out a breath like she had been holding it, and sagged a bit against the counter. "Would you?"

"Of course, Camilla," I said, my eyebrows drawing together in confusion. "Why were you worried about asking me?"

"Well, this trip is a personal matter, and I know that personal things have been getting in the way of work here, lately."

"Like I would let you go off to Brazil alone when either your brother or your uncle or maybe both want you dead," I said, indignant.

She winced slightly.

"Sorry," I said, wrinkling my nose.

"Don't be," she said. "This is why I need you along. I need someone who isn't personally involved watching my back."

"No problem," I said. "Let me see if Hyde and Howard are interested in a little Brazil action."

I didn't mention Frankie. I was still hoping that she would show up, but I didn't know if her pride would allow it.

She arrived in the evening, when Howard and I were sitting in the conference room. A tone from the security system told us that someone had driven into the parking lot. Our heads snapped over to the monitors, as if we had been sitting there just waiting for this. Which, if either of us were being honest, we were. Frankie was wearing a sheath dress and heels, and had her thick dark hair pulled back into a tight bun at the base of her neck. We watched her on the security monitors. She used her key to enter the antique store above us, but then took a seat on a velvet settee to wait.

I took a deep breath. I realized that my hands were shaking a little, and I balled them into fists to keep them still.

"What are you going to do?" Howard asked.

I watched Frankie on the monitor. "I really haven't decided yet."

I took my time up the stairs, thinking about what I would ask her. When her eyes met mine, it looked like she wasn't wearing any makeup except for mascara. I could see the deep bags under her eyes that were so dark they looked almost like bruises. She stood and took a deep breath, then held out a hand for me to shake.

"I'm here to apply for the tech position," she said after I shook her hand.

We both sat on the small sofa and sunk into an awkward silence. Her eyes were cast down, towards fingers that were tightly threaded together.

"I don't know how this works," I admitted.

"Me neither." Her voice was thick with tears.

"Well, I already know your prior work history," I said in as professional a voice as I could muster. "So tell me why you were let go from your last position."

She took a deep breath, then swallowed. "I went behind my team's back and released confidential case information. This betrayal broke the trust of those closest to me, and could have put the team in danger."

"Why did you do it?"

She met my eyes. "I couldn't let the case go. There was a victim that I couldn't forget."

"Would you do it the same way again?"

"Knowing what I know now? Absolutely not."

"Why not?"

Her brow furrowed. "Because the cost was too high, and the case would have been resolved anyway if I would have just waited."

"What do you view as the cost of your mistake?" I asked. I hated talking to her like she was a wayward child, but I needed to know.

"My relationship with Howard," she said. "The trust of my team leader and my team members. The lives of two good men who were just trying to help."

"Do you think it was my fault that Hyde was shot?"

Her chin lifted, like she was trying to get courage. "Maybe. If you would have listened to your team members, maybe it wouldn't have happened that way. But I also know that there were a million things that could have gone differently."

I nodded. "Do you think it was partly my fault that Beck and Edwards were shot?"

She took a deep breath. "I think it was mainly my fault, but I would be lying if I didn't think that you had a small influence in what happened."

Her shoulders slumped like she thought the interview was over.

"I agree," I said.

Her eyes found mine, and I saw surprise.

I said, "If I had been clearer with you, I think a lot of this mess could have been avoided. So let me be clear now: I do not think that you running off to share case secrets with the media is excusable by anything I did."

She nodded.

"But I understand what it's like to have a case linger, to not be able to get it out of your head. I should have told you that if you ever come across a case like that, you have to be patient. I should have told you that there would be resolution, even if it doesn't happen on your schedule."

"What do you mean?"

"The reason that we couldn't act is because we didn't have enough information. We didn't know what the intentions were behind the shootings, but most importantly, we didn't know who was behind those shootings. There was a case, years ago..." I took a moment to compose myself. "A girl in Minnesota. Shana Crowne. She was found in a lake. No suspects, no actionable evidence. She is still a thorn in my heart. Of all the thousands of victims, she is the one I see in my mind more than any other."

"Did you ever find out who did it?"

"No. There's nothing to go on. That case isn't the point, Frankie. The point is, I know how it feels to be obsessed with a case, and I should have told you that. I should have told you that if you ever feel that way about an investigation, then we will keep it on the radar until it is resolved. I can't promise you that you will be happy with the outcome, or that it will be a quick resolution, or that you will like what I decide regarding who we go after, but we will see it through until it's done."

She nodded.

"But I need to know that you are on my team, and not out for yourself."

"I know. I'm sorry. And I'm so sorry for what I said about Hyde. I was hurting, but that's no excuse. Just sitting across from Howard, with him not even caring, not even hurting... it made me break."

"As much as I wish I could fix things between you, I can't get involved in that. You guys are going to have to figure that out," I said. "Are you going to be able to work alongside him even if you never get back together?"

"Yes," she said. "Does that mean I have a job again?"

"Yes, but you need to understand that it will take time for me to trust you completely."

"I know that." She paused. "It was my cousin, Nalini." Frankie took a shuddering breath.

My body went tense, but I tried not to show it. The moment was like standing on a very high ledge the second before you fell, or watching that dumbass blonde in the horror film set her small hand on the basement doorknob. Something terrible was coming, something painful and inevitable.

"She was like my sister. I was five when her mother died in a car accident. Nalini was just a baby, so the family sent her to live with us. She was eight when her father remarried, and she went to visit him back in India for a month one summer."

She winced against what was coming next, and I forced a swallow down my sandpaper-lined throat.

"It was no one's fault," Frankie said, gesturing with a limp hand. "The police went next door to arrest a low-level drug dealer, and they got far more than they anticipated. It was a meeting with a wanted drug lord present."

She drew her thin arms up around her chest as if for protection. "They got him, but not without a firefight. Nalini... Nalini was playing with the dollhouse her father had bought her. It was pushed against the wall between the two apartments. She was hit by a stray bullet. No one ever bothered to find out if it was the bullets from the police or the dealers who got her."

She met my stricken eyes with large brown eyes that watered. "They kept saying how lucky they were, to be there at the right time to catch him. The papers all wrote it up as a success. No one went so far as to say that Nalini was an acceptable loss, but it was obvious they all thought so. The police didn't even bother to pretend that they were sorry. One even told Nalini's father how many lives they were going to save with him off the streets. Like my uncle should have been happy to make that trade, like he had done his civic duty by sacrificing Nalini."

I didn't realize I had been holding my breath until it left me in a rush. "I am so sorry, Frankie. I didn't know."

"She didn't even like dolls anymore," Frankie said, staring off with glazed eyes. "She liked pulling things apart and putting them back together, seeing how things worked. But I had told her to try and get along with her father when she told me she didn't want to go."

She continued. "If I hadn't told her that... hadn't told her that it was only a month and to try and please him... would she have been knelt by that stupid doll-house to begin with? Or would she have been sulking in her bedroom or trying to take apart the remote control in the living room? Would she have been safe if I hadn't told her to get along?"

Suddenly, Frankie's argument that Hyde's gunshot wound was my fault made more sense. I clasped her cold hand in my warm one until she met my eyes. Frankie looked several hundred miles away for many moments, then she blinked... once, twice, and I could tell her attention had returned to the here and now.

"Frankie, I am so sorry," I repeated. "I didn't know."

She barked a harsh laugh. "Apparently, I didn't know, either. I thought I was over that years ago."

"There are some scars that always hurt."

She nodded, then took a deep breath. "Still, I realize that I was... inserting the emotions that I felt when Nalini died into the team's case. I couldn't get any justice for her. I wanted some for Mikayla."

"That's the dirty little secret in our world, that there isn't any justice to be had, not for the victims. There's only revenge." I grasped her hand. "Frankie, it's only a matter of time before you come across another case like that, one that seems to affect you more than anyone else. Just promise me that you will talk to me about it. You can't go outside of our team."

"I know."

"Good. Now head downstairs and start packing. We are headed to Brazil."

Acknowledgements

Hi!

First off, thanks to Jesus who is powerful enough to redeem anyone and loving enough to offer that salvation to everyone. If you haven't met Him yet, you should.

Thanks to Adam, the love of my life, for supporting me in all ways. Thanks for being patient, because I am not. Thanks for your endless encouragement and for your belief that this silly little dream of mine is worth protecting.

Thanks to Kari Joy Hodgen for the amazing cover art. You take my meager ideas and my "I don't knows" and transform them into a cover that gets tons of compliments. Thank you!

Thanks to my amazing beta readers: Jenny James, Kari Hodgen, Jamie Weatherfield, Melissa O'Malley-Richard, Babs Veneman, and Adam. You guys are amazing, and I could not do it without you. You catch all of my stupid mistakes and ask great questions about character development and motivation.

Thanks specifically to Jamie for medical advice, Jenny for her meticulous grammar skills, Melissa and Kari for helping me work through my Frankie issues, Adam for his gun and math talents, and to Babs for her assertion that this book is better than my first. You guys are better than strawberry jam on a fresh-baked biscuit.

Thanks to Red for all the company while I wrote, even if it was a little gassy.

And last but not at all least... thanks to all of my readers! The response to the first book was amazing. You guys told your friends, left reviews on Amazon, and begged to know when the next book was coming out. (Sorry it took longer than I thought.) Thanks for enjoying these characters as much as I do.

Much love,
Jill

Dear Reader

Thanks to you, whoever you are, for reading my book. It is my sincere hope that you were entertained, that maybe you even laughed. That was my goal.

As a self-published author, I don't have a marketing and advertising team. I have you, the reader. If you enjoyed this book, will you please leave a positive review on Amazon or Goodreads? Would you consider recommending this book to a friend? I would really appreciate it.

If you want to know when future books of mine become available, consider visiting my website at jillmbeene.com, and signing up for my newsletter. I hate spam, so I will only send one out when I have something worth saying.

If you find an error, have a question, or just want to chat, shoot me an email at jillmbeene@gmail.com.

Once again, thank you,
Jill